p. 213/215 ?

7. Thesis Proposal @ End -1

7. light.... p. 91 → 101

8. Saint John of Gods p. 213/215.

9. Trying to Escape - cupit... p. 123, 125, 133

10. The lethal injection

11. Tales of Telepathy p. 211, p. 240

12. Therlon.

13 Battle of The Bulge.

14. Christmas Blues

15 Yoga TTC

16 mum's anniversary.

17. The never-Ending universe p. 248, 251.

18 Brain Scan.

19. Korea land. → 1950s.
                    pic:

Philippe Petit walks a tightrope.
Between The TT in 1974

C. Living - games - use to take 70 mes

Headspace.
Immunity to thirb

Vietnamese Voices

Mary Ellen Guiney

authorHOUSE®

AuthorHouse™ UK
1663 Liberty Drive
Bloomington, IN 47403 USA
www.authorhouse.co.uk
Phone: 0800.197.4150

© 2016 Mary Ellen Guiney. All rights reserved.

No part of this book may be reproduced, stored in a retrieval system, or transmitted by any means without the written permission of the author.

Published by AuthorHouse 01/31/2017

ISBN: 978-1-5246-6311-7 (sc)
ISBN: 978-1-5246-6312-4 (hc)
ISBN: 978-1-5246-6310-0 (e)

Print information available on the last page.

Any people depicted in stock imagery provided by Thinkstock are models, and such images are being used for illustrative purposes only. Certain stock imagery © Thinkstock.

This book is printed on acid-free paper.

Because of the dynamic nature of the Internet, any web addresses or links contained in this book may have changed since publication and may no longer be valid. The views expressed in this work are solely those of the author and do not necessarily reflect the views of the publisher, and the publisher hereby disclaims any responsibility for them.

Contents

Chapter 1   Baby Steps Forward 1
Chapter 2   The Death Trap 21
Chapter 3   Corfu 31
Chapter 4   The Wacky Diet 40
Chapter 5   Thailand 52
Chapter 6   Lanzarote 65
Chapter 7   Light at the End of a Dark Tunnel 79
Chapter 8   My Thesis Proposal 91
Chapter 9   Saint John of God's 104
Chapter 10   Website work 123
Chapter 11   The Lethal Injection 135
Chapter 12   The Clear Out 157
Chapter 13   Reminiscing and Moving Forward 178
Chapter 14   Travel 194
Chapter 15   Exorcism 222
Chapter 16   Moving and aGrooving for the Chan Zuckerberg Initiative 236

Chapter 1

Baby Steps Forward

It all started in October of 2011. I was getting the boot from my boyfriend of two and a half years. We had both lost communication with each other and had fallen out of love gradually as we spent less time doing things together. Friday night dinners and frozen yogurt dates in London would be gone. I took this break up on the chin and said it was time to move on. I continued on with my job in JP Morgan and became even busier as we had to do write-ups for our securities and European limited entities. So, I was happy to have a busy mind. I was also taking on the Europe, Middle East and Africa balance sheet for the firm where I analysed the liquidity risk position for all of the European branches. I was sad that I was regularly taking one bite out of my lunch and throwing it in the bin, but hey I guess it was better to lose my appetite from heart ache rather than gain a tonne of weight. I also felt that it was time to throw myself massively back into exercise to get those natural endorphins back and to put myself first. I started bikram yoga, running nine miles in and out of work and also bought a bike. I signed up for a dating website called e-Harmony and met an English guy, who was lovely but not my cup of tea. On the bright side he was kind enough to bring me a signed Brian O' Driscoll jersey on our first date. I still have it and it reads, *"To Mary, very best wishes, Brian O' Driscoll X"*.

At that same time, towards the end of November, I heard my dad had tightening in his chest which lasted over thirty minutes. My mum rang the Blackrock Clinic straight away and Dr. Brian Maurer (God rest his soul now) said to send my dad in immediately. He needed not a triple bypass, but five bypasses and sure enough that legendary doctor saved his life again. My dad had seen Dr. Maurer in 1997 when he had angina. He developed angina while out in Manila doing retail business in the Philippines. Seeing as Manila is the most densely populated city in the world and there are extremes of poverty and wealth in the country, he must have gotten a culture shock and his heart started to cave. Either that or else it was a cuisine difference. My dad doesn't acclimatise well to Eastern food and even had a dodgy stomach when he visited my sister Anna in Nepal when she worked for the United Nations years ago. I was eleven at the time and saw the worry on my mum's face at the other end of the phone so they decided to book Dad a flight home from the hospital in Manila to see our doctor here in the Blackrock Clinic. My dad still has notes from the doctor in Manila, Dr. Kuala was her name. One of the notes was dated July 29th and reads *"Dear Mr. Guiney, Thank you very much for the roses, a gesture of your appreciation which makes doctoring fulfilling and heart warming. Take care not to overdo your activities on the way home. Eat frequently and in small portions, and not three big meals. If Bill can get you a wheel chair at Hong Kong airport, or if you can walk that would be much better. Do not worry"*. There was another note which was talking about the nurse or doctor using a tea warmer for the tea pot. They must have had an English translator write all this down for my dad so he kind of knew what was going on. There are more notes back and forth and addressing Dr. Maurer and also a nice picture with the team from Manila. I asked my dad if he minded me putting in a note from the doctor in this book and he responded by saying, "Not at all" and "I'm sure she doesn't mind, she could be dead, for all we know!" Hopefully not.

While my dad was in hospital there, my mum took me and my brother John to a church outside of Dublin where there was a novina being said, and apparently Our Lady had appeared there recently, which was on the news. I wasn't quite sure how to pray; I just kneeled in the pew next to Mum and prayed for Dad's health to be OK. I really should have been praying for Mum as well as she looked close to distress. Thankfully all was OK and Dad came back to Dublin and went straight into the Blackrock Clinic where Dr. Maurer put stents into his heart.

In fact, I saw that doctor when I was eighteen and had pericarditis. Nothing serious, just a virus that I picked up from partying too hard in the London days when I studied veterinary science. I had been partying too hard with my friend Cathy, my best friend since we were four, who came over to visit me for a weekend. We drank beers all day long while we visited Madame Tussauds. We would take the piss out of Hitler in there and then stand next to Jennifer Aniston thinking we were celebrities. Anyway I knew my heart was fine and just had to do routine checks. I still exercised loads and ate a healthy diet. I continued to drink like a normal college student who was studying hard but experiencing the fun in life at the same time.

That Christmas in December of 2011, I came back home and saw my dad after his operation. He was recovering very well and I showed him the Brian O' Driscoll jersey in the hospital to brighten his day. "Where on earth did you get that shirt?", he asked with a huge smile.

"Oh some dude that worked alongside Brian O' Driscoll from London. I met him online."

My dad just smirked and said, "This online business lark is taking off."

I always knew how to make another person happy and how to distract them from something serious.

That Christmas was tough in our house, especially for Mum. She was worn out so we all had Roly's delivered for Christmas day. Mum also felt empathetic for me as I was going through my own break up; an even harder one when you spend two years living with someone. My legendary mother suggested a bit of talking therapy for me. The night before I had to fly back to London for work, she cracked open a large bottle of Grey Goose vodka and showed me pictures of her in her single days and even photos of when she met my dad. She told me, "Mary, you are enjoying your life and are far too young to settle down; you need more adventure."

She was delighted that I had thrown myself back into exercise and was moving on with plenty of friends and a fun life in London. The next morning, there were two sore heads and she dropped me off at the airport to carry on with my life and live my own dream and move on.

I was sharing a bed with my buddy Martin in a house of six people near Wandsworth Common. I was getting up early to go to the gym or cycle to work, do bikram yoga before work and work hard at my job. It was the best distraction. I felt like I got over my dad and the break up quickly.

One day we had news at work that Ben Ainslie, a professional sailor and past employee of JP Morgan was giving a talk to current employees. I thought to myself, *Wicked, I'm definitely going to see him.* All the questions about his goals and achievements in life amazed me and he inspired me so much. "How do you go that extra mile?", one person asked.

"Well it's all about fuel, you have to fuel your body right."

I nodded in agreement and knew that there was no way I could do two plus hours of training a day and hold down a stressful job in JP Morgan without loading my body full of pasta and the right foods. I always had a healthy appetite.

One of my neighbours was into triathlons, and he kept asking me to join him for a swim in the Serpentine in Hyde Park to get into that discipline. At the time, I never got around to it as I was purely focused on cycling and running.

It was also the summer of the 2012 Olympics and my friend Martin and I headed off to see the rowing as the two of us were and still are buzzing buddies who met through rowing in college at NUI Galway. He was studying for a masters in biomedical science, while I was doing my biochemistry degree. I loved the Olympics. There was a good vibe about the place. "Mary are we starting on the beer already?", he asked.

"Hell yeah, we're out watching posh tiddly heads row. Let's support them in style."

The rest of the games we just watched on our neighbours massive screen and I was so inspired by all of the athletes and the cool musicians at the opening ceremony. "WWW man and the Petshop Boys and David Bowie beat everyone at this Olympics", I posted to my wall on Facebook. I enjoyed the beers that night and then cycled all around Richmond Park and did a nine mile run the next day. I was on fire.

A few days later, I got Achilles tendinitis. Martin had given me a load of music to download to my I Pod, so it was encouraging me to run more and more. Nine miles into work, nine miles home from work and then a short three mile run around Battersea Park after a pasta party. I saw this as an early warning sign and just chilled more and used my bike.

A few months previous, there was a trip to Vietnam being planned. Myself and a bunch of Limerick heads were planning on jetting off. Nine of us were heading away. I had been to Thailand as a kid, when I was twelve with Mum, Dad and three older siblings and I loved it. I loved the hustle and bustle of Bangkok and then the serenity of Phuket. Bangkok was crazy. "Jesus those lights have taken seven minutes to change", Mum yelped from a tuck tuck.

We were then taken to a large warehouse where they were trying to sell my mum and dad jewellery. Mum and Dad looked in fright. I still remember the warehouse. Everyone looked worried and when the men saw my siblings and I and that we had our own family they let us go. "That was a close call, I thought they were trying to rob us", my mum said to my dad in relief.

This time, Vietnam was organised by the others who had been there a few years previous, so I let them book away. At the same time, while the flights were being booked one by one, my sister, Suzi and I were thinking of going to Nepal to trek mountains and visit our sister Anna out there. In the end, my big sister pulled out as there were too many injections to be taken and a lot of organisation needed. I still had to get injections for Vietnam and was even contemplating Japanese Encephalitis, but decided I didn't need that one in the end as I wasn't going to be hanging out with dogs with rabies or anything! Most of my buddies got the cheap antimalarials while my parents made me get malarone. Malarone is expensive but known to be safer and not cause any wacky side effects.

August came and I was ready with a rucksack to take on Vietnam, with a bit of adventure thrown in. I brought my asics with me as I had signed up for the Royal Parks Half Marathon in October 2012, and was raising money for breast cancer care. Friends kept saying that it is not the type of holiday to train in but I brought them anyway with good intentions. I wanted to eat well, lap up the sun, swim, drink beer, go to the mud baths, see some history and party all at the same time. Just to forget work for two weeks. A typical holiday. My favourite holidays are generally the adventurous ones, and I find it hard to sit on a sun lounger for longer than thirty minutes, as I'm always running in and out of the sea as I have energy to burn from my massive appetite for both food and life.

Most of the nine of us had separate flights over, and one lad Burkie was flying from Australia. I hadn't met him before and was looking forward to meeting him, as I heard tonnes about him. I flew in a duo on Thai airways with Claire. I was happy out. We had a few glasses of wine and there was a good few movies to watch. Almost Famous and the Green Mile were on. The only annoyance of the flight was that Claire kept tapping my shoulder in her drunken haze as I was trying to focus on the Green Mile. "Will I ask the air hostess for more wine?", she'd ask.

I'd take out my earphones and say, "Do if you want, back to the Green Mile for me."

Some may say I have a bipolar personality, as I'm into both thrillers and comedy. Two of my favourite movies are the Shawshank Redemption and Just friends. Quite the opposite, but hey a different mood for a different day. Also when someone asks me what music I'm into, I'd say "Everything except heavy metal and Jazz."

"You can't be into everything", they would respond.

I even more so am today with the legend that is spotify. Monday's are actually my favourite days as spotify recommend thirty new songs to me for my loyalty. Best tenner I spend. OK so back to Vietnam.

We landed in Bangkok and headed straight to the smoking lounge. Claire kept annoying me as she was more or less rat arsed from the flight. She didn't eat any of the food they gave us on the plane so the wine went straight to her head. When we landed in Ho Chi Minh, she had sobered up a bit more. "You more or less blacked out at Bangkok airport didn't you?", I asked.

"Yeah, sorry, I can't handle the wine." We both just laughed it off.

The only bit of research I had done prior to the holiday was googling one British pound into Vietnamese dong and a load of zeros came up. I thought to myself that I'd worry about that when I got there. At the time it said the exact exchange rate was 32,000 VDN to 1 GBP, so we made a quick trip to the foreign exchange counter at the airport.

Outside we picked up some smokes and the lady at the counter gave me a free fruit juice. "This is going to be the best holiday ever", I said to Claire. "Smokes and a free juice."

She just grinned at me. We then hopped into our taxi and listened to all the beep beep of the motorcycles going alongside us. We had a quick shower and changed our clothes and then the two of us sat in the sun and had some beers. They generally don't serve full pints over there so we were frequenting the bar quite a lot.

"How are you keeping on this fine day?", I asked an older English man while he was sipping his beer.

"Grand, it's good to be alive isn't it?", he answered back.

I got chatting to him for a while but Claire wasn't too impressed that I was starting up conversations with other people. I had to keep the liveliness going with her too.

I was fascinated with people passing by us, just minding their own business, either holidaying or working hard to make a living. The fruit ladies were the best. I kept buying all of these exotic fruits and taking pictures with the kind Vietnamese as I wanted their cool hat in some photos. Later I got googling that the conical hat is a symbol of love. It's something to represent that they had moved on from the Vietnam war and that they wanted all types of tourism coming into their country. I tried to communicate about our history and the IRA and invasion with the Brits but I was getting nowhere due to language barriers. I would sip my beer, nod and smile and purchase more fruit to keep me hydrated.

After a few drinks, my friend and I noticed that there was a tattoo parlour just over the road. Claire already had a few tattoos and I kind of wanted to get one. With a bit of Dutch courage, I decided to get a small 'Daniel' tattoo on my ankle. The two guys in the parlour laughed at me as I came in in a drunken haze. They told me that there was no Daniel in Vietnamese. They recommended that I get it done in Thai. "You're joking", I remarked, "Where is the internet?"

I kind of believed them but used my other best friend google to make sure. Anyway, ten minutes later and the tattoo was done in Thai with zero pain; thank God for beer. The reason behind Daniel was because it was my mum's father's name, my brother's name and if I ever had a boy I would name my first born Daniel.

A few hours later we met three other buddies who were hanging in Saigon too. We headed out, had a laugh and then booked train tickets to head up to Nha Trang the next day. The train part was my favourite. We were allowed smoke out the window. It was also so chilled being able to listen to beats on my I pod and watch the country go by at high speed. All the greenery amazed me; no wonder they get monsoons; sure it's no different to Ireland, just a lot friendlier.

It brings me back to Thailand when I was twelve. After that holiday we were all tired and had dinner in the Step Inn. "Bit different to Phuket," my dad remarked.

My mum nodded, "Sure Michael the Thai know how to welcome people as they live a much happier life on a lot less money."

I just absorbed everything they said and agreed.

Vietnam was the same. It had more culture and friendly faces than you would find on a miserable tube in London. You may as well stick your butt out at the next ignorant person you walk by in London or Dublin and think to yourself, *What a miserable shit having a bad day.* I have just learned to smile back at anyone being rude to me as that pisses them off more. There are a lot of friendly people in Ireland, don't get me wrong, but you do come across a fair few twats who just give out about the weather all day long and moan about their jobs. Spend more money so in that savings account that you have and book a god damn holiday.

Nha Trang was good craic. It had the beach, lots of parties and good restaurants with good food. Because there were so many of us travelling we generally went to more western type restaurants so I didn't get to taste proper Vietnamese dishes which was a let down. On the plus, I got to taste plenty of Vietnamese food in the bank before I headed on holidays. The traders in my team always got lots of good dishes delivered which was a bonus, and I was always more than happy to help myself to their food. "Mary you have some appetite, second lunch today is it?"

They used to laugh at me as I walked away with a serviette full of nibbles. Anyway I'd eat anything so I was happy enough. No allergies with me.

It was about this point on the holiday that I noticed I started to get sleep deprived but I didn't seem to care. There was always the night owls partying until 6am and getting up at 6pm, or else the early risers. For the times when I was alone not being able to sleep, I had my I pod with me so I had plenty of music to keep me entertained. I had made a promise to myself before leaving for Vietnam that I didn't want to get too drunk and start losing things so I drank plenty of water to keep me sober but high on life and beer at the same time. This was a lesson I actually learned from my ex. I think he used to worry that I was out partying too much in London, so when we broke up I made sure to still head out with my crew and have a laugh but drink a pint of water after every two pints of beer and I haven't blacked out to this day. "You're not doing yourself any good by drinking water on a night out. Sure beer is heavily watered down", one friend remarked.

I just laughed this off as I thought it was nonsense.

Nha Trang was great. We came across a Dutch guy outside one of the bars, and I started doing the robot dance with him. I always loved Dutch guys as I think they have a wacky sarcastic sense of humour, which I totally get. Sarcasm runs in the Guiney family. Anyway he was dishing out drugs and a few buddies were taking them but I was steering clear and just enjoying good old reliable beer.

One night, I headed down to the beach with a few buddies at 6am, and we buried our bags in the sand and took a quick dip. The Vietnamese ladies and men were up at that hour practising yoga. It was class. I was trying to do yoga with them and one of them actually gave me her swim cap which I still have. I couldn't really do yoga, as one of the girls was bitching over who is scoring who on the holiday and other typical shit. She wasn't happy that another one of the girls on the trip was with a guy that she fancied. I used to just listen and let my mind ignore that crap. At the age of twenty six you think you would be over that bullshit.

"Mary he's mad about you, score him for crying out loud," Martin said to me.

There was a guy called Wayne who kept coming up to me in the sea and hassling me for a kiss. To get rid of him I gave him a quick kiss and said adiós. Martin was in hysterics. "You're mad, he was hot", Martin cried. I shrugged. I think Martin wished he was gay.

That morning our wallets and a few cameras got stolen by young boys. There was a woman in on it too and she was getting them to rob us. My friends went off to get the Vietnamese police involved. I just shrugged it off because the young boy robbed all of my cash and flung my wallet with my bank cards back at my forehead. While the others went with the police, I chilled on the beach with my wallet and smokes.

As the sun came up more and more, we all collected as a group on that same beach. I was pretty wrecked at this stage and was able to actually lie there for a while and get burnt to a crisp. I pointed over to my friends and said, "Hey, there's the lady that robbed our stuff last night, cameras and all if you're interested in approaching her yourself." They shrugged and had more or less forgotten about it at that stage.

The next night it was another beach night, after dinner and the pubs. This time we decided to get jet skis. It was just me and three of the lads on a jet ski each. It was class craic and thank God for no injuries, but I still had to exert energy somewhere as I hadn't managed to fit in a run yet on the holiday. One of the lads fell off his and couldn't get back on for a good ten minutes. It was quite funny to watch. Even though I was sleep deprived at this stage I still had plenty of energy as I know how to fuel my body right. I also did para gliding over the sea that morning with Pa.

I was supposed to head off to Hoi An the next day with a few of the group, but decided I'd hang in Nha Trang for another two days with three of the others. I booked a new domestic flight which was cheap. I think it was no more than sixty dollars. The flights don't go by inflation or crap over there, you can book a last minute flight and still get bang for your buck.

The next morning, Pa and I were lying in our room next to each other in the bed. There was four of us sharing a room.

"Guines, are you awake?", Pa asked me.

"Hell yeah, are we ready for the mud baths?", I replied.

Burkie turned around and immediately said, "I'm in."

We left Kathy, the sleeping beauty behind us as she liked to laze around and wait until night time came. I had great craic with her.

After a quick breakfast, we hopped into a taxi to go to the mud baths. This was class. We could finally get some pampering in and massages for next to nothing. The three of us hopped into our own tub, waited for it to fill up with mud and then showered down and went to the steam room. Pa looked like he was about to vomit. "It's good for you lads, it's part of ozone therapy, we all need to detox the system by sweating it out," I grinned.

They both laughed and we agreed it was time for some massages. They walk all over your back in Vietnam which is class. We weren't getting a happy ending or anything, just some tension release in our bodies to take out all of the nots. I still get Thai massages here in Dublin, every month and I bear the pain as I know it's good for athletes.

I could hear the Vietnamese lady saying to Pa, "Is that Mary in the next hut getting a massage?" She then giggled.

I started wondering, how on earth she knew my name.

It was at this point that I said to Pa, "I think I can hear Martin talking to someone about me in the rowing days."

He burst out laughing and said, "Martin's in Hoi An, would ya go away Mare."

I just laughed and ignored it. We had another night to kill there before our flight to Hanoi. I was on my own on the flight as I had booked separate to the others. On the flight I got chatting to this couple next to me. The boyfriend was trying to calm his girlfriend down as there was smoke coming out along the aisles. This is part of the routine on domestic flights. I hadn't seen it before but love flying, so I got chatting to the couple and this seemed to make her a bit more relaxed. After we landed and got off the plane, Pa shouted out, "Who are your new buddies Mare?"

"They're sharing a cab with us to Vietnamese backpackers," I shouted back.

We all hopped into a taxi and got there safe and sound.

I love chatting to new people when travelling and went to Kos on my own when I was twenty two for two months. This was before I enrolled for a masters in Finance. I decided to experience some culture and went to Greece alone rather than doing a typical J1 to the States. Travelling solo is the best sometimes as you have the freedom to do your own thing and I learned that again on my swimming holiday last July with Strel Swimming Adventures in Croatia. I'll come to that later.

We got to the hostel and were due to meet the rest of the crew later that day. Pa, Burkie and Kathy went out exploring a bit and I chilled in our room. It was a room for nine people. I don't care where I sleep really, I loved the chaos of it all to be honest. In the room I started noticing my face breaking out. I wasn't sure if it was mosquito bites or the lack of sleep. I think I double dosed on malarone that day. Nothing to harm me, just making sure I wasn't getting malaria on that holiday. I also made sure to cover my skin in deet. I didn't care if it wrecked my clothes or not. I just wanted to stay safe for fear I had to tell my mum I had malaria.

An hour later the door knocked. "Miss, there is someone here to see you," one of the Vietnamese workers said. "Do you know a young man from Australia?"

"Who, Burkie?", I replied.

He let the dude meet me as there seemed to be a language barrier going on. It was actually one of Burkie's friends. I met him and he was plastered. I told him to wait around for an hour or so and that I would chill with him as Burkie would be back soon. He just said "laters" and headed off. I laughed, closed the door and thought to myself that there was a fat chance of him finding Burkie!

I tried to get some rest as I was lying on the bed. Pa came back and I jumped up out of the bed. "How's it going Guiney? You should venture out a bit. It's class out there," he said looking pleased with himself.

"Pa, my face is going all funny, and I can't seem to rest at all on this trip. I feel like I'm in over drive," I cried at him.

"Relax, you're face is grand. Just try chill out more." Pa reassured me and the two of us discussed Halong bay.

That night, all nine of us got glammed up and we headed to a late bar down the road. It was packed, so I decided to get myself a bucket. It was my only bucket on the trip, but I thought it made sense as it meant I didn't have to queue for the bar often. We met some cool people in there, some nice dudes from Sri Lanka, Taiwan and China and also a girl from Kazakhstan. I loved and still do love chatting to different cultures. Plus, I wanted to get outside the click of our group a bit. I was wearing my sailor dress and three of the other lads were wearing sailor tops as well. I needed to get a few snaps of that.

The night was getting mad and it was busy, so I headed back to the hostel early enough with one of the girls. She was moaning about losing her key for her locker. I told her that they'll replace it for two dollars or something. Panic over. We chilled outside the hostel and chatted a bit about the night. I had to remind her to keep quiet as there were lots of signs to say keep noise levels down to respect neighbours. But sure no one was paying attention to any of this.

Off to the room we went, and she passed out like a lemon. I was of course wide awake just listening to my I pod. One by one each of the group came back and passed out. I waited for 6am to arrive when I could get up, shower and throw all of my bikinis and shorts into a bag and hit Halong bay. Ready to go, I was the first one down for breakfast and getting excited about Halong bay. Everyone was coming down after me with massive bags packed, and they were remarking on mine. I said "We're off to a bay for two days, what do you expect me to pack?"

It was like chalk and cheese. A lot of them had packed a tonne of clothes and lots of make up. I even saw a few suitcases lying around. I wasn't bothered; possibly the lack of sleep made me care less. Plus my mother got me over the paranoia of needing to wear make up from a very young age. I like to wear it when hitting the town or if I look hungover but a lot of the time I'm either in training gear or sleeping so I like to have my face out.

Halong bay was class. We all had little huts, long benches to eat our food and lots of water activities. We played the game buffalo while on the boat going over there. Essentially we all had to drink our beers with our left hand and if were caught drinking with our right hand then buffalo was shouted. Martin was rubbish at this

Vietnamese Voices

game and got caught with a buffalo a fair few times, so he had to down his beer. We had to sign these little pieces of cardboard, just for insurance purposes when participating in any of the activities. There was nothing dangerous there anyway, it was just the fast doughnuts, wake boarding and rock climbing, all with experienced instructors. The rock climb instructor was a huge black dude. He was about 6ft 9 and had an Aussie lady instructor with him. I had to try it. I listened patiently, but half way up I kept hearing bitching going on in the sea. It was Claire's voice saying, "What is this Mary fucking Guiney thing about?"

I looked around and saw Craig sitting patiently in the sea waiting to rock climb. I still tried to climb more as the Aussie girl was saying, "You're a good listener, you can do it."

I was listening to her and was adamant to get up that wall, but the noise was a bit distracting. I eventually gave up and abseiled back down.

Next on the list was the doughnuts. That was great craic and nothing new to me seeing as I had done them in Greece when I was twenty two. Zoe, from Canada, who was travelling alone banged her head pretty bad on the doughnuts and had to rest in the huts for the next two days.

The next challenge was wake boarding. I watched the instructor Ben do it and he was class. I then watched the other Vietnamese instructor do it and he was even better! This gave me the motivation to go. I got out there and filled my boots. It took me a good ten minutes to finally stand up but at the same time I kept hearing voices, but this time it was encouraging voices, "she's class" I heard. It felt like there was a bit of a love buzz going on. I was a bit confused as to how I could hear the guys, considering the distance there was between me and the boat. I just ignored it and tried to do more wake boarding. After about twenty minutes I gave up and gave Martin a go. He was just as rubbish as me. At least Martin kicked Pa's ass climbing the rocks. I'd love to see them compete today.

— 15 —

That day was filled with food, beer and lots of activity. I loved it. At dinner one of my buddies gave another dude that was on the trip a type of golden shower. He pulled down his shorts and stuck his crotch into the lads face while pouring a can of beer into his face! Fair enough, as he had won the swim race that day so torture was needed in revenge. I was thinking at that time what the hell are the Vietnamese going to think of this. Laughing my head off, I went over to the other table where there were six Vietnamese having their dinner. I wanted to say hi. They were eating eye balls and rotten looking things, and I couldn't understand a word they were saying, so I went back to the bar.

"Slut banger one, slut banger two, slut banger three", one of the lads screamed at three random girls who were on the trip. I couldn't stop laughing inside. One of them got his sense of humour, but the other two looked horrified for being called a slut banger.

The bar had a "family box" where I left my wallet, so anytime they saw me dip my hand into the family box they knew it was me reaching in for my wallet to pay for beers. I wasn't hearing anything unusual at this point because there were so many of us enjoying the music and the party so I just carried on with my energy. I was also drinking tonnes of water on the trip to keep fully hydrated in the sun.

Later that night, a load of people headed in to go skinny dipping and people started dropping like flies one by one to hit the huts and go to sleep. I remember one of the guys on the trip took Craig's waterproof camera and hopped into the sea with it. I was about to kill him as there had already been about five cameras lost or stolen from the trip already, so I ran after him and grabbed it. The last thing we wanted, was another camera lost and I think Craig got some pretty good snaps from that trip.

Come 5am, and everyone was hitting the hay by that stage. I went to lie down beside Craig, who wasn't part of our group, but in the hut next to my buddies. The reasoning behind this was that I started hearing bitching going on between my buddies. I kept hearing shouting and screaming going on amongst a few of them. I could hear Claire saying, "This fucking Mary Guiney thing is ridiculous. Look she's over there in a shower trying to sleep with a Vietnamese boy."

Kathy responded by saying, "Shut up, Mary Guiney is sound."

This arguing was going on for about five minutes. So, I tried to wake Craig up to see if he could hear them but he was passed out.

I then screamed out loud, "Shut the hell up."

I couldn't see any of my friends and didn't want to go into their hut, so I got up, grabbed for a smoke and went over to one of the huts and asked this young Vietnamese dude for a lighter. Not to have sex with me of course! He was playing Nintendo in his little hut, so I was glad at least someone else was awake. Nintendo and the Play Station were two things I was a whiz kid at when I was a teenager. I got chicken pox quite late in life, when I was thirteen and had to take two weeks off from school. My mum used to make me sandwiches and tea while I sat all day long playing tomb raider, donkey kong and micro machines. Playing games like that is also really good for maths, so it's no wonder I was quite good at the subject in school. Games like that are good for reasoning and logic.

Back to Halong Bay. I sat there a bit bemused, smoked my cigarette and then headed into the sea with the early rise of the sun. I swam for a good forty minutes or so. It was so peaceful and I couldn't hear a thing. Probably because I was away from everyone and doing my own thing. Being mindful and focused on the moment I was in.

The boat trip back to Hanoi is where it started to hit home. Everyone was drinking and there was loud music on the boat. I was downstairs on the boat trying to get some sleep. I reckon it must have been seven nights sleep deprivation at this stage, so I was trying to have a bit of sense so I could enjoy the rest of the trip. Claire kept coming down and she could see I was in a bit of distress, but she kept turning the music up louder and didn't bother coming over to see if I was OK. We got off the boat and waited for ages for the bus. I remember Ben turning around to me and pointing to the bus, but he didn't know what was going on in my head. I was simply over tired and wanted more water, but the shop was closed.

The bus is the part where I didn't know what the hell was going on and voices started to really kick off. It was very faint voices of guys on the bus scrunching up their nose as if to say I smelled. This was going on for about an hour. I'd look around, and most of the lads were awake. I'd then look back at my group down the back of the bus, but they were all passed out because they were taking Valium and Xanax to sleep throughout the trip and help with any anxiety they had. I was the only one not taking these drugs and had never heard about them until the trip. I don't suffer from anxiety or sleep problems generally so didn't bother taking anything.

After about an hour, I heard the girl behind me saying, "Yeah she smells of pee."

I looked around and she was awake but I didn't know why the fuck she was saying it. At this point I started getting paranoid and I could actually smell pee off me. I was wondering how did this happen. I showered in my bikini at Halong Bay and borrowed some toiletries while I was there, so I started thinking I was unhygienic. I started thinking that this girl was a bitch. Especially since the nice blonde girls that were travelling with her, told me that she cheats on her boyfriend back home all of the time. She, was in fact, the girl that didn't mind being called a slut banger, while the other two nice blonde chicks did. I was talking to the blonde girls quite a bit in Halong Bay and we all got on very well and we added each other on Facebook, but I'm not friends with the bitch who cheats.

Eventually we got back to the hostel, and I apologised to the bus driver for thinking I had wrecked his seat. I had tears in my eyes at this stage because I was so paranoid that everyone was talking about me. The group of us headed upstairs, and Pa brought me into a new room and said, "Freshen up Guiney, have a shower and come back and meet us."

I did that, and then when I came out of the shower I was paranoid there were cameras everywhere and that the TV had a camera in it and could see me naked in my room. I quickly threw my towel back on. I sat in front of the TV on my own and it was saying "Britney beers." I started thinking what the fuck, I know I like beer and I've been told I look like Britney Spears before but how on earth is the TV talking to me now. At that point, Pa came back in and ripped the cord out of the TV and said, "No cameras Mare, you're starting to freak me out."

He reassured me, so I got dressed and headed back to the balcony where everyone was.

At this point, I kept smiling to myself because I was glad that the bus part was over and that it was just a blip of paranoia. It was tough to get on with things myself though, as everyone was concerned and more or less staring at me and kept asking was I OK. This was only making shit worse. I kept saying I was fine, and that I wanted to get on with things.

I had some food in the hostel and laughed away at some of the Vietnamese workers who had t-shirts saying, "Same same but different." They were walking around with slutty short skirts on and the t-shirts. I was thinking in my head who is copying who, and where is this same same but different logo coming from. Anytime I would say something to friends about rock climbing or rowing they would respond with a "same" remark, even though they had never rowed in their life. I knew the Vietnamese liked me and I kept having to auto correct them and say that I was Irish. I've been confused a few times before for having a thick American accent. I don't give a shit about that.

That night was the night before we were due to head to Laos, and people started getting worried because I still hadn't slept. I felt grand in the hostel though and was happy out to continue the holiday. Sara and Rebecca made me feel very relaxed. The experience I was having at this stage was a very positive one where I was enjoying myself, but in a lot of instances people can have negative psychosis where others are unsure if they are going to harm themselves or not. I've heard of stories where people can have an extremely negative psychotic episode where they think groups are after them with shotguns and want them dead. It seems to affect 3% of the population and can generally be quite a frightening experience.

While in the hostel, anytime I went up to pay for water, I could hear "Vietnamese ding dong" and I splashed out the cash I had. At one point I was making my way back up to my room, and another girl staying in the hostel turned around to me and asked, "Is Martin the loud one in your group? We could all here him come in."

I smiled back and said, "Ah yeah we're a loud enough bunch."

I started thinking at this point, that there was some running joke going on in the hostel. The elevator got to my floor and I hopped out. The Vietnamese workers and the lady were laughing at me and I shouted back, "Great trip, I love the hustle and bustle of this crazy city."

That night, without me knowing, one of the lads spiked my water bottle with a Valium in the hope that I would sleep. I did go to sleep that night but apparently I was saying a load of weird shit in my sleep which I don't remember. I hopped out of bed and straight away put on Burkie's grey tracksuit pants as I started getting paranoid about cameras again. I tried to chill outside and enjoy a smoke with Sara. At that point, a random Vietnamese dude, no more than twenty years of age came up to me and high fived me in the middle of the street. Sara and I laughed and she said, "Go Guiney." I liked chatting to Sara at this point, because she made me feel comfortable and she was just getting on with having fun on the holiday.

Chapter 2

The Death Trap

Six of the crew headed off to Laos the next day, and Martin and Alice decided to stay on in Hanoi to take me to the hospital. "Does she have any Dublin friends?", I heard a voice say, as we were lounging around the hostel. I just shrugged this off and knew that it was untrue, as I have a tonne of friends from all over the world, Dublin especially. I wanted to roam in and out of clothing stores and hand my laundry into the laundrettes, but Alice kept following me around so I felt like I had no freedom at all to do anything on my own. All of the clothes stores were right next to the hostel so I was a bit bemused as to why I couldn't just venture in there alone and buy things for myself.

Later that night, they decided to take me to the hospital. We passed an internet cafe and I saw a bunch of Vietnamese men pissing themselves laughing at a load of computer screens. I started thinking in my head *wow that's cool, they can read my mind and they're having fun inside of it.*

After about ten minutes we got to the French hospital. Martin went into a private room to speak to a doctor and then came out with a crutch. He was hopping around on the crutch and explained to me that he had to cut the holiday short as his toe was infected. He had stood on coral out in Halong bay. "Will you get on an emergency flight back with me Mary?", he asked.

— 21 —

I refused to get on a flight home with him, as I started to have a spiritual connection with the Vietnamese and I felt like they wanted to keep me in the country.

After about twenty minutes, Martin sent me in to see a psychiatrist. I didn't realise she was a psychiatrist at the time, as Martin wanted to keep that hidden from me. He thought I would freak out if I knew I was having psychosis. I remember being in the room with her, and she asked me to draw out a list of our group travelling in order of importance. I listed everyone out and had to draw a bubble to represent how much each of them meant to me. At the end of this she said, "That's only eight people, where do you come?"

I laughed and said, "I completely forgot about myself."

She gave me a smile and a shrug as if to say, that's part of the problem. I wasn't putting myself first on the holiday, but it was difficult to, as I prefer to travel solo, so I have the freedom to do my own thing and meet new people.

She told Martin that there was nothing they could do for me in that hospital, so she recommended a different one. The three of us went from one end of Hanoi to another, in the middle of the night. I was in the middle of them in the taxi and I felt like the radio was talking to me. I could hear boys voices saying, "Keep this going, it's hilarious", and then a girl saying, "This is so unfair, she can't handle this."

I could then hear more boy's voices saying, "No it's like a horror movie, keep it going."

I was trying to ignore this and kept my I pod in. I had David Gray playing at this point, but it wasn't helping drown out the noise from the radio. At one point, I thought the boys from the radio were telling us to turn around because the place we were heading was not very safe. I asked the taxi driver to stop. He pulled in at the side of the road. I pushed Martin out of the taxi, and then jumped out myself. I was crying hysterically at this stage. Martin tried to reassure me, and explained that we had to get back into the taxi. We were in the middle of nowhere at this stage.

I could see Martin and Alice getting extremely worried at this point, but couldn't for the life of me explain what was going on. We got to the hospital eventually, and I handed Martin my passport, but made sure to keep my I pod. It was the craziest hospital and I wasn't sure what was going to happen to me as it looked more like a prison in the middle of a field. It was pitch black.

Martin and Alice headed off back to the hostel and I was left in the middle of the prison type place not having a clue where I was. There were two Vietnamese dudes, just drinking a few beers and having some smokes. They had no English. I was left sitting in a chair with prison gates surrounding me. I was wondering what the men were going to do to me.

I saw a sign on the wall which looked like a lethal injection. I felt a little bit reassured and assumed that they were going to remove a micro chip from my brain.

The men knew I was in a bit of a panic state, so they handed me some smokes and a beer to calm me down. I sat there pensive for a while and pointed to the injection on the wall and then pointed to my brain. I thought there was a micro chip in my brain so I started giving them the hint to remove it. "They can see through my eyes", I heard again, as I was sitting on the chair. I had heard this when I was in the hostel just after going to the loo, and I was wondering who on earth can see through my eyes.

The Vietnamese didn't know what I was on about, when I pointed to the picture of the injection on the wall, so I chilled in a chair and listened to my I pod and reflected on my life. I thought back to my finance masters and the strategic management course that I did. I remember our lecturer saying that some day soon, technology will be so advanced, that they will put micro chips into our brains. Essentially people will walk into pubs and shops, and they will simply scan their hands over a device, which will take money out from their bank accounts.

It started making sense to me. I reflected a bit on the holiday, and quite often I was being asked by people I was travelling with, could I lend them more money. I'm generous and good at dishing out money but I only worked for a bank, I wasn't a bank. I was sick of transferring money to people in London every weekend. I was paid well in JP Morgan to build up a little bit of savings but nowhere near what the equities guys would get, but I was happy with the amount I was earning and the success I made for myself through my own education. I sat there and reflected more.

About an hour later, they opened more gates and brought me into this square patched field which had separate rooms bordering it. Each room looked like a prison cell, metal gate type doors. They brought me into my cell and put a mosquito net over me when I went to sleep. Whatever drugs they gave me, they seemed to work. I slept like a log that night.

I woke up to a Vietnamese nurse who pointed to say fully clothed. I nodded and gave the thumbs up. I was wearing a black one piece, so I knew I wasn't attacked, plus they had separate locks for each of the doors.

The next day, Martin and Alice arrived and insisted that I show the doctors and nurses my malarone tablets, as they were convinced it was these that caused me to go psychotic. The nurses didn't seem to agree. I think the nurses assumed that I had been taking drugs on the trip, but Martin kept arguing back at them to say that I wasn't.

At this point it was decided to phone my family and get them involved. Being a whiz kid with numbers, I had all of my siblings and parents numbers off by heart. I was throwing out the numbers from memory.

I was left on my own that day in the sweltering heat. At one point, while I was in my cell, another Vietnamese male patient came over to my cell. I was listening to my I pod at that time and he stared at me with a stereo on his shoulder, as if to exchange the two. I wasn't quite sure what was going on. He passed in the stereo through the gate type door and I handed him my I pod. He then handed me some tiger balm in exchange and attempted to give me a neck massage through the gates. This man was quite emaciated looking and I wasn't quite sure why he was in hospital. I used some of the tiger balm on

Vietnamese Voices

my temples to try and relax, but voices seemed to be getting louder, and this time it was a female voice following me around. I might have put two and two together and thought that it was the Irish Embassy that were talking to me through the cell, as they were involved with looking after me at this stage.

Later that day, I came out from my cell, and wandered around the small hospital square in the immense humidity. They brought food out at lunch time. I wasn't quite sure what it was – just buckets of grub where each patient would dig their hand in and help themselves. I wasn't sure what was going on but was still paranoid about cameras being everywhere. At one point, I started thinking that there were cameras in each of the cells. As I sat there, eating my food, I just eyed up each of the patients and they all stared at me. I started thinking that other patient's were looking at cameras of me, while I was in my cell. I couldn't communicate with any of them as none of them had a word of English.

Bored out of my head, I wandered around the hospital looking into each cell to see where the rest of the patients were. After two rounds of this, I got extremely bored and was fed up of being banged up abroad. I screamed out loudly and threw my bag and flip flops onto the ground. I tried to escape at this point, but was armed down by three Vietnamese men.

Another nurse at this point, seemed quite worried and came over to me. She had a bit of English. She spoke about moving me to the French hospital, where her father would look after me. She assured me that I had to trust her, and that I would be looked after better there. I was starting to go mad as I felt like I was being locked away for no reason, so I agreed to move hospitals. My two buddies came back the next day, and we all headed off in an ambulance to the French hospital in the centre of Hanoi.

I was showed to my room which was more along the lines of a Western hospital. It had a nice bed and an en suite. There was a phone beside me so I was happy. I would ring the hostel in my "high" state to see was everyone having good banter back there, because I sure as

— 25 —

hell was. At this stage, I felt very relaxed, because I was freed from the first hospital.

Mum phoned later. "Mary, your father and I are going to come over to see how you're doing, how is everything your end in the hospital?"

"I'm grand Mum, just in the hostel enjoying myself, no need to fly over, I know the distance is too long for you."

"OK Mary take care, I'll send Daniel to you."

We hung up the phone, and I was happy that I reassured my mum that all was fine. The last communication I had with her was emailing her from Vietnamese backpackers to say, "Holiday going great, we're all doing fine."

I kept on going outside of the hospital, to sit on the steps and have a smoke. I was trying to communicate with the voices I was hearing. I started getting a spiritual connection with one of them again, and I felt as though God was speaking to me. It was very reassuring. I felt like it was the most mind blowing experience ever.

I had fun with some of the Vietnamese nurses, who allowed me to more or less wander the hospital and go on Facebook at their computers whenever I felt like it. I started looking up posts from Mark Zuckerberg and then started googling facts about mind reading. Being online, however sparked worry in Alice, as she would see from the hostel that I was online. This provoked her to come straight back over to the hospital, to make sure I was sedated and back asleep. While I was in the bathroom, I could hear someone say, "She's trying to puke her tablets up."

I shouted out, "I cannot puke them up."

The next day, I had the arrival of my brother Daniel and brother in Law. I was delighted to see them. Daniel and Jerry had flown on last minute flights from Dublin to Hanoi, to take me back home. They had booked into a nice hotel down the road, but decided to stay in the hospital room with me and get some sleep on two chairs. Daniel looked particularly worried. I started going into the bathroom, or slightly away from them, and I would look up and start communicating with the voices. At this point, I thought I was talking to Sara, who had gone up to Laos already.

"Mary, chill out, the exact same thing is happening up here. We're going through the same thing in Laos", I heard her say faintly.

I nodded, and then went back to speak to my brother.

The doctor came in, and handed Daniel a bill for the hospital. I ripped it up, and told Daniel that there was nothing wrong with me. "He's similar to doctor Giggles in that movie Daniel, he's just acting", I said to my brother.

Daniel nodded in confusion. He wasn't quite sure what was going on, and thought like the rest of my buddies that I had a bad reaction to the malarone.

"She's about to hit the red carpet", I heard loudly when I left the room to get some water. At this point, I was overly elated, as I thought that the joke was over, and that everyone from the trip was around the corner and clapping with me for putting up with the joke for so long. As I turned the corner, there was no red carpet. I couldn't see anyone from the hostel either. I looked up at the Vietnamese nurses at their computers, and they kept smiling at me.

Shortly after this, I was convinced that Craig was about to come visit me with a big bunch of flowers. But he never arrived.

It was time for my brother in law to get booking a flight back for the three of us to Dublin. The whole experience was starting to scare them a bit, and they felt like I would get better treatment back in Dublin. My parents also wanted me back pretty urgently to make sure everything was OK. Three tickets were booked last minute, and the three of us headed back to the hostel to get my rucksack. I was still quite smily and laughing all of the time, as the experience in my head was a positive one. I was glad that I was away from the prison type place.

I wasn't quite sure who or why people were talking to me, but I switched it all into a positive experience so as not to scare myself.

"Where are your things?", Daniel asked when we got to the hostel.

"Oh the room that Martin is in, just upstairs, let's all head up and get my rucksack."

We all headed upstairs and I saw a bottle of vodka in their room. I went to take the vodka, because at this stage I thought I just needed to black out on the trip to remove any micro chip or mind reading that was going on. Martin quickly grabbed the bottle off me.

"Jesus, your brother will think we're lunatics Mary."

I laughed back at him and said, "enjoy the rest of the trip lads."

It was when we got to the airport, that I could see Daniel had a bit of urgency about him. He was worried we were about to miss our flight. I felt like the monitors and radios around the airport were communicating with me.

"You're gate is this way", a kind Vietnamese air stewardess said with a big smile.

I smiled back and the three of us headed off for our flight.

We had to firstly get a connecting flight to Bangkok. Daniel and I had a smoke in Bangkok airport, and I tried to reassure him that all was OK. I told him that he was the best for coming out to get me. "I have your name plastered on my ankle in Thai", I uttered.

He felt a bit more relaxed at this stage and was happy that we were away from Hanoi and we were finally en route home.

"Jesus, Mary that city would make anyone go mad with all the beep beep and craziness of it." "That's definitely not it Daniel, I can handle the craziness, I'll get to the bottom of this", I remarked.

On the second flight back, Jerry handed me a load of drugs and sleeping pills. I more or less passed out for the entire flight home. When I got home, my parents were quite worried, especially my mum. She had a smile on her face when I showed her my Daniel tattoo, however. She was touched that I got her father's and son's name tattooed on my ankle.

My sister had her psychiatrist friend at the house. I burst out crying as I explained about the trip back from Halong bay. They took me into Vincent's hospital straight away for a check up. After about three hours, we got seen to.

"Can I check your bag Mary?", one of the nurses asked.

She pulled out my pyjamas, moisturiser, toothbrush, shampoo and razor and she ticked everything off one by one.

"Give me that", my mum said looking horrified at the razor. I think all of the communication back and forth between friends and family had made my mum so paranoid that I was going to harm myself.

"Mum, I'm literally packed in preparation to stay over night in Vincent's, you know I would never do anything to harm myself." I reassured her and she gave me back the razor.

In Vincent's general hospital, there was nothing much they could do for me, so they referred me to Cluain Mhuire mental health clinic. I stayed the night at home and went in to see a psychiatrist the next day. He listened to me for about fifteen minutes, and then decided to prescribe a course of Haloperidol, which is a first generation anti-psychotic. In the meantime, the psychiatrist spoke to friends who were on the trip with me and they assured him that I wasn't taking drugs on the trip, just malarone.

About a week later, after seeing the psychiatrist, he wanted to have a meeting with my mum and Dad, which I was obliging to. He brought up the seriousness of taking drugs, which I had already mentioned I wasn't going near, and he also brought up the fact that I was taking Larium. I reminded him that it was malarone that I was taking, so he obviously wasn't writing down correctly the antimalarials that I was taking. Luckily, I do know that CCTV is in every room in hospitals and clinics that we walk into and if anyone wants the truth of this story out then maybe we will be able to tap into IT intelligence and make a movie about this to highlight the seriousness of mental health.

This psychiatrist had gotten all of his facts wrong from what he was told.

Malarone is known to have very little side effects, and only 1% of people taking the medication will experience psychosis. Larium, the cheaper form of the drug, is known to have a higher incidence of psychotic tendencies.

When my parents and I left, my mum laughed at me and said, "the cheek of him bringing up drugs and not writing down correctly what you told him. The bugger wasn't listening to you. I trust you Mary."

He didn't listen very much, he only prescribed Haloperidol in a very high dose to me to take for eighteen months, with check ups every month. The psychiatrist did not list off any of the nasty side effects of the drug that I was going to experience over the next few months either. Haloperidol causes heart problems, huge amounts of weight gain, diabetes and is also known to cause tardive dyskinesia, as it hugely lowers the dopamine levels in the brain. This can lead to Parkinson's disease in some people as dopamine can get lowered to an unsafe level. I never looked any of this up at the time and just assumed that the psychiatrist knew what he was doing. It is unfortunate however, that they do not list these side effects off, as it should be made known to the individual what risk they are taking on from taking the drugs.

Chapter 3

Corfu

Mum, Dad and I needed a break from the stress of it all, so we headed up to Johnnie Foxes for a glass of wine. We were silent in the car journey home. I then spoke out. "Mum, I need to see a priest about this, those doctors don't have a clue here."

"Mary, no priest is ever going to understand your story, you're just going to have to get on with it. Write down your experience girl. You were a whiz kid at Mavis Beacon, so I know you are a fast typer."

I sat there silently and absorbed every word my mum said.

Over the next month, I found myself sleeping roughly twenty hours a day, and eating a massive 4,000 plus calories a day, with huge cravings for chocolate and refined carbohydrate. Being massively into running and cycling, I tried to fight the weight gain by continuing to exercise but much less capable than I had been pre-Vietnam. My cycles were only five or six miles and short three mile runs. I tried to keep up this routine, but became more and more lethargic as the time went on. Within five weeks, around mid October 2012, I had shot up on the scales from nine stone to ten stone five pounds. I felt like there was nothing I could do to control it, as I was advised not to go back to work so I was just extremely bored sitting at home.

I kept saying to the psychiatrist, that I still wanted to run in the Royal Parks Half Marathon in London in October. I had raised money for breast cancer care. He didn't think it was a great idea, but

I knew that I would get my mind into driving gear and just run it. I had done all of the training before the holiday. I flew over to London to go back to work early in October, and decided to run the half marathon. I successfully completed it in two hours and five minutes, which was a lot slower than the one hour and fifty minutes I had anticipated. However, I managed to complete it drugged up heavily on the medication.

"I wish I was in Vietnam with you babe", my house mate Emily remarked one evening.

"I know, I'm not sure it would have made any difference though", I replied.

We both went silent and she told me that it was my own experience, and I can't ignore the elephant in the room. I replied by saying that I was an elephant as I had recalled everything that had happened with my sharp memory.

One evening, Martin said, "Oh Mary, Ben is asking for you, he was really worried, I'll let him know you're OK now."

"What's his surname Martin? I'll try add him on Facebook."

I looked for him on Facebook quickly, but couldn't find him. I shrugged this off and headed to my room. For some reason, I thought that Ben might have had a better idea as to what had happened to me, as he was in charge of our trip out to Halong bay. I was also still a little bit confused about the experience, and wasn't sure whether there was a running joke going on with the Vietnamese.

I worked for three weeks in JP Morgan, but then started to suffer a massive low. It is known that post-psychotic depression is quite common after psychosis, as I was on an extreme high in Vietnam. "I'm starting to feel depressed", I said to my psychiatrist over the phone from work.

"Yes, post-psychotic depression is common", he replied.

He then advised that I could get a prescription for an anti-depressant. Seeing as my mum had told me that it took her fifteen years to find an anti-depressant that suited her, I didn't bother getting one. That was the end of that conversation and I hung up the phone, and went back to my desk. I have come to realise what isn't noted on anti-psychotics and anti-depressants in Ireland, is a side effect of depression from taking the medication. It is however listed as a side effect in the UK.

My boss in work even said to me that I wasn't the bubbly Mary that she knew around the office.

In work, I had less jobs to do, and found myself roaming to the vending machine every hour to fulfil my chocolate cravings. Canary Wharf also has a great selection of restaurants and deli's, so on some days that I was working late, I would get two large burritos and at this stage I had stopped cycling or running home from work. I was nervous going in to tell my boss that I needed to take November off from work to go back to Dublin and spend time with my mum. She was more than obliging, and knew that I wasn't myself.

I weighed myself when I got back to Dublin and it was the last week in October and I had gained a massive twenty pounds of pure fat since Vietnam. A woman who has a huge appetite managed to put on some amount of weight in such a short space of time. The tablets made me depressed, as it would any woman who felt unattractive and lost her bubbly personality. I had to just deal with it, and luckily at the time, I had a legendary mother to come home to.

At this stage, I had written a book describing step by step what had happened to me in Vietnam. It was about thirty pages long, and described what happened from the flight over, to the point in Halong Bay. I gave it to my mum to read. It had listed names of my friends and people who were taking Valium, Xanax and street drugs. She read it in delight, and encouraged me to keep writing. At this point, however, I was starting to lose complete motivation and lost pleasure in doing anything. I was lethargic, still getting on my bike but not to the same level.

Instead, I used to ask my mum to drive up to the shop to get me super noodles. I used to lace them in cheese and eat copious amounts of shitty refined carbohydrate, chocolate and not burn a single calorie off. I turned into a slob. I was literally binging on food to a disgusting level. My mum looked so worried, as to how much I could eat in one sitting. I think she was wondering what sort of heavy duty drug I was taking. I couldn't even stomach fruit or vegetables for ages, as I had no desire to eat healthy food. It's no wonder that diabetes is a side effect of the medication as well.

It was at this point, I started googling diets and I came to realise that there was 3,500 calories in a pound of fat. I thought, wow, a lot of work to go for me.

"Mary you need to look after your self-image more", my dad remarked when we were in the car one day. "It's very important to put more effort in and wear nice clothes to feel good about yourself."

I just shrugged and said, "tracksuit bottoms will do me."

All I wanted to wear at the time was baggy tracksuit bottoms and a hoodie. I didn't feel attractive, so I gave up on tight or glamorous clothes. I didn't bother wearing any make up for months. I also stopped going out with my friends. I went out the odd night, if I had the energy to, but I didn't get much pleasure from it as I was dealing with depression. I also felt quite restless when talking in a group, and couldn't hack listening to a conversation for more than five minutes.

By about mid November, I stopped gaining weight and remained around ten stone seven pounds. I recalled in my head that the only time I was a bit heavier was in third year in college. I was rowing at the time and doing a lot of weight training. We were encouraged to eat carbohydrates like they were going out of fashion. "Quinoa is the best carbohydrate source for you girls, and it's packed full of protein", I still remember our coach saying.

Unfortunately, I was also eating chips and curry sauce like it was going out of fashion after a night on the tiles. That summer, after champs, I moved home from Galway and worked in a restaurant as a summer job. I dropped the weight in an instant. When I came back to NUI Galway for final year there were rumours going around that I had gotten a boob job. I just laughed it off and was happy that none of the weight fell off my boobs.

My metabolism was a lot higher post-Vietnam, as I had put on so much fat by that stage. At this point I had a few more meetings to go to before going back to work and one of the nurses recommended that I get a brain scan done. I was delighted. Yay, open myself up to science and see what is going on with my mush mash grey matter. I'm still waiting for a fucking brain scan after reminding them this year. Three and a half years, and healthcare in Ireland couldn't fix your elbow let alone your brain.

December 5th came, and I knew I was ready to take on London again. I headed back over as miserable as shit, but knew that the distraction of work would help. My mum was proud that I wanted to get back into the swing of things so soon after Vietnam. I thought this time, I was ready and would just have to stick it out no matter if I felt low or not. I was home two weeks later for Christmas. My colleague at the time was class, he used to always give me Christmas time off as he didn't mind working it. Looking back now, I almost wish I had worked over Christmas. It was a second rubbish Christmas for me. I was at the stage now where I was trying to desperately lose the weight I had gained, but of course so many temptations were around. I just ate the shit food and didn't bother going out much as I was still on a low. On a positive note, my energy was coming back slightly. I didn't bother exercising much over Christmas. I promised myself that I would get back into it from January. I didn't have long at home, just a week or so, and then I went straight back into Canary Wharf at the end of December.

By this stage, I had decided to move out of the five bed house I was living in in London, as I needed more space on my own. I rented a one bed apartment for myself in Battersea. It was expensive but worth it, as I had more freedom to myself. I was back cycling on my trek the nine miles in and out of work, doing a lot of walking and three runs mostly at the weekends around Battersea park. The most strenuous part of the cycle was carrying that heavy lump of a bike three flights up the stairs to land it outside my door. Looking back now, I would never cycle on a hybrid again. I have a new boyfriend. My specialized road bike which I'm in love with and I'll get more to that later.

I couldn't manage to lose any weight as I still had a massive appetite for burritos and chocolate, but at least I was building my fitness back up. I was back into a structured routine and going out with my friends in London. I was a bit happier. However, exercise and nights out just didn't feel the same as they did before Vietnam. I almost felt like I had to force myself to engage in those activities.

I had my own apartment, so I could just chill in the evenings, watch shitty soaps and go for runs when I wanted to. I used to stock up my fridge and cupboards with plenty of nutritious food and treats. I also took back up yoga in Clapham Common, so that was another thing I could cycle to after work.

One evening, when I cycled to yoga, one of those annoying dudes outside the station was eyeing me up and shouting "hey pretty". I threw him daggers, because at that stage I wanted to chuck my bike at someone, as I was finding it much more tedious to cycle. I didn't seem to get the same endorphin kick out of cycling. I locked up my bike and headed off to yoga in a rage.

Sure enough, my wheel was robbed when I came back out. I knew it was because I wasn't happy go lucky back at that dude and he probably did it or coaxed someone else to rob it. I thought fair enough, I was ignorant back to him for calling me pretty. I had to carry that piece of shit on a bus back to my apartment. I got the wheel replaced about a week later, as I tested out the running lark into work more.

At this point, I decided it was time for a colonic irrigation. I had eaten so much crap, so I decided I needed to clean out my bowels. I had heard that Elvis died with twenty pounds of crap in his intestine. I needed to clear out the rubbish.

"This is quite satisfying", I said to the lady as I watched my colon being emptied into a tube.

"Yeah they're becoming more and more popular."

We got to talking about diet then.

"I have a very healthy diet normally and my mum would be a firm believer that the body self cleanses and we don't need colonics if we follow a good enough diet, but I am drugged up on medication which makes me crave shit food."

"Each to their own", she replied.

"What is your opinion on chia seeds?", she then asked.

"Oh I love them, I sprinkle them all over my porridge, they're excellent for endurance sport and full of omega 3s. I use them a lot for long distance running and learned about them in the book 'Born to Run'."

She replied, "Wow, that good but they're quite fattening aren't they?"

"Ha, not fattening", I said, "They have a lot of calories but calorie counting is dangerous, you deprive your body when you do it."

It was good to share information again.

February to May felt a little bit better. A colleague next to me was trying all sorts of diets to lose weight for her wedding and I was doing Atkins two days a week and then carbohydrate loading the rest. I wasn't really on any diet. I just can't do it, as I love food too much. I didn't care so much any more as I had my fitness regime back and wanted to become an even better athlete. Triathlons were still on my mind at this stage. I just never got into gear to head off to a fifty meter pool in London.

"There is an opportunity for an employee to take up a role in Sydney, Australia", my manager said to me one day.

"This is a rare opportunity, and I think you would be crazy not to apply Mary."

I started dreaming about travel again. I thought about Australia, and what my mum had said before. "Australia is grand, but there isn't much culture to the place, just sun, sand and sea", she said to me when I was about eighteen, as I was questioning why we had never travelled there before.

I started thinking it would be a good place to get myself settled for a while, and enjoy the beach every day after work, as I felt I had experienced London enough. The only off putting thing for me would be the big spiders. "Spiders are a sign of luck", my mum used to say to me. Anytime I saw a large black widow in my bedroom, I used to get my mum or Dad to remove it. I would probably shit my pants if I was faced with an Australian spider staring at me.

"So do you know who got the Sydney job?", I asked a trader one day in the bar.

"Mary I don't have a clue, but I can see you really want it", I just smiled back and sipped my beer. All of the traders were lovely, but they could see that I had a passion for travel, and that I didn't want to stay put in London any more. Three weeks later, I found out that another man on the team got the Sydney job. I just moved on with my current role and kept tipping away.

May came, and my mum decided it was time to go on a holiday to Corfu. Just my mum, Dad, brother and I. I flew in from London and met the other three there. I remember our first meal, I ordered a large Greek salad by the pool, while the other three had three large burgers. I was happy out. I love Greek salads, plus I'm not a massive burger person. I mentioned to my mum and Dad that I had just come off my medication, Haloperidol fat pills that is, as I was back to myself and wanted to shift the weight I had gained. They thought fair enough, and knew I was back to myself on that trip.

The trip was fine, but I noticed my mum smoking the electronic cigarette, so I thought to myself there was something wrong there. I kept asking her why she wasn't smoking any more. She used to have the odd one or two with me but mostly the electronic. She told me nothing was wrong, but I knew she was lying to me. I also noticed she was quite out of breath climbing the hills on that holiday. Anyway, Mum and I both being best buddies, were always quite silent with each other when it came to worrying the other person. She wasn't herself on that holiday, and started to develop a dry cough. Of course, I put two and two together, and lung cancer screamed out at me. None of us mentioned anything, and carried on with enjoying the holiday.

The restaurants were great there. Parmigiana with feta cheese, meatballs in tomato sauce, pasta and plenty of seafood. It was nice to be enjoying some relaxing time with family. I remember going to one of the bars on the strip with Mum and Dad. They weren't mad about those bars as the music can be too loud, so there were no late nights. We just had some nice beers and the odd cocktail each night after dinner.

Mum bought me a nice pair of gold Havaianas on that trip with a little diamonte on them.

Mum went to bed early one of the nights, so it was just me and Dad in the hotel bar.

"I really want to travel the world, and visit every country out there", I grunted.

He smirked and said, "You won't be going to Afghanistan that's for sure."

"I want to be the best athlete I can, and run around the globe with a little back pack, and meet so many more people in life", I replied.

"You can't run around the globe Mary", he said in confusion.

Dad used to row for Neptune back in his day, but he packed it in quickly, as he hated the running training. I, on the other hand love all forms of exercise and think that we were all "born to run". This was a book that was recommended to me by a colleague in JP Morgan. It discusses the Tarahumara tribe of north western Mexico who love to eat chia seeds for endurance running. I was on a high again with the adventure planned in my head. Life is too short.

Chapter 4

The Wacky Diet

Back to London I went after a week off, and I was clearly worried about my mum. When I got home in the evenings after work, I looked up the signs of lung cancer and sure enough lethargy and a dry cough came up. It only made sense, seeing as my mum smoked for over forty five years. She had an extremely healthy diet all the way up in life, very balanced, nothing eliminated but healthy foods and treats every now and again. Something remarkable for a woman that was born the youngest of twelve kids, and never had a mother of her own, as Gretta Grogan passed away giving birth to my mum. She learned all of her culinary skills from Auntie Mary, who acted as her mother figure, and was twenty years her senior.

Unfortunately my mum was put on anti-depressants at the age of forty six, and slowly but surely her cravings for sugar got bigger, and she gained weight gradually as she ate more refined foods. I understand all of this now, seeing as the drugs did the exact same thing to me.

The more I was googling, the more worried I was getting. I was on the phone back and forth to my dad every day. He would tell me that Mum was in bed, and that they're still seeing doctors, but that no diagnosis had been given.

At this point, Claire was talking about a trip to Thailand in August, and I just booked away without thinking about anything. I knew I would need escape at some point.

"You're not seriously going to Thailand with Claire?", Rory asked me in the pub one evening. "Yeah, sure look Rory lightning never strikes twice in the same spot, nothing bad will happen." "Seriously Mary, make sure you'll be OK, I don't trust the two of you going together, she's not going to look out for you if anything goes wrong."

I just smirked at him and had a sip of my beer.

It got towards the end of June, and I was getting impatient about my mum not having any diagnosis. I went online and booked a one way flight back to Dublin. I mentioned to my boss, that I needed a few days at home, and she was fine about it. I booked a flight back for the 25th of June. Sure enough, the day I arrived home, was the day my parents got back from the doctor, and the diagnosis of lung cancer had been given. This was even worse news for my parents, as it was their wedding anniversary. I didn't know what to say.

My sister gave my dad a big hug, and I just listened to my mum give out about chemotherapy and having to go through it, as she had seen several siblings pass away from cancer or diabetes, and one in particular where chemotherapy did absolutely nothing for pancreatic cancer. Chemotherapy can be good in cases of breast cancer but for the vigorous kinds like bowel, pancreatic and lung cancer it has very little help.

I listened, said nothing and headed out into my back yard for a smoke. I thought what the fuck am I going to do about this. I knew from watching the movie the Stepmom, that weed was good for cancer patients. It also chilled them out and made them forget their worries. It is also known to be an anti-inflammatory, a muscle relaxant, a pain killer and a natural steroid to open up the lungs. I had weed on my mind instead of chemotherapy. It is also known to boost someone's appetite, so I preferred to think of a natural plant boosting her appetite rather than nasty steroids. I came back inside, and Mum went back to bed.

The next day, my dad took out barbecue spare ribs from the fridge. "Who are you giving them to?", I asked.

"Dinner for everyone", he remarked in confusion.

"You can eat them but by no means is Mum", I said with a frank looking face.

Bless him. I didn't realise, but Mum was eating barbecue spare ribs and crap for a while. Easy things which were stress free and can be thrown into the oven. I guess what was my dad supposed to do, he was just as stressed as the time my mum was when he was in Manila or had his five bypasses years later. I thought to myself it's lucky I came home at this point.

For the next six weeks, google was my best friend, and I was going to be pulling all nighters glued to the internet. I bought a carrot juicer and a Vitamix straight away. At least I knew carrot and ginger juices would be great for her health and also green juices and berry smoothies in the Vitamix.

"Mary those carrot and ginger juices are delicious", my mum remarked one day.

"Don't give me too many of those horrible green juices though."

I just laughed it off, "You're having both whether you like it or not."

I also made sure we got plenty of fish, salmon and mackerel in and lots of whole vegetables, fruit and potatoes. Every morning, I juiced my mum freshly squeezed orange juice and brought her down tea, eggs, porridge, berries and toast.

The first thing I learned while googling diet for cancer, was that cancer thrives on sugar. It absolutely loves it. Anything from refined carbohydrates, chocolate and sweets had to go. I thought, only complex carbohydrates and plenty of fruit and vegetables, and mostly fish as the protein source. My mum was getting sick of salmon and mackerel at one point, but I knew it was one of the best as we needed to boost her omega 3s.

There is plenty of research done on cancer which shows that omega 3s are highly beneficial in the diet. In fact, in the Western world, our omega 6:3 ratio is completely skewed. We have tonnes more omega 6 in our body, which comes from a lot of different oils such as plant oils and sunflower oils. It is this imbalance which accelerates cancer growth. So the main aim was to give her plenty of fish, which my mum was used to, as we were brought up to eat fish skin and everything as kids. She spent a lot of money getting nutritious food for us, so we were made eat it all. I remember as a kid, if I didn't like the fish skin, I would back wash it into the milk glass and feed it to the dog. But hey that's just developing an acquired taste for this stuff as a kid. We also got plenty of breaded cod and fish fingers so we could be happy with a good balance.

That was the next thing I googled. Mum would definitely not be having anything breaded, as the breaded fish contains so many trans fats, which again cause a host of problems with any chronic disease. It was easy for me to fix up her diet, as on numerous occasions in London, while at the bank, I had contemplated doing a nutrition masters, as I have a passion for cooking and healthy foods. Now was the time to be looking into a masters, once I got my mum's health back on track.

I found an article online, which was entitled "Eleven natural ways to kill cancer". It was about a 200 page document which I got my brother to print off in work and bring home. There was so much alternative treatments in it, but I understood the bulk of what it was saying, seeing as I have a biochemistry degree. I'm pretty well in tune when it comes to learning about the mechanics of how the cell works. My undergraduate thesis was entitled, "*The Mechanisms of Triplet Repeat DNA mutagenesis*", which explores the reasoning behind neurodegenerative diseases. That's the essence of biochemistry. It's all about molecular biology and the functioning of each of our cells. Every organ, bone and fluid within our bodies are made up of millions of cells.

The two main things I took from this read, was oxygen therapy and deuterium depleted water. I knew at this point, that I couldn't interfere with what our doctors were saying, but I did read that deuterium depleted water can be used in conjunction with chemotherapy to be more potent at killing off cancer cells. Essentially, normal water has a high level of deuterium in it, which is only really good at flushing out toxins in the body, but cannot do anything to destroy cancer cells. Deuterium depleted water, on the other hand, has this molecule extracted during fine dilution processes, and when this molecule is lowered it attaches itself to the cancer cell and destroys it. It works like a positive and negative charge, so it causes a chemical reaction within the body. Say for example this water is negative, and the cancer cell is positive, this allows for an explosion within the cancer cell. Numerous cases have found that the treatment of simply drinking this water, while receiving chemotherapy enhances lifespan greatly. We hadn't gotten to the chemotherapy part yet, but I was doing all of my alternative research along with a good diet.

I found out straight away where I could purchase this water. I knew it was safe, and don't believe in efficacy bullshit when it comes to simply drinking water. This was bookmarked. The next thing was oxygen therapy. I just thought, by simply getting my mum's strength back up, then she could take long walks with me in Marlay Park and that would be a good start.

I had to get a little help with this. My cousin Marian had told me that she saw an article in the daily mail about an eighty year old man from Middlesbrough, who had this wacky diet and cured his incurable colon cancer through his diet, without receiving conventional medicine. I was happy out. It was all the stuff I had researched. Plenty of fruit and vegetables, wheat grass and he cut out red meat, but there was a catch. He was taking apricot kernels. I hadn't heard of these before so I googled it.

Apricot kernels obviously come from a plant, and they're literally just the seed from the fruit, but you need to buy them from a health food store. They contain laetrile, which is present in the apple core, the seeds which everyone throws away. I got the number of this man, who had lost his daughter to cancer and didn't want the same thing for him. There were a few phone calls and emails back and forth between him and I, and he was telling me he was taking forty kernels a day when he was eating the most. I was reading mixed reviews about these kernels, like the food and drug administration saying we can only eat two a day, as they contain cyanide. But if this eighty year old man was eating forty a day and he killed off his cancer then

I thought I'd build my mum up gradually and I'd take them too. She started on five and then over the course of about two months, she built up to a massive sixty. I was eating about twenty a day, and still do as a preventative measure. I buy them from Kernel Power UK as they have the more potent forms. Here is an article I wrote for the Irish Independent two years ago, but they wouldn't publish it for me as it contradicts mainstream therapies.

Laetrile (vitamin B17)

A kernel of truth

Cancer is unheard of in the Hunza Tribe which is on the northwestern border of Pakistan. Huge interest in their diet has therefore mounted in recent years. They follow a very balanced diet with plenty of fruit and vegetables and very little sugar. They are also renowned for grazing on apricot kernels all day long. Hunzas are known for consuming 200 times more nitrilosides than the average American. Nitrilosides are not only present in apricot kernels but also in the seeds of the apple core (which most Westerners tend to throw away). Apricot kernels contain laetrile, also known as vitamin B17 and consuming seven or eight daily is very beneficial in the prevention of a number of chronic diseases. More kernels may be ingested for the treatment of a number of cancers. Western treatments for cancer usually act only as palliative care for the most life threatening forms such as bowel, liver, brain, pancreatic and lung cancer. Laetrile contains one molecule of cyanide and one molecule of benzaldehyde which get activated at the cancer cell due to the presence of the enzyme B – glucosidase. This in turn is believed to destroy the cancer cell. Wealth in the hunza tribe is measured by how many apricot trees they own. The FDA recommend only two a day, however there is plenty of research on the web to promote their use, and Mary Ellen has been consuming twenty a day since her mother got sick by chewing on them slowly and swallowing. She built her tolerance up gradually by having five and then increasing slowly.

Mum still had loads of doctor appointments to go. I remember a conversation between the three of us in her room downstairs and Dad was asking me to hang on and delay work in London for a while.

"Mary has her own life to live Michael", she groaned.

"I'd rather be here, I'll update work after the next doctor trip", I responded.

The next day we headed back into Vincent's hospital. The doctor gave us more bad news and said that the cancer had spread to the liver. My mum and Dad sat there in silence. I started talking about laetrile and deuterium depleted water. She looked at me rudely and asked, "Are you some sort of expert in this field?"

"No", I replied. "But I've done two weeks solid research on alternative cancer treatments with no sleep so I'm just giving my input."

We headed home, and I phoned my boss at JP Morgan straight away and resigned.

I found out that the deuterium depleted water got produced by HYD limited in Budapest, and they call it Preventa. The woman selling the water was very helpful and said that my mum needed to start out on a a level of 105 parts per million (ppm). She then needed to lower down to 85 ppm and then we could order more down the line. I ordered a six week supply of 105 ppm and six week supply of 85 ppm. Mum was doing great. Everything seemed to be working, so pretty soon I was ordering lower levels of deuterium down to the point of 45ppm.

Now this water is expensive; a two litre bottle is ten euro, but it was worth it. Something that should be on the Irish Health Care system but sure this country is as backward as a cow's arse. Health care is an absolute joke. I could bang on about the Irish government right now but that's going off track. At least I have a caricature painting at home that I bought my dad for Christmas of four politicians heads on cow's bodies. Enda Kenney is one, Mary Lou Mc Donald, Claire Daly and Mick Wallace are the other three. They try, but they have a very odd sense of showing that they care for this country.

"Wow, I thought you were going to be some wacky mad woman with a bag of cats", the caricaturist said when I came to his door.

I just laughed, strolled in and picked up the painting. €400 for the painting or €100 per cow. It was worth it. Anyway back to my story.

Before any chemotherapy was decided, I was doing more research. Mum was doing good. She was out of bed, going for short walks, drinking carrot and ginger juices, green juices, freshly squeezed orange juice, berry smoothies, lots of white fish, risotto, salmon and spuds, plates of bell peppers, radishes, tomatoes and broccoli. I knew she had to eat a good diet but I wouldn't allow her sweets. Just dark chocolate and a glass of red wine to chill out in the evening. This also suited me down to the ground, as I wanted to shift the dumb ass weight from the retarded tablets a doctor prescribed me back here for psychosis. Not only do they cause weight gain but I had to get ECGs, blood tests and blood pressure taken all of the time, because they affect your heart in a bad way. They also are known to cause locked jaw and a host of other problems, but I found out in John of God's this year from another patient that chocolate helps prevent locked jaw. It's no wonder I was eating five bars a day. Looking back, I am happy I was listening to my body's cravings rather than end up with something more serious.

The next thing I researched was the Oasis of Hope. I read that lung cancer survival rates over there were 50% chance of survival after three years. While here, with chemotherapy it is 1%. I thought bullshit to chemotherapy for lung cancer, it doesn't fucking work. I got on the phone to this clinic and was back and forth with them about putting my mum on a plane. I think her head was a little wrecked, as the oncologists here were advising the chemotherapy route. I forgot about the Oasis of Hope, but found out from a friend's mother about a herbalist and naturopath in Dublin who is excellent at giving nutrition advice. His name is John Doran, and he was brilliant.

Mum and I went to see him twice, and she could see that we shared a similar passion. I was telling him things he didn't know and he was giving me articles on lung cancer survival rates on salvestrols and omega 3 to 6 balance and all this jazz. He advised not to give Mum the salvestrols however, as I was already giving her laetrile. He also wanted to advise me on a dietetics course for myself but that was at the back of my mind. I was only focused on my mum's health. College and work are the least important things in life when someone dear to you is that ill. I read all of the articles and I was pleased. I was doing everything right and he advised again that sugar was the big NO NO. He also gave me advice on Chinese herbs such as astragalus and high dose of vitamin C and vitamin D3. I got everything he said and made sure my mum took them. Her immunity and strength was building back up before any western cancer treatment was administered.

John Doran also put me in touch with Dr. Ralph Moss in the States, and I had an hour long conversation with him over the phone. He had a lot of advice, and recommended sodium bicarbonate, which is essentially bread soda. I soon discovered there was a nun down the road by my old school, Mount Anville, who sold a special bread soda which was more potent at making the blood stream more alkaline. Cancer loves acidic environments which comes from a lot of food, but it hates an alkaline pH. Cancer cells make the body even more acidic as they produce lactic acid. Taking action to make the body more alkaline is vital in the battle against cancer. A lot of meat, grains and sugar are very acidic and fruit and vegetables make the bloodstream more alkaline. I had my mum on this bread soda straight away. She was taking an even wackier diet than the dude from Middlesbrough, but it seemed to be working.

Funnily enough, I even recall a conversation with my sister Suzi.

"What does the BS on Mum's calendar mean Mary?", she asked.

I looked over and Mum had put BS on the calendar five days on and five days off to remind her to take the bread soda.

"Oh that's just a reminder about taking the bread soda Suzi", I replied.

Suzi just laughed and said, "I thought it was Mum saying bullshit in her head."

I also made sure that she was drinking sencha green tea from Japan and matcha green tea, as I had read that it was more potent than regular Chinese green tea.

I started thinking about ketogenic diets for my mum, seeing as sugar is cancer's best friend. I pondered this for a while and then thought that she needed plenty of fruit and vegetables for all of the antioxidant benefits to actually fight the mother fucker. Ketogenic diets are essentially an Atkins type diet, but because fruit and vegetables contain sugar you are not supposed to eat many of them. I then started to think back to my mum's weight. She was put on anti-depressants at the age of forty six and her desire for sweet things and refined foods had gradually crept up. She still kept up a balanced nutritious diet but her weight had slowly started to increase since being put on the medication. She was always thin as a whistle after each of her seven pregnancies, as she was very active and ate very well. I knew this was a similar thing to me and had she not been put on anti-depressants and increase her sugar intake so much, then maybe she wouldn't have had a diagnoses at all. This is where big pharma can be nasty. I see a lot of individuals who are clinically obese and taking anti-depressants smoke a large amount because there is simply nothing else to do. Even in John of God's, individuals are put in there who have given up smoking and because they are locked in wards with very little to do day by day they start smoking again. They need heart rate and blood pressure taken four times a day. It's all just ludicrous in my opinion.

At the same time, I was googling other nutritionists in Dublin and I came across a personal trainer, Damien from Westwood. He is obviously working in both fields, but after speaking to him about my mum for ten minutes he asked, "Are you Suzi Guiney's sister?"

"Yeah", I replied.

"I met you before, you live down in Sandyford right?"

I remembered him then, and said congratulations on the new role. He advised me not to go too crazy with juicing real wheat grass and to just give the powdered form, as I was probably taking on too much. I continued to juice the wheatgrass fresh but after tasting both dried and juiced myself, I thought the dried shots tasted better, so I decided that was better for my mum's taste buds. Mum and I used to take a shot first thing in the morning, and she would put on her scowl face, and then we'd fire the shot glasses into the dish washer.

I also had her drink numerous turmeric teas, which when I look back on now, they tasted awful. I was using the dried spice and mixing it with black pepper in boiling water, as black pepper and turmeric together are known to be a potent killer of any chronic disease, specifically cancer and joint pain; anything to do with inflammation. Today, the shop up the road from me has the real turmeric and it tastes an awful lot better. I throw it into tea or just eat the mother fucker raw and don't give a shit about yellow teeth after wards. I'd eat anything if I knew it was good for me, except liver, that's one thing my mother could never get me to eat. Liver is one thing my dad had her eating after her brain aneurysm in 1998, I'll come to that later.

Anytime I gave my mum green tea, I would mix it with lemon. And broccoli I would give her with tomatoes, as the two work well in synergy. Tomatoes are also one vegetable which is better for you cooked, as the lycopene gets released. I read about ten different books on cancer treatments such as Patrick Holford "Say no to cancer" and "Life over cancer" by Keith I Block and "Alive and Well" by Philip E Binzel.

Anyway, even dealing with all of this, it was good to be spending some quality time with my best friend in life. I was also back in Westwood, and this time rather than doing just steady state cardio, I got a personal trainer to recommend high intensity interval training (HIIT) and weights. I did all of the long distance, HIIT and weights, had a great diet and was happy my mum was doing better. I was also re reading a lot of books which I read in my college days when I used to row. Such as "The First Twenty Minutes", how to exercise better, train smarter and live longer. "A lifetime in a race" by Matthew Pinset to encourage me to get back rowing, and "Mind over Water". I also read a new book called "The Psychopathology of Every Day Life" which was putting me on a more positive note. By about August, I was down to nine stone seven pounds. I was in shape and obviously heavier than in Vietnam, due to the muscle building up in my body.

At this point, Mum was getting her first round of chemotherapy at Blackrock Clinic and I was by her side for every step of it, of course with carrot and ginger juices, celery and broccoli in my bag. I thought it was a disgrace seeing all of the scones and biscuits inside a hospital for people going through chemotherapy. But as it's been said before, every doctor should study nutrition but I guess they just are so closed minded to that and think nutrition is wacky. Then what on earth are we doing on this planet if nutrition is wacky? Some oncologists really piss me off. Our doctor at the time gave Mum three months to live. He only told me as my mum and Dad didn't want to know. I kept it quiet from them but siblings were asking me for updates so I told them, but said to keep it hush from Mum and Dad. I also reckoned that she would do better with all of this diet, herbs and basically good food that I had researched. Passion from Delia spread to a passion of Mary's.

I look back and still remember eating beetroot and periwinkles with my mum at the kitchen table at the age of four. What four year old eats that? Well someone who loves the fun and games with her mother and knows that she's just trying to build up my strength and appetite for good food. Going off track, but my dad still laughs at the time a rat pissed on my baby bottle. When he brought it inside, my mum said, "Ah a quick rinse will do Michael." The woman knew how to build up a strong immune system from a young age. There is too much paranoia these days over sterilising bottles and who is breast feeding and for how long. You just do what feels right.

At this point, we decided to buy a new English mastiff, as Mum really wanted a dog. I enjoyed going for walks in Marlay Park, just the three of us.

Chapter 5

Thailand

I was feeling better and so was my mum. It was time to tell my folks that I had booked a holiday to Thailand in August to take a break. I was contemplating cancelling it and phoned the airline to get a refund on my flight but they wouldn't return the fee, so I decided to head away.

This time, I was going with just three others and I wasn't going to be taking antimalarials. I got travel insurance this time, as I wasn't covered in Vietnam, and it cost my parents the guts of €12 grand to send people left right and centre on last minute flights, hospital bills and drugs.

I was ready to take on Thailand, and needed a bloody break after everything I was going through. I also remember coming back from the Step Inn with my sister Anna and saying, "I swear on Mum's life I wasn't taking drugs in Vietnam." She believed me and responded by saying "Go enjoy yourself and there's plenty of us to look after Mum. You can check in with me all of the time."

Don't get me wrong, while studying biochemistry and rowing in NUI Galway, I was a bit mischievous and tried MDMA a good few times. The buzz off it was class, but the come down the next day was just horrendous. I used to have an upside down smiley face on me for about ten hours the next day. A lot of people nowadays seem to be taking coke, which is wrecking havoc in people's minds. It's the greedy man drug which causes a lot of fights on nights out. I tried it once with a group of friends, and just thought it was the dumbest thing ever. A greedy man stupid drug that causes fucked up broken septum's and shit. Ha, I laugh now, as I was telling a buddy about wanting to do ironman last year and he said, "That shit is bad for your heart."

He snorted a line of coke as he said that to me.

I have to laugh, as I think there are a lot more things worse for someone's heart. Plus, with all of the adequate training, you are unlikely to put your body through strain if you use common sense. I wouldn't want to mention too much of what I think in front of people, or else I'll get a big fat argument thrown back into my face about smoking or something. Sure half of my friends are addicted to Valium, Xanax and anti-anxiety pills and they see nothing wrong with it. I actually have a heart rate of forty two beats per minute which is sinus bradycardia, and a sign of extreme fitness, so I couldn't give a shit as to what they think of me. I'm doing triathlons, rowing on the indoor erg, hill walking and I'm fitter than I ever was in my life. I enjoy beer, red wine but I'm well tune with both sports and normal nutrition. And hey everyone needs some sort of vice. I promised myself I'd give up smoking when I want to start a family, so if that day comes, then I'll give up for the right man. The rest of the world can shut the hell up right now. Anyway, I've researched that smoking actually stimulates brain tissue so it's no wonder I was good at studying and my mother was a fucking genius at writing. And lets not forget the writer Carrie Bradshaw from Sex and the City or the legend David Bowie. Musicians, writers, artistic people, triathletes, athletes, a lot of them smoke. Enough said.

Off to Thailand I went. Three of us, and a newbie Sam who had taken over my room in London when I moved out. Pa was there too. We landed in Bangkok. Ready for one night on the tiles and then onto Phi Phi, Ko Samui and Ko Tao. I remember as we were roaming the streets, Claire and I came across a guy playing some wacky instrument on the street. She was in a hurry to go meet Sam, and I just shouted back, "I didn't come over for just a drinking holiday, I want to see some excitement and culture too."

That was the problem in Vietnam, everyone wanting to do different things or wanting to travel in groups so it just turned into a drinking holiday. I really wanted to actually see stuff here, as I didn't get to in Vietnam. Although at least I got the mud baths and Halong Bay part into it. That was cool.

We hurried on to meet Sam and get ready for a night out. Bangkok is just pretty much a load of people drinking on the side of the streets, good craic, but the beach is obviously much better. Claire and I got chatting to about ten guys at a table outside a pub, and one of them was coming onto me straight away after only five minutes. I told him that I was a lesbian. He looked horrified and then ended up scoring Claire. I just laughed. It's the same shit like with Tinder back in Dublin. Lads just want to know girls for five minutes and then sleep with them. I see so many friends still going through it. I've been on a few tinder dates for dinner or drinks and it rarely turns into a second, as I know within minutes whether I'm mad about them or not. Plus, college was the time for me to mess around a bit more and luckily I got it out of my system then. I think my virginity has grown back at this stage. Tinder got deactivated from my phone a long time ago as it was just head wrecking. I wasn't interested in talking the same bullshit to another person. "Hi, how are you, what do you do?"

I always said to myself that my only two things in a guy was height and banter. I wanted fun and zest in a guy and the height thing might be about being a good athlete or maybe just someone tall enough to protect me, and I could still wear heels and not look funny next to them. I never cared about their job or how much money they had, and hated that bullshit in London when a guy would approach me and ask what do I do.

"I work in JP Morgan."

They'd lose interest. Probably because they were threatened by me. And to be frank, I couldn't give one shit if anyone felt threatened. I'd just order more beers and continue chatting to my friends more who I was having fun with.

I'd much prefer to be happy alone than with the wrong person. As my mum used to say and I firmly agree with the quirky woman, "You're born into this world alone, and you die alone."

I look back on a swimming holiday in Croatia last summer on my own, and I visited a graveyard (with spotify blaring into my ears) and it was the death of a mother and father and son. I cried for a bit and thought that will be Mum, Dad and I up in Johnnie Foxes. I then said to myself, if so, so what. So I say this now, when I die, I want my organs to go to science (I'm already an organ donor so that's fine), and I want my body cremated and thrown into the sea. No time for this urn bullshit, straight into the sea and then my name can be plastered beside Mum's and Dad's up at Johnnie Foxes grave. Bags that space for my name.

Or hang on, if the sea doesn't work out and people are arguing, you can preserve me and put me beside Lenin in St. Petersburg in Russia. I saw him in his tombstone when Mum and Dad took me and my brother on an Eastern European holiday and it was class. I was so excited as I did my special topic in history in secondary school on Krupskaya, Lenin's wife. Yes Hitler was a bad man, but I had a lot of time for Russian history. Forget Stalin, go Lenin. It's no wonder he is preserved.

Back to Thailand. The next day we arrived in Phi Phi. We met our friend Pa there. He was coming in from Australia and we just randomly met him along with Sam, while Claire and I were having dinner. I was delighted to see him again. The four of us sat, had dinner, a few beers and discussed scuba diving. This was something I hadn't done before but really wanted to, seeing as I have a passion for the water. Pa said he had done his paddy license in Australia before, but we were going with professionals so all was good.

We ate and drank that night and then signed up for scuba diving.

"Are you sure you Irish lot are ready for scuba diving?", the paddy instructor asked.

I responded with a big "hell yeah."

— 55 —

We chilled for the evening, and then Sam headed on home, because he had been scuba diving loads before. Pa also took an early night, so Claire and I roamed the streets of Phi Phi more. At one point we landed in a restaurant and there was a monkey in a pair of nappies. I got a load of snaps with him.

Claire and I headed back to our hotel early enough and we sat on our balcony and had a beer each. She was asking was I OK as I wasn't as chatty on the way home.

I said, "I'm having fun and will take everything as it comes."

She was silent. I then started chatting about my mum and how I missed her and I was worried she was going to die. She listened and told me to get some rest before scuba diving. Seeing as Claire was taking Valium on the trip, I decided to take one to make sure I got a good nights rest.

Anytime my dad wanted to contact me he was contacting Mary Phi Phi from his phone. Seeing as my Samsung phone got lost in Vietnam, I decided to bring a Nokia with me and put a Thai SIM into it.

The next morning, the three of us headed scuba diving. Claire and I had a quick breakfast and then decided on our lunch on the boat. Ham and cheese toasties all around in my head and tuna baguettes. No toasties though, as we were on a boat.

We got on and Sam the instructor explained everything in detail. I was taking it all in with excitement. We all got chatting to each other and Sam was asking what I did. He said he was a carpenter back home. I joked and asked, "Does that mean you lay carpets?", he just laughed at me. Anyway, time to fly down under water and see fishes. Claire got in but couldn't manage any of it. I hopped in and went down with Sam and his crew. I only managed about ten meters as I started freaking out that I wouldn't see my mother or father again. Just in case the tank decided to explode in my face. I came back up and Sam followed me. I told him to go back down and look after the rest that he was instructing.

I don't know why, but I had this crazy vision as I was trying to enjoy life that I wouldn't see my parents again. I hopped back onto the boat and chilled and enjoyed myself. Claire jumped into the water and shouted, "I feel a million dollars, jump in."

I didn't feel like jumping in at that point so I chilled on the boat.

While I was sunbathing on the boat I could hear my friend Martin saying, "Mary is into rowing", in a really faint voice. I knew straight off that this was baloney as he was in Japan at the time, so I just decided to ignore it. I started thinking, what the fuck is wrong with me and being on boats in the sun. I thought to myself that everything should be fine and if I felt like psychosis was emerging that I would know how to deal with it.

On the way back to the land, others on the boat were remarking on my T shirt which had a picture of a dog getting a tattoo. I told them that I picked it up in Bangkok. We got back and I asked Claire could I get a tampon off her. She started getting all freaked out, and was saying that I needed to be over for the meeting with the rest of the crew. I just said, "Emergency here, not my fault my body decided to period in the sea."

She handed me one, and I headed to the loo.

That day, I wanted to head out to meet Sam and the other instructors for lunch, but Claire thought it was a bit much and that I needed to chill out after the long day. Being the energy woman I am, I didn't think it was a long day at all. The three of us sat and had some pizza, and I ordered a carrot, apple and ginger juice. I left Pa and Claire to go off and climb some hill, while I headed back to my room. When I got back to my room I could see Sam doing weights over in the next gym. I waved up at him and just chilled in my room. I was missing my mum but at the same time wanting to enjoy life, but I felt a bit more out of place on this holiday. I went along with the flow and the four of us headed out that night. While we were dancing on the beach I took off my flip flops and said to Pa, "No one can steal these, they're the pair my mum bought me."

He laughed at me and thought I was acting like a princess.

The next day we arrived in Ko Samui. I was delighted this time that I had brought a suitcase. When I went to Vietnam, I was throwing everything out of my ruck sack and kept losing things.

The four of us kept venturing along and then Claire was saying to Pa that I was out of character because I kept laughing to myself. Something I quite regularly do alone is laugh to myself when I think of funny things. I was high on life but people kept misinterpreting things. I was sleeping fine and didn't hear a single voice except for that one of Martin's on the boat. When Pa came up worried, I said I was fine and not to get my family involved and that they were going through enough with my mum having lung cancer. It was advised that I take some Valium to make sure I chilled more, so I did that.

Later that night I kept lathering my body in after sun so that they would know I was OK, but Pa was genuinely worried at this stage.

"Hey do you know where the 7 11 is?", a Spanish guy asked us in the middle of the street.

"Please can you just go away, we're in the middle of something important", the other two shouted. I knew right then and there that I was back to square one, so anxiety started building up in me.

The two of them agreed that it was time to get my parents and family involved.

I just said, "Here's my phone, call them all you want, I'm going to an internet cafe to apply for my nutrition masters."

I left them with my phone and rocked up to an internet cafe, and decided to look up nutrition courses, as that is what was on my mind at the time. I didn't feel like I was having psychosis, but my mind felt like it was going into overdrive, as I was finding it difficult to relax at this point. I headed up to the internet cafe and started looking up online courses in the UK. Pa and Claire came up to me in the internet cafe and said, "Time for you to go to hospital."

There was nothing I could do at this point, so the two of them roped me into a taxi and lumbered me into the nearest hospital.

Pa tried to explain at the speed of light what had happened to me in Vietnam, and the doctor classified me as schizophrenic. He looked quite empathetic towards me but I just kept quiet and let Pa do all of the talking. I took it on the chin and lay down in a hospital bed and allowed them to inject me with whatever drugs they wanted. Valium, Xanax, everything under the sun. I had no choice in the matter. They injected me with a concoction.

At one point, the drugs made me think I was on a boat going back to Phi Phi to see Sam the instructor. I felt like I was unstable in the hospital room, and almost like the building was on water. I also visually hallucinated loads from all of the Valium and started seeing spiders crawl up my arms in the hospital bed.

I remember Pa and Sam coming in to visit me and at one point I hopped out of the bed and said to Pa, "Have a bucket on me", with a huge smile. I was kind of enjoying the Valium buzz.

He laughed and said, "Go away Mare, I'll be onto your Dad pretty soon, I can't have any buckets."

Little did I know, my sister Suzi was on her way out to get me from Ko Samui.

On the flight back, I was out of it and don't remember much. I was in a haze of in and out when we landed in Hong Kong airport. All I remember is that we had about three hours to kill at Hong Kong airport, so the two of us decided to go to Milanos to get a lasagne. I was hungry thirty minutes after this and inhaled a fourteen piece sushi set. After that I ate half of a large toblerone. I didn't give a crap at the time.

We still had spare time, so we decided to go into Zara. I was clearly drugged up but still trying on clothes to fit my new frame. Maybe subconsciously I wanted to make sure I was buying new clothes to fit the figure I had tried so hard to work at and I knew at the back of my mind that round two of weight gain was going to happen with the medication. I remember it so clearly. I bought a few tops and a pair of red striped trousers. They were rotten but Suzi let me buy them anyway.

Onto Heathrow we went, and all I remember is Suzi saying, "Come on Mary, you're walking so slow."

I don't remember much else of the trip back. We obviously had to fly to Dublin, but the Valium and drugs must have been kicking

— 59 —

in more. All I remember is when I got back to my house, my mum was sitting up with a bright smile on her face, glad to have me home. I was delighted to see her and thought round two of chemotherapy must be treating her well.

Again, I had a round of psychiatrist appointments to go to. This time, luckily the psychiatrist was much nicer and actually understood that I had experienced post-psychotic depression before.

"Your bloods are back Mary and everything looks fine." I just nodded.

"Jesus, I have never seen cholesterol as low as yours in my life", he remarked.

"Well my diet was super healthy before going to Thailand, so I guess that might be the reasoning behind it."

Looking back on it now, perhaps my cholesterol was too low as I was doing a lot of juicing and perhaps not taking in enough fat. Mono-unsaturated fats and especially polyunsaturated fats are essential to the health of the cell. I was getting plenty of these from oils and nuts and fish but perhaps I wasn't eating enough saturated fat. Cholesterol, especially high density lipoproteins are essential to the body. It is low density lipoproteins that need to be lowered in the circulatory system. "These tests don't split out my high density and low density lipoproteins so I cannot see the ratio of fat in my bloodstream", I said to him.

"Oh that's just the reading we get with the results."

Again, nutrition isn't a thing to be discussed with doctors.

Since then I have upped my saturated fat intake and of course will eat real butter rather than that plant sterol crap that tastes like air. You need a bit of indulgence or else your body will feel deprived. On a bright note, I eat plenty of fruit and vegetables so there's plenty of plants going into my body. I don't need that weight watchers shit.

Daniel and his family took me to Cabinteely Park to go to a fun fair with the kids a few days later. It was fun and I decided to buy Mum a nice necklace at it. Daniel and I got talking about philosophy and he was eager to understand more as to what happened in Thailand and Vietnam.

"Do you believe in brain washing?", I asked Daniel.

He was silent. "OK put it this way, do you believe in reverse psychology?", I then asked him.

We talked a bit about psychology and some of the philosophical books Daniel has read over the years, but I couldn't for the life of me explain it.

"Why reverse psychology Mary?", he asked.

"Anytime I thought in my head that I wanted a beer, the Thai held up a two litre bottle of water in the shop, and anytime I wanted more water, they held up a beer. It was mad."

"Amelia come back", he shouted.

He was distracted with his kids so we just got on with our day.

I phoned Martin the next day to let him know I was OK.

"What is going on with you Mary?", he asked worried.

"Oh I don't know, I heard you banging on about me rowing again while I was on the boat trying to scuba dive. I then got jacked up on copious amounts of Valium and started hallucinating and seeing spiders float up my arms."

"That's mad", he gasped.

"Yeah I know, back to this shit, OK Mum's calling I have to go."

As a treat, Mum decided to take me to Monart health spa in Wexford to unwind.

"You really should get reiki done, it will do you wonders", she said on the way down.

Reiki is simply a treatment where a therapist holds their hands over your head without touching it, but they can feel a lot of energy moving around from the scalp.

"You really have a lot of thoughts buzzing around in your head, I can feel a sharp energy moving around in there", the therapist remarked after an hour long session.

I just nodded and said that there was a lot going on since 2012 for me.

"Yes, you seem like you are not the happiest girl over the last two years and that there is something holding you back from moving forward and doing what you want in life."

By holding her hands over my scalp, she examined the seven chakras of my body to observe energy movements. I was wondering at the time, why she said I wasn't the happiest girl over the last two years, as I only really felt miserable since after Vietnam. Then I thought, maybe I was still dealing with a bit of heart break, while I threw myself into intense training in London in 2012.

Mum also treated me to a head massage and a body massage, but I still found it difficult to relax properly.

This time, I was adamant to fight it and not going to let depression or weight gain affect me. Because I had a horrendous experience with Haloperidol, I decided to try other drugs on the market. Abilify was recommended to me and the psychiatrist said that it didn't have as nasty a side effect as Haloperidol, as it was a newer drug.

I also decided to practice a ten week course of cognitive behavioural therapy with a group who were going through all different types of mental health problems. I remember walking into the Centre for Living one day and laughing to myself. "What are you laughing at? There's nothing funny about mental health", one patient remarked.

"Oh I don't mean to be offensive, but I had a very positive experience while in South East Asia. Not all psychotic episodes are bad."

"What do you mean?", she asked.

"I heard positive voices in my head and anytime I heard bitching going on I filtered it out."

I had purely reflected on Vietnam at this stage.

She walked away looking bemused.

I did the art therapy courses at the Centre for Living as well, and the teacher made me open up and cry in front of people, as she made me talk about what I was taking on with my mother's illness at the same time as to having psychosis in South East Asia. I hate crying in front of people and never do. The only time you'd see tears coming down my eyes is if I'm out for a run and the wind is blowing strong against my face. I cried quite a bit on my own when my mum had her diagnosis and listened to others crying to me. The only time I actually opened up and cried was in front of my dad when we went into Vincent's for the first time for a check up on Mum and I burst out crying while talking about Auntie Mary who passed away from pancreatic cancer. I was telling him that chemotherapy just doesn't seem to work for aggressive forms of cancer.

Anyway, back to cognitive behavioural therapy. I didn't do much talking in this class but a hell of a lot of listening. As always, I'm a good listener when it comes to other people's problems, and I don't open up much about my own. This is where writing comes in handy three and a half years later. One girl in the class pointed out that she gets paranoid with what's app. She gets paranoid that people have seen her message and not responded. I had to but in and say a lot of the time people have read your message but they're just too busy to get back at that point in time. I could see what she meant though, as it can be quite rude sometimes if someone just doesn't respond at all to a message. So essentially, the gist of what I got from that class was that people suffer paranoia sometimes due to phones and the new form of messenger. I think myself and another dude were the only ones dealing with psychosis, while a lot of others were dealing with anxiety and depression.

I asked the teacher to recommend a good book to me and she recommended, "Undress me in the Temple of Heaven", which was written in 1986, the year I was born.

I was adamant to continue going to the gym, but found doing weights next to impossible. The drugs had zapped my strength and energy completely. I laid off it for a while, for fear of dropping dead. While still attending cognitive behavioural therapy and looking after my mum's health at the same time, I decided it was time to read the book. It's about two friends who travel to The People's Republic of China and one of them experiences a psychotic episode. The gist of the book is that one of the travelling buddies undresses physically on holidays, while the other one undresses psychologically. It made me reflect on Vietnam where people were sleeping around somewhat but I was just trying to enjoy time with friends, zone out and mind my own business. I liked the book, but I didn't like the way it was written from the so called "normal" friends point of view. I wanted something written from the girl's point of view who actually had psychosis.

At this time, I read the thirty pages I had written after Vietnam and thought about continuing to write, but Abilify was knocking on my door. I started to lose motivation for life again. I had signed up for a nutrition masters in UCD, a bit late at this stage, but signed up in October and carried on with my modules that I was allowed sit at the time.

November came, and I decided to volunteer on Dulra Organic farm just outside of Dublin. I drove there twice a week and helped out with planting and weeding, while I learned a lot about organic farming. I learned that commercial farming is concerned about the large amount of nitrogen, potassium and phosphorous in the soil. Large amounts of potassium are getting leaked into the sea through the loss in our urine, so the land is becoming more depleted in this mineral. As a result, seaweed accumulates a lot of these minerals. To counteract this at Dulra, they recycle potassium by chopping vegetables and planting on new growth.

"Can we get a poly tunnel?", I asked my mum when I got home one Tuesday.

"You won't keep up the maintenance of growing fruit and vegetables in it, don't bother."

I just shrugged. I wanted to grow all of our own vegetables and at least this way it would save me having to go to Blackrock to buy organic fruit and vegetables all of the time. I didn't bother in the end. I guess I had a lot going on at the time anyway.

Chapter 6

Lanzarote

Around this time, Mum and I were in the cash and carry filling up the trolley with lots of food for Christmas, and copious amounts of chocolate. At this stage, I had gained five or six pounds since Thailand, but come December, I was having chocolate parties in my pants while studying my masters. I was eating radishes, bell peppers and cherry tomatoes for snacks, so at least I was getting some healthy food in, but the chocolate fetish just got worse.

"Mary you're never in Westwood any more, and I don't see you out running", Mum remarked one evening.

I just shrugged and said, "Not for me right now."

I promised myself I'd pick back up the pace with exercise again in January. I just had to sit through another shitty Christmas for now.

My friend came over to visit me and she knew I was feeling depressed again. I reflected on Thailand and told her that I had a little crush on our paddy instructor, Sam. I told her that he was a carpenter in the UK and that he was probably back in the UK at that stage.

"Do you know his surname?", she asked.

"No. But I could text Pa and ask him for the name of the place we went scuba diving."

I texted Pa and he gave me the name. Within five minutes, my friend found out his surname and found him on Facebook. I added him straight away, but he didn't seem to accept my friend request.

By the time January came, I was back up to ten stone seven pounds. I decided, fuck this, I'm going back to Haloperidol. At least that drug is much cheaper on the market and I didn't want my parents paying €160 for a piece of shit drug every month that was making me miserable.

I switched, and there was no change as expected.

The psychiatrist at this time, recommended weight watchers to me. I threw my eyes up to heaven. "That shitty diet, are you serious?".

Of course psychiatrists know nothing about nutrition. Weight watchers is one of the worst you can do, as you eliminate one of the major food groups, fat. Fat and water make up the bulk of our cells and it is needed for cognitive function. So a psychiatrist recommending weight watchers is just ludicrous, as psychiatry is all related to the brain function and fat is essential in the diet.

I thought to myself, that I would give it a stab anyway to see what all the fuss was about. I went twice. First time for weigh in and to listen to a load of baloney. Second time to lose four pounds. I never went again as my body was starved.

The week I was trying weight watchers, my divil of a mother suggested Roly's for dinner. We went, but I knew she was testing me out as she knew I was one to never go on stupid fucking diets before. I still remember having some tasty chicken on an off day.

"Mary get the steak, never mind that dull and dry meat."

I just nodded and ate away at my chicken.

Mum was done with chemotherapy by January. The next thing, I was driving her to Vincent's once every two weeks for radiotherapy treatment. At this stage, the oncologist who had given Mum three months to live since July, said that the cancer had shrunk in both lungs and the liver by a massive 80%, but that it had metastasised to the brain. We needed a bit of radiotherapy to target any remaining cancer on the lungs.

"Definitely the chemotherapy is making me feel better, but I put most of my improvement down to Mary's diet", Mum said to Dad, as I sat in the back of the car. She was thrilled when we got this news and we decided to stop off in a pub in Blackrock. I watched my mum with devil eyes as she lapped up a big ice cream in celebration!

While driving Mum to radiotherapy, I was trying the Atkins diet again. At least I did my typical thing of distracting from a major issue, by focusing on my own problems post Thailand. I used to sit outside the radiographer appointment, and think about my next low carbohydrate meal and what sort of mileage running I was going to clock up for the day.

Mum took all of this on the chin, and in fact preferred the treatment at Vincent's, as the doctor, who was foreign, was much nicer than the previous oncologists we had seen. He was kind and empathetic, and explained that he lost a son to cancer, but that he was going to do his best. I'm not going to dish out doctors names now but I know exactly who treated my mother with respect and who didn't. I was getting treated like dirt anytime I brought up nutrition but that's neither here nor there.

Atkins didn't last long. I'd get ketosis, which meant I was burning fat and I'd lose a shed load of weight within a week. One gram of carbohydrate attracts four molecules of water, so I was essentially losing water weight. One week later, I was back to a pasta binge.

I started dreaming of water fasts then. I read on google that there was a guy in the States who was clinically obese, and he lived on water for a whole year. Nothing else, just water and his accumulation of adipose tissue. He dropped a massive fifteen stone. I decided to give it a go. The longest I lasted on a water fast was six days, and then I would go back to normal eating. I used to dream about going back to the prison type hospital in Vietnam, and I could just lie in the sun and drink water, as I would have had no interest in the food they dished out in tubs there. Too much fucking temptation in the developed world. Ding ding ding obesity problems. Not like fat tax or sugar tax is solving any of those issues.

Atkins was gone, seeing as I'm a carbohydrate addict and athlete, weight watchers can go fuck off and water fasting was just ridiculous for someone who had maybe a stone to lose. At least with water fasting, the hunger goes after two days and you feel like you are cleansing your body. It's quite meditative actually, and you feel an inner peace as the digestive system is given a complete break.

Anyway, none of that was for me. I started googling fat loss programmes and purchased a long paged document on the internet called, "Venus Fat Loss Programme". It was a huge list of dieting tactics to lose weight. I didn't follow any of the guidelines and couldn't believe I had spent the guts of €200 to purchase nutrition advice. Three weeks later, Allied Irish Bank rang me, to inform me that I was scammed by €6,000 from my bank account. I put two and two together and knew it was some scamster over the web, who had hacked my account when trying to purchase nutrition information. Luckily I got refunded every penny.

By February it was decided that Dad, Mum and I would take a trip to Lanzarote. This is where shit really hit the fan. I brought my lap top, as I had modules to study and I threw myself into runs and long walks. I still ate like a king. I remember asking the chamber maid for more of those nice chocolates they put on the pillow, and she brought in about twenty of them. I devoured them within five minutes.

"Give me one you greedy mare", Mum remarked. That would be my hour long run gone out the window.

Mum started going downhill. I distracted myself by writing down in my phone that I could do two hours plus of exercise a day, as triathlon was still a big dream of mine. One evening before dinner, Mum came over to my door as I was in the middle of an online exam.

"Delia leave her alone she's doing an exam", Dad remarked.

I just laughed when I saw her and closed the door, so I could do well in chemistry of nutrients.

Before dinner, the three of us drank Coole Swan, which we bought in the airport. It's similar to baileys. We needed something to celebrate to keep us going.

"Give us a drag of that smoke", Mum asked one evening.

I couldn't let her have any. It seems cruel that I still smoked, but I needed some sort of stress buster to deal with everything going on in my life.

I have to say, hats off to my mum. For someone who smoked for so many years, she knocked it straight on the chin on June 25th 2013, the day she was diagnosed. She was adamant to fight this. That woman was the biggest fighter I know.

I still remember the holiday to Bermuda when I was twelve, like the back of my hand. The eight of us, one brother missing in action in a bank in London, had an Indian dinner the night before travelling to Bermuda. It was a dinner out with retail suppliers who my mum and Dad were dealing with at the time. Mum wasn't herself afterwards and she was singing odd words to songs in the kitchen. We still got on with it and flew over.

"Who's having a Bermuda burger?", Gretta asked. We all jumped in and lapped up the nice burgers by the pool.

"Your mother's not feeling great", Dad remarked.

I remember going into her room. It was 1998 and the sun was out. Her room was all dark with the curtains drawn and I was sitting beside her as she sang, "Somewhere over the rainbow." I was playing on her bed and staring at her wondering was I going to lose her then and there.

The next day, she was flown air ambulance over to Canada. My sister Anna and my dad flew with her, while Gretta minded us younger brats. We carried on with our holiday in Bermuda like nothing was wrong. It's funny looking back now, but I remember Daniel getting served alcohol even though he was two years under age, while Gretta had to go back to her room to get her passport. Gretta is six years older than Daniel. The difference in girls versus boys I guess.

Auntie Jenny was in Canada to help along the way, and she visited Mum, Dad and Anna all of the time. Mum had a ruptured brain aneurysm.

Serious brain surgery, and a chip put into the back of her head and Mum was flown back to Ireland safe and sound. She was advised to give up smoking then, but couldn't manage to knock it on the chin then. I remember getting a whiff of smoke from her bathroom downstairs, as she used to sneak behind us in her own house.

"Canada have the best brain surgeons in the world, due to skiing accidents", my mother proudly said after making a full recovery. She was back to work within six months.

Back to Lanzarote. Things were getting worse, and we needed a wheelchair most evenings to go around the hotel.

"Where's Michael, where's my bag?", Mum kept asking as I pushed her.

I would angrily say, "Dad is right behind us, and your bag is sitting on you."

The radiotherapy was affecting her and I knew it was making her go a bit mad. Either that or the chemotherapy, which killed off her immunity altogether.

I was still buying plenty of juices for Mum but they were much sweeter and probably had plenty of fructose in them. They weren't as potent as the ones I made laced in ginger at home.

One day while lying by the pool, Dad and I decided to take a quick dip in the sea. I was excited as swimming was the one discipline I wanted to get back into. I couldn't swim. I just lapped up the waves and enjoyed a bit of time with Dad. About twenty minutes later, we came back to Mum and she was passed out in the sun, with three random Spanish people around her. I felt pretty guilty.

"I'm grand", she grunted.

Dad and I helped her up and we went back to the room. Mum always said she was grand and never complained about a thing in life even though she went through a lot.

A few nights later, we had dinner in a fancy Italian with the best pasta as far as I can remember. Mum headed off to the loo in the middle of dinner.

"Your mother is taking quite a while", Dad grunted, after about ten minutes.

Up I got straight away to investigate. The cubicle door was locked and I called at Mum from outside. "I'm on the floor and can't get up", she moaned.

Vietnamese Voices

"Put all of your weight onto your hands and shimmy your body off the floor", I replied.

She just couldn't get up. I went out to the waiter and explained. They started hammering at the lock and we got to her eventually.

I went out for a smoke and phoned Gretta. "Back in a minute Dad." His steak was arriving at that stage. I tried to explain what was going on, but it was hard for Gretta to understand. She phoned Suzi, and we decided that it was time to book a flight home early, and get the hell out of the sun. Some may say the sun got to her head but I'd like to believe it was those stupid false UV rays from radiotherapy and not the natural ones from the sun.

The flight back was horrendous. Anytime Mum needed the bathroom, I had to go with her and squeeze my body in to make sure she didn't flush herself down the toilet. At least the two of us were laughing about the situation. Two little brats who got each other's sense of humour and commitment to each other.

We got back to Dublin at the end of February, and Mum was getting worse. She was not interested in my food input any more. I couldn't blame her. I was next to giving up at this stage, so I kept on a brave face and continued into the UCD library. I was learning all about chronic disease, obesity, cancer, cystic fibrosis. For the love of me, I just wanted to fucking kill some of the oncologists out there. I had offered to give Mum one of my lungs at the initial diagnosis, but the oncologist wouldn't allow it. He was probably well aware that the cancer was aggressive and would spread to every part of the body. Looking back now, it's a blessing in disguise. If I had given her a lung, I wouldn't be able to run, swim or cycle the way I do today.

Mum was still driving and doing the food shopping, while I was venturing in and out of the library. On a few occasions, a call would come through from Superquinn, in Rathfarnham, "Is this Mary, Delia's daughter?"

"Yes, give me a second", I would whisper, as I walked out of the library.

"Your mother is here and has forgotten where her car is."

— 71 —

I phoned my dad then and there and asked him to take over, as I was tired of being heavily involved in this while trying to do my masters.

At this point, I decided it was time to move back to London. I had looked up a few banking roles in Dublin, but none of them suited me. I got offered a role in the Bank of England by the end of March.

"Mary that's great news, you know I used to work for the bank on Threadneedle street?", my mum said in delight.

She knew I was going to get a good job, with a great pension and some security in life. I was finally putting myself first. I felt guilty, but I felt like there was nothing I could do any more for Mum.

I dyed my hair dark, the way Mum loved it, and my bags were packed. I was off to London at the end of April to start work at the Central Bank in the beginning of May. I gave myself a week to do viewings all over London to find the right apartment. I was sick of Battersea and Clapham, so I settled for a nice two bed with a Canadian girl in Queensway, right beside Hyde Park. I was ready to start afresh with my life. My masters is also online so I could continue to study while in the UK.

I started walking the five miles in and out of work along Oxford Street. I wasn't ready for running back in, plus looking back on it now, the Bank of England didn't have any showers like they did in the good old JP Morgan days. I kept up a good diet, lots of green tea, sushi, pasta, pod nori wraps and enjoying the healthier selection of food London had to offer. I went for my first run around Hyde Park. It was good but could have been better with some beats in my ear. I started building back up my fitness and would do two laps of the park. It still wasn't the same as the good nine miler I used to do around Richmond park with the deer, but it was fine as it was on my doorstep.

While getting on with work and getting on with my own life, I was back and forth on the phone to my sister Anna. I was enquiring about the apricot kernels and other stuff I was giving Mum previously.

"She's just not really taking them any more Mary, and she seems to just want beans on toast."

I'd hang up the phone and just think about my own situation. I would think about how I wanted to feel within myself.

Work was getting hard and I started having suicidal thoughts, as I hated my job and the situation at home. I hated that I had left my mum for a job that meant nothing to me. No amount of money can compare to someone else's life.

I thought at the time, it was a good idea to distract myself with tinder. I went on two tinder dates, just first ones, as it's tough for a guy to get onto the second one. I seem to hold up a barrier of my problems. Not once did I mention any of my problems, but they could see how passionate I was about nutrition. They were surprised I was working in banking.

On one of my tinder dates, I went to the Churchill arms in Notting Hill. This pub was located just a ten minutes stroll from my apartment. I met my date and was instantly not attracted. I had a few beers however. By the end, my date started ordering shots for us. At this point, I started chatting to a random dude in the bar, to get away from my date. My date was trying to coax me home with him. I got absolutely twisted and then fell outside of the pub and jumped into a taxi. The taxi journey should have been no more than five minutes, however I spent the guts of an hour in the taxi. We were outside my apartment complex and I wasn't sure if it was my home or not. I phoned Martin and put him onto the taxi driver.

"Are you sitting outside a row of white houses?", Martin asked the taxi driver.

"Yes", he responded.

"Tell Mary to get out of the taxi and go in. She lives there."

Sixty pounds later, I made it home safe and sound.

I phoned in sick once or twice to work, and headed off to the local pub to meet some random people and talk about fun stuff while sitting in the sun. This was the best way I could distract myself from the shitness of life at the time.

Within seven weeks I started contemplating handing in my notice, but didn't know how to phrase it. Eventually after a week, I plucked up the courage to go to my manager. I cried about my mum's health.

"We will definitely leave the job open for you Mary, and you can take a month or two to think about it."

"I've thought about it", I responded. "I won't be coming back."

I got home at the end of June, and left my apartment in London open until September, so that I could go back and forth to visit and get things. This was the one and only time that my mum didn't come to the door to greet me. I walked into the living room and she was sitting backward in an electronic chair unable to really move. She still had a big smile and was glad to see me. I scratched my head and headed out off to the Blue Light pub with a friend just for two or three drinks.

"Are you sure you can't get up and walk down the stairs with me by your side?", I heard my dad say as I came in the door.

I went over straight away and said, "Leave her, bring her back into the living room, she's not ready to go down."

Mum nodded and said, "Exactly, I'm not ready."

Dad and I sat up with her for another hour or so until we eventually managed to get her down the stairs to bed. She liked being in her bed and liked reading the affirmations I wrote out for her on a large posted on the wall. Those affirmations are still there and read:

> *"I lovingly forgive and release all of the past. I choose to fill my world with Joy. I love and approve of myself"*

The next one reads:

> *"Every day in every way I am getting better and better"*

I made my mum read them over and over from the time she got diagnosed.

It was around this time, that a lot of fuss started happening in the house. The idea of bringing her to a hospice was brought up.

"I'm not going to let that happen, as it will be like I have given up on her", my dad said.

For me personally, I was thinking a hospice was a good idea, because I was literally sick to death of this shit. I didn't want chemotherapy, steroids, a billion anti-nausea drugs or radiotherapy, as I knew it didn't work for lung cancer. I wanted weed, herbal plants, Tibetan mushroom, laetrile, the best diet unimaginable. But of course I couldn't get my way. Christ, I had to write out a list longer than the biggest shopping list before going to Thailand, of not only the things I was advising to give her, but also the shitty drugs that doctors here were advising. Looking back now, I'm happy we went with my dad's decision to keep her at home.

A few days later, the fire brigade arrived at our house, and six fire men lifted Mum out of the bed from downstairs to a hospital bed up in our drawing room. Her body was weak, and the effect of muscle wasting and sarcopenia had kicked in. The woman was simply immobile since I left to go back to London. At least her hospital bed was beside my piano, and it's now replaced with a new shiny erg that I bought from the indoor rowing championships in December last year. I always know how to move on with my life and I've replaced the shitty memory of that room with a gym. A treadmill that was bought when my dad had five bypasses, and an erg for me and any other rowers that want to use it and break that bad bitch in for me. I find triathlon relatively easy, but I find the rower extremely challenging. It's time for me to get back that rowing fitness I had in college. Prodigy and Deadmousse will be blaring, as I get back into that sort of training. Sodium bicarbonate will become my new best friend as my aim is to lactate late, with less pain running through my thighs. The last thing I want is sarcopenia. It starts to kick in after the age of thirty, according to Brendan Egan, who knows his shit on exercise and nutrition. I attended a conference with the Irish Society for Clinical Nutrition and Metabolism last year, and I asked him a good few questions about sarcopenia and the importance of high intensity interval training, weights and branched chain amino acids. I was purely focused on myself at the time. At this conference, I also learned about GEDS. A ninety year old man in the pool on one of Brendan Egan's slides, swears by genetics, exercise, diet and spirit. Back to Mum.

"Hi I'm Frances." This was some outside help that we needed from the hospice at last. Dad started staying at home more, as I think it hit home with people that this was it.

"Do you think Mum is going to die?", a few siblings asked me on occasion.

Either they're gone blind or I am.

"Yes", I responded. "It's quite obvious."

I'm a no bullshit character who knows what is laid down in front of her, and I know when hope is lost. But who can't say I tried my fucking best.

Frances was great. I used to go out and get coffees for the three of us, while she sat with Mum. Anna was trying her best to help but she was pregnant at the time so she couldn't lift a dead weight.

The next two months, Frances and I spent our time cleaning Mum, sometimes in the shower, sometimes in the bed, taking her to the loo and just sitting with her. Suzi was good at reading books to her and the others were good at feeding her.

"Can you make that nice dish your mother likes Mary?", Dad asked me one day.

"What are you on about, risotto is it?", I had a million other things on my mind. I cooked the mushroom risotto, fed it to Mum and that was the last meal I gave her.

"Do you feel like a slave?", Mike asked me one day grinning.

"Yes, I sort of do Mike."

I was cooking meals for everyone that was coming up to the house, all of the siblings and in laws and grand kids. I felt like fucking crap.

"Have you always wanted to be a nurse?", my mum asked on numerous occasions. I'd grunt at her and just carry on. This was torture for Mum and I. I just sat with her in silence and watched her as she pondered on life. It was wrecking my head not knowing what is going through her mind. I needed a distraction.

I went back on tinder. I met a nice guy, who funnily enough lived in Australia for a few years, but experienced psychosis while out there. I decided it was time to give this guy a chance. I went on about five dates with him, but it just didn't feel right. One day, when I was heading out to meet him, I said to Mum, "Off to meet my tinder date."

"What's he like?", my dad asked.

"Yeah nice, but he could be a bit taller."

Mum, in her morphine riddled state laughed and said, "As long as he knows where to put it."

Dad went red and I left the room.

I couldn't sleep with this guy. At the time he was just some nice company to deflect from what was going on in my life. A proper gentleman. I also look back, and think that someone who has experienced psychosis is probably not a good match for me. Who the fuck knows what would happen to the two of us! He would think that the mafia are out to get him, and I would think that there are cameras all over the place.

29th of August came and I decided that I was still going to Electric Picnic, which is a music festival in county Laois. This is what my mum would have wanted. I was excited, and geared up and ready to let my hair down. I got to county Laois, and my sister phoned me to ask me to return home. This was it, my mum was about to pass away. I hopped out of the car and decided to sell my ticket, cash in hand to some random dude.

Not thinking at the time, the car park filled up loads before I could track my move back and hit the road. I met Crunchy in the meantime, one of my brother's friends. I just said, "I can't find Mum's car, I need to go home to her."

He smiled and said best of luck with that. I couldn't get through to any of my friends, as the networks were all down. I got through to my sister eventually who was driving back from Tipperary, and she agreed to pick me up. For the next two hours, I just hung out with random people and had a beer to pass the time.

Mum was unconscious when I got back, and I was pissed off that I missed my last words with her. The last she saw of me was a happy go lucky girl off to a festival, so I was a bit reassured by that. She knew I had done so much work for her, like she did for me. We got her last rights said and then one by one people started going to bed. I wanted to stay up. I sat with Mum and held her hand to the very last minute. I drank beer while beside her to numb my own pain. Her last breath was around ten in the morning and I was happy she was eventually free of pain.

Chapter 7

Light at the End of a Dark Tunnel

The funeral came around a few days later and I chose to say a prayer to Frances. I wanted to pray to someone who had helped us a lot towards the end. No tears, but that's just how I roll. We all headed up to Johnnie Foxes where we buried Mum, and afterwards I enjoyed a good few drinks with friends and family, the exact way Mum would have wanted it.

"It was so nice to see one of Mary's friends cry at the funeral", my older brother said to my dad. My friend Cathy cried, but I just couldn't.

"Mary I remember how sound she was when she used to take Michelle and I to Superquinn for food shopping when you would be at singing lessons. She used to let us throw any sorts of treats into the trolley. Also the times she took us to Marlay to feed the ducks."

"I know", I smirked.

That's probably why I still frequent Marlay Park a lot, because I have fond memories of my mum of when she was both well and also trying to recover from illness.

I found out a few quirky things about Mum from others talking about her and discussions with the priest. I did some maths and calculations as to when they met and when they got married. It was a shot gun wedding more or less. They fell in love within the moment of seeing each other and were married within three months to go on and have seven children. They got married much later in life, my mum was twenty eight and my dad was twenty nine, which was late for their time. The average age back then seemed to be about twenty four. It was also a great love story of meeting on Saint Paddy's day and my dad asking my mum to buy him a six pack of Guinness. He chased her and chased her until she decided to give him a shot. I look at Dad and think he is "the cat that got the cream". I still pray for Dad and want him to move on in a more positive light the exact way I have.

It was around this time, I started seeing a psychotherapist. I started work in the family business, took on a job in a restaurant, continued my masters and got back into training slowly. I had a lot to focus on, and as they say *"out of sight, out of mind"*; or *"a busy mind is a happy mind"*.

Every Monday, I went to see this psychotherapist in the gestalt centre on Leeson street. I was happy. Seeing someone who's not going to force drugs on you and just listen to problems for an hour. I was still taking my medication post Thailand but was weaning off them slowly. I had to pay €80 to see this person but it was worth it. Well, initially I thought it was a load of bollox. She kept bringing up my mum, but I kept wanting to discuss Vietnam and try and explain what happened then. A psychotherapist is supposed to be quite experienced in psychosis, so I thought she might get to the root cause of my episode. I was discussing my weight with her a lot and that I still had issues with binge eating disorder which I had post Vietnam. This time however, I was binging and then purging my food maybe three times a week. I wouldn't be able to stick my fingers down my throat but I would drink a lot of water after a binge episode, and then puke in the toilet. This is something which I had never done before in my life. It was mostly water that I was puking up, but it made me feel better to jump on the scales after a purge episode. I wanted to discuss this with the psychotherapist, but she wanted to discuss my mum, so in the end I was mostly silent for the first four sessions.

Session five came and after she did some homework on me, she wanted to get to the nitty gritty of Vietnam. I tried to explain my reasoning behind my psychotic episode and explained that a few people kept bitching to me about others on the trip and that my energy levels seemed to be all over the place. She couldn't really understand the root cause of it all, but knew I was still fighting food addiction. I took a great tip from this psychotherapist. Epsom salts. She advised that soaking my feet in them will help with my chocolate cravings, as chocolate addiction is a sign of magnesium deficiency. Magnesium gets absorbed best through the skin rather than diet. Epsom salts also aid in recovery after any form of strenuous activity.

During session six, seven, eight and nine, I spoke more, but not about my mum, about me, and my training abilities. By January, I had my last session with her. I told her that I was doing bootcamp, trekking mountains with my University, I had a new personal trainer and that I was travelling to different places to buy retail for work. I didn't need her any more and I was eventually off my stupid fat pills.

I dropped down to nine stone ten pounds by February, and was extremely fit. I was probably only eating 1800 calories a day, which is very little for someone doing so much exercise. I lost my periods. This was a side effect of the fucking medication as well. My periods were all over the place post Vietnam and Thailand, and I swear the drugs can make anyone infertile. Hello population control Mr. pharmaceutical drugs.

Anyway, I kept asking my personal trainer was I doing too much or did I need to eat more because amenorrhoea is a severe problem in women who just don't eat enough. My personal trainer recommended that I go see Danny Lennon from Sigma Nutrition, and discuss this with him. I didn't bother going at that point. I just used my head and bunked my calories up slowly. Over the course of a month, I was gone from 1800 calories a day to 3000 calories. Within that time frame my periods came back. This was May. I was eating carrot and ginger juices with a tub of cottage cheese, plenty of berries, nuts, or porridge for breakfast. I was eating tuna sandwiches and omelettes for lunch and then big hearty dinners with lost of nutritious snacks in between. I would also regularly enjoy some 90% dark chocolate or just the milk variety with a glass of red wine in the evenings.

While I had missed my periods between February and May, I asked a few friends about this issue and they told me they miss theirs all of the time. I thought to myself, that it's not normal to be missing periods, but sure half of my friends self medicate with anti-anxiety drugs and think that is normal. May came and I had my periods back. I knew that now was time to sign up for this bloody triathlon that had been on my mind pre Vietnam.

I signed up. Dublin Vodafone City Olympic triathlon. I knew I was capable. The distance is a 1.5 kilometre swim in the river Liffey, followed by a 40 kilometre cycle around the Phoenix park and then a 10 kilometre run. I signed up, bought myself a specialized road bike and joined the fifty meter pool at UCD. Life was great. I was back to cycling nine miles in and out of work, continuing to study nutrition and training hard. I had two personal training sessions a week, did twenty miles of running, three kilometres of swimming and lots of cycling. I loved the sessions with the personal trainer, as he would do weights and high intensity interval work which involved the rower. My bitch face worst nightmare, but I loved the challenge and pain of it all.

I all of a sudden came back to life after my mum passing away and we both bounced positivity off each other. He would take body fat measurements and weight every now and again and mine didn't seem to shift much. We both decided to throw my scales in the bin and just be happy with a ten stone frame. I have gained easily ten pounds of muscle since the Vietnam days and am even fitter than when I used to row in college.

"Mary you seem to be eating a fair amount and doing a lot of intense training, you should check out Michael Phelps' diet, he eats a massive 12,000 calories a day. I'm not saying you should eat that much, but it's worth looking up."

I googled it the next day and was amazed that Phelps ate several breakfasts, lots of eggs, a full kilogram of pasta a day, ham and cheese toasties and pizza. The man was burning roughly 1,000 calories each hour of swimming. I thought to myself that I'd love to train more and eat more and get up to four to five hours of training in a day. Of course during Phelps' intense training and diet regime he needed to get blood tests and triglycerides measured frequently. Everything was in check as he was burning off all of the sugar.

In preparation for my first triathlon, I wanted to practice open water swimming. I booked a last minute trip to Croatia on my own. An island called Krapanj. This was the best holiday to date. I was free to live my own dream, and I could swim over four kilometres each day from island to island.

At the airport, I stopped in at a bookshop and landed in front of a pocket book on mindfulness. It's short and has all of these quotes on positive thinking. I read a few quotes and thought to myself that this is exactly how I feel. I was extremely happy again and felt like I had overcome post-psychotic depression and grief at last. I reflected back on my mum at that point, and thought, "How did she practice the Mona Lisa smile?". She was such a positive individual, especially in her latter years, as I think the suffering of depression had made her a much stronger character. Luckily for me, my depression only lasted two and a half years post Vietnam.

I booked the holiday with Strel swimming adventures, and met the best crew of people ever. There were nine of us on the boat. Nine seems to be the magic number. There were nine in Vietnam, nine in Croatia and nine in my family. There was a mixed cultural group on this trip. They were from England, Lithuania, Australia, Slovenia and Sweden. I got chatting to them all but also enjoyed chill time on my own listening to music. I was having issues with my two year old I phone's battery life back in Ireland, where I needed to charge it twice a day, but while in Croatia, the sun juiced that bad boy up and I only needed to charge it every second day. I was on a high again.

"My father has swam the length of the Amazon river", Borut told me one day.

"Wow what distance is that?", I asked.

I all of a sudden started having dreams of doing marathon swims across the sea.

One evening, after dinner I asked could I swim across the lake back to our hotel.

"You're mad", Helen remarked. "That's about one kilometre and you've had a few beers."

I jumped in in my clothes and chilled for a while. We got the boat back to our hotel, and all of us decided to strip down and jump into the sea. "Ugh, I stood on something", I said to myself. I wasn't sure what was in my foot but just headed straight to bed.

The next morning, I was jumping around like a mad thing in my room. I went down for breakfast and Helen was there.

"What's up Mary?", she asked.

I sat down at the breakfast table and said there was something in my foot. Helen being a nurse decided to examine my foot.

"You have a bit of sea urchin in your foot, place it up here and I'll get it out for you."

I rested my foot on the chair while she hammered at my foot.

"Julius can you get me some eggs and toast and a coffee?", I asked as Julius went by.

"Yes, anything else?".

"Oh and throw in a some yogurt and grapefruit juice."

"Why are you ordering me around Mary?", he asked a bit confused.

"I can't move, Helen is getting sea urchin out of my foot."

He sat down next to me and laughed at me.

Julius is a legend and I kept asking him does he know of underwater headphones for spotify.

"Mary I don't use spotify, you have to get an MP3", he said.

He was the fastest at swimming in our group and had all of the gadgets to track distances done with GPS and was listening to beats as he went along underwater. I was slightly envious of him. Next on my list is to find the technology for spotify so I can do high intensity intervals better at the pool. I googled it later and found out that the best Olympic athletes use headphones in all forms of their training to give them that extra push. No surprise there.

"I can't wait for this swim", Vlasta said when she came down. "We do an island crossing today", she added.

"So rather than swim along the islands we actually cross over?", I asked.

"Yep", she nodded and smiled back.

Vlasta is an absolute hero and does cross-fit and long distance swimming with a trainer back in Slovenia. We keep in touch about our travel and swim plans on a regular basis.

"Mary check out the water bottle", Adeline said on the boat to me later that day. The label read:

Do more in life of what makes you happy

All nine of us were happy. We couldn't have asked for a better holiday. I then saw Ironman 70.3 plastered on the Swedish ladies bag. I took a quick snap. 70.3 miles is the half Ironman and it involves a 2.2 kilometre swim, 90 kilometre cycle and a half marathon at the end. Even before my first triathlon, I had half Ironman on my mind.

Borut is a legend, and I am going to Turkey on another swim holiday with him this year. I asked him to write me a testimonial for my website and he wrote the following:

I met Mary on a swimming holiday in Croatia
and she turned out to be a very positive thinker,
hard working and passionate about her beliefs.
We all enjoyed her charismatic personality.

Borut Strel
Strel Swimming Adventures

I got another testimonial from a keen Irish adventurer and enthusiastic health advocate who I met last year:

Mary Guiney is a very self motivated, hard driven young
woman with a lot to offer! Her passion for nutrition has

developed for a long time which was invigorated even further during her mother's illness! This kind of passion and thirst for more is what will fuel this new age of world nutritional revolution ideals that are ongoing. With obesity levels in the developed world skyrocketing and so many nutritional related problems from cancer to depression we need people like Mary to lead the charge and keep this revolution growing. Only with passion and knowledge will we succeed to turn the tide and Mary Guiney encapsulates both!

Karl A. Greene
Health & Nutritional Enthusiast

Karl was telling me all about the sky dives he has done and we were sharing our passions over a nice Thai dinner. After meeting him I wanted more adventure again.

I also got another review from an Irish man I met hill walking in April:

Positive mental health is something we are all entitled to. I was inspired by Mary's openness and honesty in this area the minute I met her; her experiences in life seem to be propelling her forward now and it is clear she has driven an ambition to help others and improve people's lives. With this spirit, I have no doubt that her path will have a positive impact on all those she meets.

Ed Clarke
Accountant

Ed was telling me that he wants to travel a bit and would love to go to Cambodia. He emailed me later to say that work have a placement for him in the Philippines. I told him that he would be mad to miss out on that opportunity, and that travel is very important. People who travel seem to be more open minded in my opinion.

The Croatian holiday was in July, and my triathlon was in August. Adeline came to visit Dublin as she was travelling the world while she took a break from her job back in Australia.

"Mary I'll meet you at Sea Point and do the 1.5 kilometre route with you in preparation for your triathlon."

We swam it together and then I took her to my house to meet my dad. The three of us headed up to Johnnie Foxes where my mum's grave is to have a beer and a whiskey. Adeline stayed the night and then I headed off to work the next day.

I was extremely euphoric the morning of the triathlon. I listened to beats on my phone while changing into my wetsuit. Most of the people racing were in groups or with company, but I was happy to do it alone and get chatting to random people. My group was called out and I put my phone and headphones away.

"You're about to miss it, hurry up", one of the organisers shouted.

"Have you done one of these before?", I asked the girl next to me.

"I've done a sprint triathlon but this is my first Olympic", she said.

I looked away and thought to myself why on earth is this girl wearing a full face of make up. She was about to jump into the river Liffey, and had mascara and foundation on her. I just laughed to myself.

I nailed it. It was pissing rain on the day, but I gave it a good stab, also without music which I was horrified about. I jumped into the Liffey and seemed to be quite strong going upstream, but then I noticed a good few girls passing me out going downstream. I don't seem to notice the difference between up and downstream. I hopped out of the Liffey and ran to my station where my bike was. It seemed to take me about five minutes at transition one, as I scampered to get my wetsuit off in a hurry. I jumped on my bike and I was instantly out of breath. I hadn't practised this transition before as I did all of my own training with no triathlon clubs. I never risked leaving my bike down at Seapoint for fear of it getting robbed. Within about ten minutes I finally settled into a good rhythm on the bike and completed the five laps. I ran straight back to transition two with my bike and spent about two minutes in total, until I was on my feet again to begin the run. I completed it all in two hours and fifty minutes. The swim took twenty nine minutes which I was thrilled at, the bike was one hour and twenty six minutes and the run took me forty nine minutes. It was strange. I had estimated two hours and fifty minutes a few weeks before the event. I'm all about numbers and timing sometimes. It also pissed rain that day, so I hadn't exactly estimated for going slower on the bike. The bike comes easy to most but it's probably my most challenging as my crotch gets pretty damn sore after about an hour in the saddle. The euphoria was high.

I got straight back to work the next day and cycled. It was pissing rain again and I fell off the bike going over the luas tracks. I got straight back on the bike to avoid embarrassment, and I cycled home with blood running down my knees. It didn't phase me.

Ironman was on my mind at this stage. I wanted more. I signed up for the Ironman swim at Glendalough Lake in early September. While we were all in the lake waiting for the horn to go off, I got chatting to two older ladies who do long distance swimming quite regularly. The horn went and I swam off in a panic state. My breath seemed to be completely out of sync for the first ten minutes and my groin started to bother me as I was kicking way too fast. I eventually got my rhythm, and my breathing became more relaxed. I swam the two laps of the lake and completed the 3.9 kilometres in one hour and twenty minutes. I could picture a 180 kilometre cycle and a marathon after it and thought to myself that I was ready to take on that feat next year.

I signed up for the Dublin Marathon in October and the half marathon at the end of September. I couldn't run the half marathon as my hip was bothering me a bit. I'm not sure if it was the dead-lift at the personal trainer or else the fact that I had groin pain throughout the Ironman swim. Anyway, I bailed on the race as it would have been dumb to run it. To ensure I didn't run, I decided to go on the piss the night before it instead.

At the end of September I was looking up Ironman tattoos, and found a nice swim bike run one that I wanted. There was all this bollox on google about how sad it would be to get one before actually completing the feat, but I thought to myself that it was all in the mind. I was tempted to get the 140.6 plastered at the bottom of it.

At the same time, I was contemplating getting my mum's bird tattoo. I wanted it on the other side of my ankle just underneath my birthmark. My mum used to draw this simple bird picture and put it on letters when we were kids. She said the symbol opened up the doors to communication. I couldn't for the love of me find a note with her bird, so I copied it as best from memory and headed off to snake bite on my lunch break.

"How much for this tattoo in small?" I asked the artist.

"Oh you're looking at sixty euro for that size."

"And if I wanted two tattoos?"

"That's cheaper. Two for eighty quid."

While he was drawing my mum's bird, I was distracting from the pain by yapping about the Ironman tattoo that I wanted. He laughed and asked, "Where do you want it? It's a busy leg you have."

I pondered for a while and then decided to think about it more. The artist was also telling me about a woman who wanted her boyfriends name tattooed in her private area. He told her on numerous occasions to go away and think about it, but in the end she was adamant to have it.

"I presume you're not using the same needle?", I asked him with a grin.

"Mary, that tattoo looks like the twitter logo", my brother Mike said to me when he saw my leg. "Haha, I never thought about that, maybe twitter and Mum put logger heads together, along with the world wide web to open the doors to communication in this crazy world."

I had wanted to get this bird tattoo in Croatia when swimming but it was a crazy storm on our last day and the tattoo parlour was closed.

While I was doing a lot of erg sessions at my personal trainer, I also wanted to experience rowing on the river again. One of my brother's in law is a keen rower, and does a lot of training before work and at the weekends. He used to have the fastest erg time in Ireland and almost qualified for the Olympics in 2008. While we sat in the pub discussing megalithic man, we also talked about rowing.

"Yes Mary, you got everyone at the motor neuron charity dinner talking about megalithic man, let's just sign up now."

Megalithic man is a challenging run followed by a cycle and a run up the mountain with your bike on your shoulders followed by another cycle. We both signed up to the fast wave.

"Sean, I wouldn't mind trying rowing with you on the river as well, can we go out in a double one of the days, maybe next weekend?", I asked.

"Yeah sure, just let me know when suits."

We finished our pints and headed home.

One week later I stood by the banks of the river and waited to hop into the double with Sean. He went in bow and I went in stroke.

"You already want to go in?", he asked after thirty minutes.

"Yeah I'm not sure I have the patience for it, I think I prefer triathlon."

We stayed on the river for another fifteen minutes and then pulled into the bank. I reflected a bit, and think I preferred the spins on the river that I did on my own. I could stop and start whenever I wanted and not worry about getting the rhythm 100% correct.

At one of my sessions with the personal trainer, he recommended that I watch Bressi's Ironmind because I was so dedicated to triathlon.

"Who on earth is he?" I asked.

"Niall Breslin. He does the voice of Ireland and coaches triathlons, but he suffered from depression before. All of the women are mad about him."

My friend had at the time actually recorded one of his shows for me.

One evening, I decided to put on Bressi's Ironmind. He was encouraging four athletes to do their very first Olympic triathlon. These were all athletes who had suffered from different forms of mental health. At the time, I had forgotten that I had even suffered mental health as I was purely living in the present moment. I enjoyed watching the show and was happy I kicked all of their asses. This provided more encouragement to keep going and train harder.

Chapter 8

My Thesis Proposal

It was around this time that we had to start thinking about what topic we were going to pick for our thesis. I knew I had wanted to do mine centred around the psychological versus habitual intake of food and how anti-depressants and anti-psychotics can actually cause eating disorders as they did in me. They are renowned for contributing to the obesity crises. The title I had come up with was:

> "The impact of secondary ailments with the use of olanzapine on the emotional well-being of schizophrenic patients who are within a healthy BMI at baseline".

My proposal that I handed in before Christmas went like this.

Overview

Obesity has been shown to be more prevalent in individuals experiencing mental health issues, specifically schizophrenia. This is largely due to the complexity of their genotype, their surrounding environment and the use of anti-psychotic drugs (Holt, 2009). It it thought that treatment with second generation anti-psychotics (SGAs) improves the dopamine reward response but at the same time heightens the hedonic impact of food (Elman, 2006) which leads to over-eating and poor food choices based on increased perception of the palatability of food.

The desire to consume food is driven by two different pathways: The homeostatic route controls energy balance and drives individuals to eat following energy depletion, while the hedonic route is based around reward mechanisms (Lutter, 2009). Research has shown that the use of drugs / drug therapy (Lutter, 2009) can elicit changes in brain biochemistry which impacts the hedonic intake of food. It is well documented that adiposity is tightly controlled by the cortico-limbic system, the hypothalamus and the gastrointestinal tract (Holt, 2009).

Neuro-biological mechanisms have evolved to ensure adequate consumption of nutrients and the maintenance of energy balance which leads to ideal amounts of adiposity (Zheng, 2009). Since the hunter gatherer days and with the increased production of processed foods, refined grains and sugar, individuals are provoked by appetising hunger cues which naturally offsets the neuronal/hormonal regulation of food intake. This also creates leptin resistance in individuals as they have a constant supply of energy dense food. This means that the cortico-limbic region of the brain becomes disrupted and high levels of leptin no longer provide satiety due to the surrounding environment (Zheng, 2009). Low levels of leptin, in response to a reduced intake of nutrients is thought to signal the reward mechanism and consequently affect the behaviour of the individual to consume more food (Zheng, 2009).

Project Objective

Secondary ailments associated with SGAs which increase the risk of metabolic disease account for 20% of the shorter life expectancy in schizophrenic patients compared with the rest of the population (Panariello, 2010). While numerous studies address the physical aspects of drug therapy, there is less research on the emotional well being of the individual with regard to weight gain.

Several randomised controlled trials have shown that intervention with drug treatment, such as metformin and dietary education are most efficacious at reducing risk factors while taking SGAs (Wu, 2008). Other studies using intervention with metformin alone have showed its efficacy in reducing insulin sensitivity and glucose intolerance and have demonstrated that drug treatment is safe (Klein, 2006). Such interventions are only considered for individuals who are overweight or obese, while those who are within a healthy BMI are generally not considered as problematic. The purpose of this study is to investigate the benefit of nutritional education for those undergoing drug treatment with olanzapine and who are already within a healthy BMI.

Project Outline

- Background to the Research
- Goals and Objectives
- Contributions to current research studies on the topic
- Research Methodology & Study Design
- Timeline to achieve objectives
- Required funding and budgets
- Evaluation of the results
- Discussion & how the study contributes to current knowledge
- Conclusions

Context/Relevance

Research has shown a clear link between the use of SGAs and risk factors for increased adiposity, glucose intolerance, diabetes and elevated low-density lipoproteins (LDLs). Randomized trials have showed that baseline screening and continued monitoring of secondary ailments associated with drug therapy are essential in risk reduction of obesity and metabolic disease (Citrome, 2011), however few studies have focused on the quality of life of the patient, specifically their level of satisfaction while receiving treatment.

Certain studies have investigated the use of behavioural intervention in the treatment of weight gain and associated cardio-metabolic risk. One such study found that behavioural interventions can significantly improve insulin regulation and if administered at the start of drug therapy that some individuals may in fact experience weight loss (Gabriele, 2009).

Cognitive behavioural therapy (CBT) has been used as an intervention to educate individuals about nutrition and physical activity and thus is aimed at motivating patients to adhere to lifestyle interventions. In 2006, a pilot study was carried out by the Diabetes Prevention Project (DPP) which involved the comparison of CBT versus drug therapy with metformin (Weber, 2006). The results were outstanding and showed that there was a significant improvement with the CBT group who lost more than four times the body weight than the control group. Another randomized study measured the efficacy of a twelve week CBT programme versus control group who were given brief nutritional education, and it found that the CBT group had better outcomes in weight related cognitions (Khazaala, 2007).

In Australia, an eighteen month naturalistic study (with adherence rates of 85%) found that ongoing education and intervention specifically with exercise at the onset of drug therapy saw a 3.5% decrease in body weight compared to the control group who experienced a 4.1% increase (Poulin, 2007). While many interventions aim to interview individuals, motivate them and educate them on nutrition and exercise (Park, 2011), they usually last only twelve weeks which may not be adequate time to alter behaviour. This study aims to compare both physical and emotional side effects of the illness across control groups and those receiving drug therapy and/or nutritional education.

Methodology

Subjects

A total of forty nine participants suffering from first episode psychosis (n=12) or schizophrenia (n=37) will be recruited. Both males (n=15) and females (n=34) will be assessed who are within a healthy BMI at baseline (mean = 21.9 + 1.4/ - 2.2).

Study Protocol

A pilot study for sixteen weeks will be used to evaluate feasibility of an intervention creating educational awareness around healthy dietary habits and exercise while taking SGAs.

The population group will be recruited via the psychiatrists who are treating patients. Psychiatrists will make individuals and guardians aware of the intervention study, what is involved, how long they will be assessed and any side effects which may be experienced. If the individual agrees to be involved in the study, they will provide written consent for participating.

Participants will be recruited from three different mental health clinics across Ireland and researchers will require approval via the psychiatrist who is treating each individual. Below shows details of each of the services selected in Dublin, Cork and Limerick.

- Cluain Mhuire Community Mental Health Services, Newtown Park Avenue, Blackrock, Co. Dublin
- Dean Clinic Cork, Citygate, Mahon, Cork
- St. Joseph's Psychiatric Hospital, Mulgrave Street, Limerick
- One group (n=22) will be assigned an intervention based around education on healthy dietary habits while also being administered olanzapine, a commonly used SGA which is

known to have several metabolic risk factors and increased adiposity associated with it

- The second group (n=17) will solely undergo standard drug treatment with olanzapine with no nutritional education and no questionnaires surrounding this
- The third group (n=10) will have less severe symptoms of psychosis and will not undergo drug therapy. They will however attend cognitive behavioural therapy (CBT) and the associated educational awareness around healthy lifestyle choices. CBT will be scheduled once a week for four hours over a sixteen week period. These individuals will have attended counselling sessions with therapists & psychiatrists both alone and with family members / parents. Parents will have given informed consent as to not use drug treatments as psychotic symptoms were either quite mild or else the individual was concerned about drug intervention due to personal views. Ethically the desire of the individual must be respected and other interventions are thus adopted.

Statistical Analysis

<u>Photographic Atlases</u> will be used to give a more concrete estimation of food intake. As of late, these strategies are proving more useful than the standard weighted approach which can leave room for error. Photographic atlases provide a memory aid for participants when involved in twenty four hour recall of food intake (Lazarte, 2012).

Laboratory Studies

<u>Blood tests:</u> These are routine measures used both at baseline and throughout drug treatment.

Individuals will give blood samples at 0m, 6w & 3m to measure fasting glucose & blood lipid profile

Body Fat: Weight & height will be measured to record BMI; however callipers will also be used to assess body composition & to record an accurate increase in adiposity in relation to lean mass. Callipers are not always accurate, however changes recorded will be accurate once the same measure is used by the health care nurse. These tools are both quick and inexpensive.

Questionnaires: Current treatment involves questionnaires at baseline (i.e. When the individual is taken into care initially and may still be in the midst of their mental illness (i.e. experiencing auditory hallucinations or else suffering from post-psychotic depression). These questionnaires are normally followed up one month into treatment and after that follow up surveys are usually not carried out for the majority of the population.
This study aims to carry out surveys at baseline, 1m, 2m, 3m & 6m.

While most questionnaires try to assess the individuals life satisfaction at the time, it can be quite intimidating to answer certain questions relating to their current mood. Of course these questions should be mandatory as they are imperative to ensure safety of the individual, however questionnaires addressing life satisfaction (such as educational awareness on healthy eating & exercise) and contentment with treatment plan and physician care are also needed.

Pre- and post intervention questionnaires will be used to measure overall satisfaction, educational awareness, attitudes and overall behaviour modification.

Impact Statement

This pilot study will add value to current research in the investigation of weight gain and associated metabolic risk factors with the use of SGAs. Past studies have reviewed the altered neurobiology when taking SGAs and have made a link between their action on biochemistry and the risk of increased adiposity and associated metabolic syndrome. These studies, however have put emphasis on the "at risk" group of individuals and those who have been in the overweight or obese category at baseline. This study only investigates individuals who are within healthy BMI at baseline and thus aims to establish overall risk both physically (metabolic) and mentally for this group.

Preclinical trials have shown that SGAs are capable of altering the insulin response and consequently lead to glucose intolerance and insulin resistance in some individuals (Elman, 2006). These ailments may either be secondary to increased adiposity or might actually influence the increase in fat mass. Studies have hypothesised that the increase in adiposity and metabolic ailments are initially uncorrelated, however with increasing fat mass the secondary conditions become more pronounced, thus establishing a viscous cycle between the two (Teff, 2011). Animal studies have shown that direct administration of SGAs does in fact impair insulin-induced glucose transport and increase lipogenesis irregardless of weight gain (Teff, 2011). On the other hand the dysfunction of leptin appears to be a consequence of the increase in adipose tissue (Elman, 2006). Observational studies have found that not only do SGAs cause an increase in food intake, but they also cause a huge reduction in physical activity due to their sedative properties (Elman, 2006).

Patient satisfaction while receiving drug treatment has been studied to some extent and one cross-sectional study found that patients were not given the necessary information on adverse effects of drug therapy (Gray, 2005) and that practitioners could have communicated this better. This study will aim to assess the well-being of this group throughout a sixteen week period who would normally not be categorised as an "at risk" group for metabolic syndrome.

My lecturer liked the idea that I was proposing, and said that it was quite unique, however she was worried that there wasn't concrete enough evidence to support the research and that I would have ethical issues with carrying out such a study.

I woke up at 5.30am to go swimming one Wednesday before going to my personal training session and thought to myself life just gets better each year. Even with my mum passing away, 2015 was the best year of my life. The only slight issue I was facing for a while was rising early, but I was still getting about seven hours of sleep and was never bored as the pool would open at 6am.

After attending a nutrition conference with Danny Lennon, I asked him a good question on water weight and not being able to sleep the full whack of eight hours.

"Very good question Mary, you might be suffering from elevated cortisol, but it's nothing major to worry about."

I started googling this and straight away went to my local doctor to get a cortisol test done. Sure enough my cortisol was elevated. I was happy enough, as I got to see that everything else in my body was in full swing like red blood cells, white blood cells and triglycerides. I was perfectly healthy so I didn't stress about it.

I try to chill out more now and load up on potassium rich foods such as bananas, sun dried tomatoes and potatoes to balance out my electrolytes.

I was also going to bed around eleven O' clock, but learned pretty quickly to put my phone onto flight mode. Team leaders from my nutrition course had set up what's app groups to help each other out with exams and assignments. I used to leave the groups and not read any other stuff as I like to study alone. That's what I wasn't mad about with my first masters – the groups. It was grand, but I did much better studying alone and on my own time frame and it goes to show seeing as I got a first in my thesis *Irrational Exuberance: A case study of investor sentiments driving market Euphoria*.

This thesis is all about the greed, inequality and corruption that starts at governments and works its way into banks and then onto individuals. Anyway not to bang on, but I've got my Pakistani dude that I hired to work on my website to put this thesis up on my website so anyone who is interested can have a read. It could be a difficult read for some, but just ignore the maths equations and logarithms and read my own writing if you're stuck. I talk about how media hype can cause manias, panics and crashes, as a lot of traders in the banking system tend to trade based on what they hear in the news. It is very difficult for some of them to detach themselves from what they hear, and they are solely after investments which make a profit for the firm.

Looking back on my masters, we were told in Strategic management about green technology and how there would be electronic pumps in garages around the country to promote green cars. That was eight years ago and I'm still waiting to see a green car in Ireland. It just goes to show, we still have these arguments about oil going on between Russia, Saudi and the States. The jig is up. That fuel source is finite. It's time to move on with the infinite resources and the advancements which the Chinese have made in technology. As we all know, both China and India have the largest populations in the world and to me they are the next super powers as they mass produce so many goods and have made a lot of discoveries in technology.

October came, and my brother was talking about the world cup rugby tickets. He suggested that Dad and I should go over to see Ireland play Argentina in Twickenham. We hadn't qualified but my brother was certain we would.

"That's the weekend of the marathon, I'm going to bail on this one", I said from the Step Inn.

My buddy who was with me at the time was furious I had the option to go. I got onto my sister in law and we agreed that I had plenty of opportunities for a marathon and that the rugby world cup is more exciting to go to.

My friend and I left that conversation and then we started talking about head transplants.

"Did you know there are some people out there who pay over a million dollars to have a head transplant if they are riddled with cancer or disease?", he said.

"What on earth do you mean?", I asked.

"Well if someone is dying of cancer and they have no disease on their brain then they can have their head transplanted. Look I googled it yesterday."

Vietnamese Voices

I may as well have told him then and there, that my mother had her head transplanted onto my body, but I thought we just went six feet under as my spiritual connection in Vietnam was long forgotten about.

Later that night I got home and reflected on Mum. I felt like I had no one to chat to about her. Five of my siblings are married and have kids so it's easier for them. Anytime I brought up funny stories about her with my dad, I could see tears in his eyes, so I would just sit alone in another room. I changed my what's app status to, "Travelling the world and heading to space". I had travel on my mind again and was fascinated by Richard Branson's updates on LinkedIn at the time. Some people are actually travelling to Mars to never return home again. Dad thinks it's nuts. But I see their side to the story.

Dad and I booked tickets over to London. Ireland didn't qualify but at least I was about to watch Australia versus Argentina at Twickenham. A weekend of beer, lots of food and I came back to Dublin zapping full of energy and ran fifteen miles at an eight minute per mile pace. Normally I'm seven and a half minutes per mile, but once it clocks over eight miles I slow down my average.

I looked up the next marathon and signed up for Clonakilty in December. It was a more challenging one with lots of hills but I had run up to my mum's grave five or six times which is quite a challenge. I was ready to take it on.

At this point I was doing lots of assignments and studying animal slaughter. I thought this lecture was grim and wanted to become a pescatarion altogether. The manufacturing of some of the beef and especially chicken in Ireland is just horrific. Battery fed chickens as my mother used to call them. I was put off meat for a good month and now just have it maybe twice a week. I'm still sometimes wondering what exactly is in the meat. The previous year I had done an assignment on the "Horsemeat scandal" which most people are aware of, but it also highlighted that there is a lot more food fraud happening along the supply chain with people trying to cut corners and cut costs on a regular basis.

By this stage, spotify was getting better. They were recommending thirty new songs to me every Monday, so I was kept excited on the music buzz. You're never alone once you have music and exercise in my opinion. "Workout more energy" was a classic by Arnold that I found on my crazy playlist. At this point my dad was getting nervous.

"You know lots of people drop dead at the end of marathons, or look at the hurlers who have sudden cardiac arrest."

To keep his mind at ease, I booked in for an ECG. €100 later and I found out I had sinus bradycardia.

They asked me at the doctors did I practice sport. My heart beats at forty two beats per minute and is only a sign of extreme fitness. I googled it to be sure, and came onto a triathlon website where it was more or less saying that people discussing slow heart rates may as well be discussing cock size. I laughed at this. Onwards and upwards. I had completed a load of assignments and my exams and was ready to hit Clonakilty with a saucepan over the head. The longest I had run was fifteen miles, but I had the mind over matter built up in my head and a lot of hill mileage built up.

I was in driving gear. Swedish House Mafia was playing on spotify and I was driving down to West Cork. A bitch on a mission ready to take on the world. I got to the bed and breakfast in Clonakilty, and the weather looked ominous. I went to the event and met party Kev. He was organising the event. I bought a woolly hat and gloves, ate a load of pasta, had a glass of red wine and went back to my room to have a jaffa cake party.

I couldn't sleep well that night, as the rain was thrashing down on the bed and breakfast. I kept logging on and off to Facebook to see was the event going ahead. "Run through anything, who cares about the weather" was one comment. The next would say "Danger Danger Danger."

I ignored this, and kept stuffing jaffa cakes into my mouth. I was ready to run through sleet at this stage.

The next morning I was all geared up on three hours of sleep. I had porridge, eggs on toast, black pudding, copious amounts of fruit, water and coffee. Thirty minutes later we found out that the event was called off. I thought screw this, so I legged it out the door and drove back to Dublin. I was still a bit euphoric so when I got home, I hopped out of the car and did a ten mile run. The weather was still quite bad, but I needed to exert my energy on the road. The next week, I carried on with work and going to my personal training sessions.

Chapter 9

Saint John of God's

I had decided to celebrate my 30th birthday bash in December, seeing as January is a shit month to celebrate it as everyone seems to be dead in the water after the chaos of Christmas. December 19th arrived, and I had a few friends fly over from London and Manchester, all of my Dublin friends and my family at it. I decided to rent out a room on Baggot street. Something similar to where I organised my brother Daniel's surprise 30th.

I took all of the empty beer bottles from our house to the dump, where they recycle things. I cleaned the house from top to bottom and changed sheets for people staying. I also prepared a massive chilli con carne and made sure there was plenty of beer, wine and nibbles in the house.

"Mary are you fucking serious, you still have the frogs from Vietnam?", Pa asked looking puzzled. "Haha, yeah sure that holiday was great even though shit hit the fan", I replied.

"You kept buying random shit off the Vietnamese and do you remember the green hammock you bought?"

"Yes", I said. "That hammock is out in the shed and the nieces and nephews love the frogs."

It is a set of three wooden frogs with a stick type thing which makes a frog sound. The kids love them. At least I managed to bring all of this stuff home with me seeing as things were getting high out there.

I got to my 30th and my brother John gave me a present of Pogs. I started crying as he gave them to me, as it reminded me of playing pogs on the kitchen floor while Mum was cooking dinner. A game that hopefully the kids might still be into.

Mum's birthday came around, the 21st of December, and I ran up to the grave and went to my personal trainer. That was the last session I did with him. Hustle and bustle was about to happen. Again, I was hosting Christmas and taking on my mum's role. It's hard sometimes, but I didn't move back with my parents because I just felt like it. I did it for them and to mind them and keep them company, while looking after their health at the same time.

Anyway, I have a large family and here we go. I was making a turkey, fry ups for breakfasts, lunches, four more dinners, cooking and cleaning. My brother Daniel was great help. He could see I was getting stressed doing all of the work for everyone and it wasn't fair, so he helped with the stuffing and cleaning the dishes. He also made me nice carrot and ginger juices when I had simply lost the energy to do anything else. His wife was great at chopping meat for me when I needed time out. I took a stroll on Christmas day to get some space and saw a full moon. I took a picture with my shitty camera and put it on Facebook entitled "Christmas got good."

I was starting to get sleep deprived, and could feel stress building up. I wasn't hearing any voices but I knew this was it again. Christmas isn't for me. I had wanted to be in another country just lapping up the sun on my own. But I was hosting this Christmas for my dad. Wrong move, and now lesson learned at last. I need to put myself first, just like my mum would have wanted. If she was alive she would have been saying that I should not be taking on such a large responsibility as a singleton.

The next day, I decided to visit my Aunt who was taken from a nursing home into a psychiatric ward in Tallaght. Dad and I got there and she was chuffed to see us, but wasn't doing too well.

"I'm paranoid about all of the nursing staff and what I'm hearing on the TV Mary", she immediately said to me.

I wasn't sure what was going through her head. We took her to lunch and then I went over to some of the black nurses and explained about her paranoia.

"You're an earth angel", they said to me.

"You're good to come visit her, we will look after her from here on in."

I had to explain to my Aunt that she had to trust the nurses in there.

Two days later, I phoned to see how she was doing and she had been moved back to the nursing home where she felt more comfortable.

I had to carry on. New Years came and went and so did my birthday. The third of January. My family took me out to Roly's for a celebratory lunch but I just wanted to be in my own company. The show must go on. I kept posting things to Facebook, just writing down my thoughts at the speed of light. No one can understand any of it. It's what my sister Anna calls the train of consciousness. She did an English degree and said that some of the best writers write in this format, but it is difficult for others to understand. You write exactly as you think and that's what I was doing on my laptop and on Facebook. Essentially trying to open up the doors of communication as to how I was feeling at the time. My thoughts were coming out at the speed of light.

One of the first things I posted was a screenshot from my phone of what I had been googling in 2015 and it was all of this information about what nice hobbies there would be for a 72 year old man to take up while he is grieving for his wife. Throughout all of 2015, I was so happy, but my heart still cried for my dad. So, when I was finished with my day, training, volunteering and working hard, I would google what stuff my dad could do in his spare time to keep him more positive. I then started posting more stuff at the speed of light.

All of a sudden, I got a notification to say that Sam, the paddy instructor from Thailand had accepted my friend request. I started thinking to myself, why on earth has he accepted my request two years later? I was thinking then and there, had he just not seen it back in 2013.

I found it hard to sleep, as I saw that the planets were all congregating the next morning, and that it would be the first time in a long time that all eight planets would be able to be seen from the naked eye. I got to bed and then rose early. I don't have experience in planet watching, but watched each of them get brighter as the sun came up. I cycled my bike around the garden and stared into the sky. My dad came out and he couldn't understand what I was up to. I lost interest and went inside.

At that moment my Uncle Donie rang me from Germany. He had been taken into hospital for a serious operation just before Christmas. I was talking on and off to his ex wife's son and gave him a lot of advice of how to care for Donie after his operation. I sent a text with a list of foods to keep his strength up. Donie was doing much better and wanted me to come visit. At this point, I had him on my mind and was listening to my playlist Kill Bill which has the song, "To Germany with love". I booked the flight and sure enough my dad started worrying about me again.

Dad decided to send me into John of God's, a stress clinic in Dublin. I was lying in bed asking him to leave me alone and he said, "trust me." I hopped out of bed and there were two Gardai in my house and an ambulance outside. I sat in my kitchen, had a smoke and stared at my tiger balm which I kept from that dude in the first hospital in Vietnam. This was the guy who I gave my I pod to in exchange. Good deal. I'm a retard at times.

I wouldn't talk to any of them and I massaged my temples with the tiger balm.

"Mary listen to me, your father is worried", the Irish Garda said.

After hearing this, I went along with it and hopped straight into the ambulance to be brought down to Blackrock Garda Station.

The French Garda had tears in his eyes while I discussed nutritional aspects of the French and how they have the eight healthiest diet in the world according to a TV show I watched a few months previous. Iceland are number one with all of their fish, and Japan somewhere like fifth. Ireland and the States are rubbish, surprise, surprise.

Anyway onwards to Blackrock Garda station and it was again another funny experience. I was in the back where they throw people in a padded cell for the evening for their sins. I was ravenous at this stage.

"Is there anywhere to get food? I haven't eaten for eight hours", I asked in confusion.

"There's a chipper down the road", said the middle aged Garda. He reached in for my bag, took my wallet out and grabbed a fifty euro note.

I was left with a junior Garda who was no more than twenty four, and we decided to add each other on Facebook. I made him laugh and we discussed education and fun stuff. The older Garda brought back food and landed a burger and chips in front of me and never gave me any change. This was the fourth of January. I have a good mind to go to the ombudsman in town because essentially I got robbed by a Garda. They can properly tap into CCTV there and this dude won't be laughing any more. I'll only do it if I have the energy to.

"Do you know the Chan Zuckerberg Initiative?", I asked the older Garda.

"Who's that?", he replied as he chomped down some food.

"It's the CEO of Facebook and his wife, they want to donate their net worth to charity. I hear my dad banging on about how generous they are all of the time and I have googled their initiatives more this Christmas."

"That Mark guy is just a greedy asshole who has too much money", he said back.

I looked at the junior Garda and said, "Don't let older cops pollute your mind, let's enjoy the burger."

Some Gardai are as corrupt and ignorant and need the fear of God put back into them.

— 108 —

It was pissing rain and the three of us headed down to the paddy wagon. I had a smoke with the middle aged Garda and he made the young one pretend to drive like a lunatic by revving the engine up and down for ages. I was pissing myself laughing.

"You know John of God's has a golf course?", the older Garda said.

"Oh I didn't realise. I know it from visiting my mum in there but didn't realise there was a golf course."

I was high as a kite and didn't give a shit where I was going as long as I had a bed to lay my head on. They drove me there safe and sound, with a lot of banter going on in the car about the disgrace of the health care system in Ireland.

I turned around and said, "Ciao for now, see ya later kiddos."

"Mind yourself", the Garda remarked.

Oh the joys of being a Garda. They catch all sorts.

The next thing, I was escorted to my ward. I know John of God's well. The coffee area that is. My mum was in and out of there for years only for a few weeks at a time. She initially suffered depression, but told me when I came back from Vietnam that it was bipolar she had.

"It took me fifteen years to find the right drug, talk to me about Vietnam young lady", was one of the first things she said to me in 2012.

All I could do was show her my book at the time. She was always glad when I opened up to her. It's a pity I didn't do it often enough.

Anyway, I took this on the chin and thought to myself that I am off to a ward to follow in my legendary mother's footsteps. Why was she in here in the first place? She raised seven children, cooked amazing dinners, cleaned and hoovered a large house from top to bottom, worked for USIT in her London days to promote travel in young people, became the first female manager in Ireland and also ran and directed Michael Guiney Limited with my dad. The woman was on fucking strike from doing so much for other people and so was I. She also made sure that our family business donated a large sum of money to UNICEF each year, a charity close to her heart.

In 2015, I was moving on with my own life, but volunteering with Spina Bifida Ireland, working in retail, doing a nutrition masters and doing triathlons. I thought I had a good healthy balance in 2015, so I just knew then and there that Christmas was the trigger. I was doing too much for such a large family. I walked up with a nurse and said, "I'm on strike."

I got to my ward, and it was about midnight at this stage. Two nurses took me in for a chat and I explained what I was doing all over Christmas. I ran into a room and jumped on a blue mattress. "You're not sleeping here", they said in confusion.

"Why not? I'm bloody wrecked."

The blue mattress reminded me of Vietnam when I simply needed to lie down but there was so much craziness going on in Hanoi at the time, that I couldn't rest. I followed them out and they said that my bed would be ready in about an hour. I just rolled with it.

I had my headphones, laces on my runners and I pod confiscated straight away. This was precaution in St. Martin's ward in case I got too high by listening to spotify in my own little bubble. OK, I can kind of see why they confiscate wires but seriously my laces? In the end I went through three pairs of headphones in there as they kept getting damaged or robbed. I had to get on with it. No bed and I was wrecked. There were lots of patients to talk to though, as none of them seemed to be able to sleep.

I got talking to Heather. She was cool and such a nice person. She was up in a pink night dress chatting to another patient. We got talking about music and she sang some songs for me on the smoking terrace. I sang for her too. I had my voice classically trained as a kid and sang the Ave Maria, Amazing Grace, Pie Jesus and a few other songs at my brother's and sister's weddings. Martin in fact came to my brother Mike's wedding and was shocked when I opened my mouth to sing.

"Jesus Mary I didn't expect that from you", he gasped.

Heather's talent was certainly there, but mine seemed to be a bit rusty.

"CCTV is watching us, they know everything we're up to, the IRA bombings went on and I own six houses and the Gardai have confiscated all of them from me."

Heather left, she felt uncomfortable. I got chatting to Norman. He was talking about CCTV and the IRA. I calmed him down by saying, "I know we're all being watched but IT intelligence is going to get the nasty fuckers. I had psychosis in Vietnam and thought there was cameras all over the place, and look I just found out that they put a huge one billion dollar investment into technology in Vietnam so I wasn't far wrong." He laughed and we got chatting.

Norman was wearing a diesel jumper and looked like fun. We got talking more and it turns out he knew my uncle who was in John of Gods for alcohol addiction and sadly passed away at the age of forty five.

"You knew Con?", I asked shocked. "Sure he was in here about twenty years ago."

"I've been locked up in this ward for eighteen years", he responded.

I was horrified. He did seem very genuine but completely institutionalised in my opinion. It wouldn't surprise you. How on earth is someone supposed to get well if they are locked in a ward for eighteen years? He continued to say that Con cracked him up and made him laugh an awful lot. Con was also a best friend to my dad, before he met my mum of course.

Con used to go on some holidays with Mum and Dad when they needed a break from the kids, and I still remember fond stories of the three of them living it up in Acapulco. My dad still has a poem from Uncle Con which he wrote to Ryan Tubridy's Dad, who is a psychiatrist. Ryan Tubridy does the talk show "The Late Late" on a Friday night. The poem from my Uncle Con was entitled "Sir Watered Scotch."

The next person I met that night was Andrew. He was roughly my age, thirty or so and was apparently admitted for having too much fun over Christmas. He was on detox tablets.

"That's just nuts, you went out a few nights over Christmas and now they have you in here on detox medication? What sort of tablet is that anyway?", I asked.

He shrugged in confusion.

"I ended up leaving a hotel room I was at, with a bunch of lads in Kilkenny after a night out, and I had no shoes on as I had accidentally left them in the hotel room. I got home that night and went straight to bed but my mother was worried about me. The next day, there were three Gardai in my house, so I decided to jump out of my bedroom window and take a long stroll to avoid all the fuss. After about fifteen minutes, I saw a police helicopter chasing me and they threw me straight in here", he told me.

I pissed myself laughing and the two of us took another drag of our smoke. He asked what my story was and I mentioned the stress of Christmas started making me go manic, but I was also trying to explain Vietnam to him as I felt like the two scenarios were connected.

One by one, people came out from their rooms and we all got chatting. It was certainly better than everyone being in isolation. There was a lot of chat going on and the nurses were asking us to keep quiet so we started writing down our experiences. Mark was nice but he was doing too much talking.

"Write down your problems, here's a pen and paper", I told him.

"I can't write", he responded.

"I bet you ten bucks you can write."

Within about ten minutes he kept writing notes to me and I read them. He also showed me photos of him before he got thrown into John of God's years ago and he was in much better shape. He said that he regularly goes on hunger strike to piss off the nurses. Five minutes later, he brought out a bag of Doritos which were hidden under his bed.

I got bored after a while, and requested my I pod back.

"There's a camera on this," the nurse said.

I reassured her that it was just used for music and had no camera. This brings back to the camera memories of Vietnam. I was thinking to myself, now who is the one getting paranoid about cameras. I hit play and we all listened to some mellow tunes as we continued to write. One by one, people started drifting off to their rooms.

I could hear a lot of shouting and yelling coming out from the isolation room.

The nursing staff had roped Mark into that room and locked him away. He didn't stop screaming.

Three hours later my bed was ready. I finally got to lie down. It was next to impossible to get any sleep as the amount of snoring going on in some of the bedrooms was intense. I could also hear Norman going up and down the ward mumbling to himself. Every hour, a nurse would come into the room and shine a bright torch in on top of our beds. This was more annoying than anything. The next four nights, I was going to be more sleep deprived than ever.

The next morning, I got up and had breakfast and then headed to the balcony for a smoke. I met Kara out there. Kara was gas. She is more along the lines of being clinically obese and has been taking medication for years which is a horrible side effect of it. She seemed to also have a really bad pulmonary infection. To me, this woman needed to be in a general hospital for physical examinations. She would sometimes sing on the smoking balcony to keep herself entertained.

"Do you play any instruments?", I asked.

"I'm very good at the piano", she replied.

"Cool, I'll get my dad to bring in my classical piano book and you can play a few tunes in the coffee area."

They have a piano downstairs which used to get played often when my mum was in there, but no one ever plays it any more as the piano is completely out of tune. It's quite a disgrace actually that they haven't bothered to tune up the piano as there seems to be quite a few talented people in John of God's. Unfortunately no one is allowed to use their talent.

The next person I met was Leo. He was sound out.

"I've been in here for three years, the same ward for three years."

He carried on smoking and so did I.

"Its a disgrace how they're treating people in here. Any idea why you're here in the first place?", I asked.

"No idea, but I get out in May and I won't be back that's for sure. I'm going to get a construction job and get fit as a fiddle again."

"Good call, right time for it and you'll lose a good bit of weight that way", I remarked.

I couldn't believe that some individuals had been locked up in that ward for years. It's no more than four hundred and fifty square foot.

I enjoyed having coffee breaks downstairs with Leo and the odd cigarette, but started to feel really sorry for everyone in the ward. I knew I had to get out as soon as I could and focus on myself. I learned from looking after my mum that you cannot do a good job of it unless you have fully started to look after yourself first. It was at this point that I started getting ideas about properly writing a book and launching a website on mental health, with of course my passion for nutrition and exercise thrown in.

"Was that your Dad, Mary?", Jane asked me.

I nodded. "I couldn't help but over hear some of your conversation, but are you Delia Guiney's daughter?", she asked with delight.

"Yeah, I'm her youngest", I replied.

"Oh my God, she is the loveliest woman ever, she advised me to go to college when I was in here years ago and sure enough I did. She also used to take me for spins in her car and bring me out for coffee and lunches."

I was glad to be hearing such great things about my mum and how she loved to help people so much.

"What did your Dad bring you in Mary?", Jane asked.

"Oh it's just a titanic book and postcard dated 2012 from my Aunt. She asked my Dad to bring it from her hospital into me. I don't know how, but she must know I would have been into the Titanic when I was a kid", I replied.

Vietnamese Voices

"Titanic was 1912 and the postcard 2012, is it just to resemble one hundred years apart?", she asked.

"Maybe, but I was also in Vietnam in 2012 and I've been reflecting loads on Vietnam over the past few days. My Aunt doesn't have a clue about Vietnam. It's random." We both went silent.

It was at this point, that I started realising that most people in John of God's were worried about work. It brought me back to a recent time in the pub with my friend Sue Roe, and we had an older man approach us and say that he was looking for plumbing work. We laughed at him and said, "How are we supposed to help with that?".

He replied by saying that he couldn't help but over hear my conversation on anti-depressants and that he was on them for fifteen years and is now looking for work.

"My son was a great journalist and sold all of his stories to the media for €25 million", he continued to tell us.

I nodded and thought in my head, that he needs to rekindle some sort of relationship with his son or maybe, his son is just a plonker for making a success of himself and then selling his stories to a media warehouse, that seems to control the world news these days. The media adds to negative press.

I started getting more signs from Mum in there by reading magazines and watching adverts on the TV. One in particular was to always look the part. Seeing as I was dressed in gym gear all of the time, I decided to start wearing jeans and dresses. They didn't like that I had gym gear on all of the time as they thought I was mad on an exercise hunt, so I toned it down a bit with regular clothes.

I also asked my sisters to bring me in make up and nail varnish so that I could glam myself up a bit. I did not want to make the third mistake of neglecting my appearance and feeling purely like shit.

I look back and laugh now, because anytime I asked my dad to bring in more underwear for me he mixed it up sometimes and brought in bikini bottoms.

"Haha, where does your Dad think you're off to, are those red bikini bottoms?", one patient asked.

"I know, but my room is full of stuff and he must have whipped them out from somewhere by mistake." We both laughed it off.

As I was watching TV, I saw that it was a leap year. I started thinking more about Mum then. "Mary, you know that a woman can propose to a man during a leap year, which comes around every four years", she used to say to me when I was younger.

I started thinking, who on earth am I going to propose to in here!

Martin's ward is the observation unit. It is tiny and there is very little room for people to move around. Everyone appears like zombies crawling up and down the tiny unit trying to stretch their legs. Patients are allowed down for coffee twice a day with nursing staff just to get a bit of fresh air and go for a smoke out in the open.

Being a triathlete and eager to continue exercising I was horrified. One of the days I was allowed out for good behaviour and I went for a thirty minute high intensity run around the grounds out the back. For the rest of the day, I ate my three meals and tried to do yoga poses and core exercises in a busy ward. There's not much else one can do.

I felt gross in the mornings. The heating was on full blast during the night, so I would wake up extremely sweaty.

"Mary you can't come out in a towel", one of the nurses remarked as she was dishing out drugs.

"I have no dressing robe and need a shower", I replied.

"The showers aren't on until eight", she angrily said.

It was 7.30am at this stage and all I wanted each morning was a shower to freshen up. With mental health, they bang on about sleep hygiene, although the stupid water doesn't start first thing in the morning. Some of the toilets are horrific in there as well, so it adds to the most unhygienic practice I have ever seen. Four days later and I was moved onto St. Luke's ward.

Luckily, in this ward, I was given my laces and headphones back and could listen to music freely. The first thing I saw on the TV was that David Bowie had died. I had my phone back at this stage so I posted to my Facebook wall, *Legends are born in January and legends die in January*. I then started listening to Heroes and the song brought me back to Croatia when I was swimming with Dolphins. My phone got confiscated again.

"Mary, why are you back on Facebook?", the psychiatrist asked.

"I posted one comment about Bowie, is there something so wrong with that?".

She said that I had posted far too much weird stuff before coming in and that I might want to delete them.

"It's about not caring so much what other people think and no one is going to be stalking me that far down, I've covered it all up with pictures of cats at this stage."

She laughed at me. I was happy I eventually got a giggle out of a psychiatrist. They usually look like they are sucking on a lemon.

St. Luke's is a much brighter and bigger ward as well.

"Hey there, what's your name?", I asked this nice looking dark haired lady.

"I'm Zoe, what on earth are you doing in here?", she asked.

"Oh who knows probably the same as you, I need to get out of here soon."

"I'm not ready", she said. "I need a few more weeks here."

Zoe in my opinion was dealing with a bit of stress from carrying on too much at home. She had kids and a husband, but it reminded me of my mum being in here for taking on too much as well. Zoe started showing me photos of her before she was admitted years ago and she was telling me how she desperately wanted her old figure back.

"I'm going to start weight watchers as soon as I get off this ward", she said.

A lot of people seemed to be carrying excess weight and were unhappy about this. I read before that the obesity epidemic started when the low fat guidelines were introduced. Well, do you know what? Obesity started when psychiatric drugs came onto the scene.

I had more freedom to go out of the ward when I wanted to grab a quick coffee. The days seemed long in there though. Grabbing a coffee at nine in the morning seemed like the biggest treat in the world.

I emailed my lecturer to let her know that I was in John of God's, but that I would easily be able to get on with my thesis and that I had it all stored in my head as to how I was going to approach it. I was also explaining to other patients what I was studying and they were more than happy to give me permission to put their scenarios and drug side effects into my thesis. Olanzapine seems to be a big one and so does librium, atomoxetine and lithium. It was advised that I postpone my thesis and will be completing it in 2017.

At night time, we were all like zombies. Everyone was queuing up for drugs as if they were about to get on a Ryanair flight. I used to take my medication last so I could avoid any queues. It's quite degrading actually. Queuing up to take pharmaceutical pills that make you fat, depressed, have heart problems, locked jaw and any sort of medical condition under the sun. Luckily my medication was a pink dissolvable fluffly tablet which tasted like mint. I call them chewing gums. Risperidone quicklets. Another Chinese man on the ward was taking the same medication.

"You're on the pink tablets, good for you", I said.

"Yeah, they do nothing", he replied.

"Yep, they don't seem to have as many nasty side effects and not very sedative. They actually make me more restless."

The other patient nodded. At the time, I thought these tablets were more along the lines of a placebo, as they didn't seem to have a sedative effect. Down the line I would find it to be a different story. Every time the nurses would hand me the tablets, they looked angry. Some of them were very rude. I have dealt with people in the public before who have been extremely rude to me, but because they are giving me business, I always smile. Some of the nurses in there, treat mental health patients like they are nothing. If they do not like the job of dishing out drugs and working night duty, then I suggest they move roles. They certainly do not help people with mental health. In fact, there was only one Irish nurse that was very nice out of all of the Irish nurses I met in this ward. The rest who were nice, were foreign. The nurses in the observation unit have a much harder job, but they are actually a lot more pleasant. I hope they get paid a lot more.

Also, a few of my friends remarked by saying that the receptionists in John of God's were very rude to them when they came in and asked which ward I was in.

Personally, I noticed that the foreign security guards were extremely friendly and in general any of the foreign staff.

Back to drugs. I've never taken any sort of headache pill, aspirin, ibuprofren or anything in my life as I believe they all act as placebos. I prefer to drink lots of water and have a healthy balanced diet. I refused to take the sleeping pills they prescribed at night as they caused a host of problems for my heart, where it would flutter and I felt like death in the mornings.

"Mary you can take the other drugs but please don't take the sleeping pills", I remember my mum saying after Vietnam. She knew the doctor here had prescribed a host of drugs which was close to horse tranquilliser. I stopped taking the sleeping pills as soon as my mum had informed me.

This year, I had numerous arguments with my psychiatrist over them. At the end of the day, it is my body and my choice in life as to whether I want to put shit into it or not. It's not the psychiatrists, or a brother or sisters body, its my fucking body and choice. I know how shit makes me feel. I chose lavender if I was having difficulty sleeping.

At least in this ward, I was given a bit more freedom, and I went to the gym twice a week. It really should be open more than that but John of God's doesn't seem to know a lot about mental health. For crying out loud the rehab clinics in the States have much better facilities I can imagine. Nice food, gyms, some sun.

To pass the time, I practised zentangle, which soldiers used after World War One and Two. It zoned them out after being through a bloody nightmare. I felt like I was in a nightmare. I did cooking and baking classes, I drew colouring books and I did plenty of runs outside. I was getting bored of the small laps though. I snook off to go to the swimming pool once or twice and bought green tea for the ward. I got into shit trouble for doing that. It's pathetic. Carrying on with my life and the moment I'm in and just a happy go lucky girl.

Anytime I handed the nursing staff my laundry, it would take them three days to return my clothes.

I was colouring in one of my books just before tea with my headphones in.

"TEA, NOW", an obese nurse shouted at me at 5.40pm.

She was pointing to the dining room. I smiled at her as I know this pisses people off more. The fucking ignorance of her. There was always stupid queues for tea and I knew to go in at around 5.45pm when the queue had died down. You'd swear I had an eating disorder and was avoiding my dinner. I was pretty pissed off with how aggressive she was and thought to myself, "If I'm in a stress clinic and one for addictions then that nurse should be in her own ward for addictions."

I decided, not being a moaner ever in my life, to post a comment in the comment box and it read:

> "I am a trained triathlete and nutritionist and do not appreciate being shouted at by an obese nurse to go for my dinner"

They are supposed to be anonymous, but I signed that piece of paper.

That evening, I found the sticker of an apple in my mashed potato. Rotten. The only nice thing about going for dinner was Dave and the Chinese lady. Dave knew I had a huge appetite and always gave me seconds. He was also dishing out oranges and apples constantly as he knew I loved fruit. The Chinese lady was very pleasant too. One morning I said, "Go on, can you not toast the brown bread for me?".

She laughed and pointed to the sign on the wall that read:

We do not toast brown bread

Are they worried that the toaster might explode because it's racist? Again, let's just shove refined carbohydrate into everyone's mouths and get people even fatter and unhealthier. Don't get me wrong, I eat white bread as I burn it off, but for more sedentary people who are in there and just too fucking sedated from their medication then they should really be eating more complex carbohydrates.

I volunteered on an organic farm when my mum was sick, volunteered for Spina Bifida Ireland in 2015, aimed to volunteer for Depaul homeless but Garda vetting restrictions got in the way, and I also wanted to volunteer in a hospital for nutrition. I thought to myself that I'm never going to be allowed volunteer in a hospital because the government are as thick, but as my dad says, "Why do Irish people moan and give donkey's bollox about the government, we're the thick fuckers that voted them in."

Anyway, I felt like I was volunteering as I started noticing more and more people eating natural yogurts, oranges, apples, bananas and nice vegetarian meals, which were generally a lot more appetising than the shitty pieces of meat they give you in hospitals. I was pretty much back to being a pescatarion while in there.

I had several doctors appointments and was accused of being high again because I like to throw my oranges up in the air while walking along the ward.

"Why are you throwing oranges in the air Mary?", the psychiatrist asked.

"Oh I do this in my kitchen at home after a run or a cycle because I'm just plain happy and it keeps me mindful and focused on the orange. Vitamin C also helps lower down cortisol post exercise." She asked me to stop talking then. Again psychiatrists get paid a billion dollars to test people out as clinical trials and prescribe a drug but they don't fucking listen to their patient's needs for long enough in my opinion. I was also baffled as to why I have seen six different psychiatrists since Vietnam and why I wasn't sticking with the same one.

Anytime I brought up Vietnam, she would ask me to stop talking. If mental health patients want to get to the root cause of their diagnoses, then it makes a lot of sense to reflect back on the first episode they have ever experienced and to try and connect the dots. I felt disjointed when talking to her.

I also remarked by saying that the risperidone was making me quite restless and I felt more agitated and elated on it. She seemed to disagree with me, and said that it will take a while for the drug to kick in. Some of them do an OK job, but some have a tendency to ask the same routine questions over and over again. That's why I much prefer psychologists. It's simply a matter of talking therapy which does not involve the use of drugs. Drugs change the balance in someone's brain to make them depressed and lethargic and crave shit food. God gave us everything on this wacky planet and it started with seed and fruit. Two weeks later I was free to go.

Chapter 10

Website work

I had to attend the Centre for Living a few times for more doctor appointments, and to make sure I was doing OK. The receptionist, Valerie, is so lovely and she looked so confused as to why I was back there again.

"I'm so sorry your mother passed away Mary, she was the most generous woman", I smiled and said, "Tell me more about her."

"She used to come in here and donate a load of lovely yoga blankets to the centre."

Later that day they tried to make me do yoga, but I wasn't interested. I'm more into bikram yoga and I was also feeling quite agitated still. The yoga there is essentially for beginners and gets the person to focus on their breathing, and try and be mindful in their approach. I got home, and all I could focus on was work.

Website website website. I bought the rights to two platforms. I have a little bit saved from the London days from working hard in both Samsung Electronics and JP Morgan for four years. It's not much to a lot of people in London or Dublin but it's enough as a back up. I liked to enjoy myself in London too. Splash out on high rent, buy nice clothes, go for nice dinners and nights out with buddies.

My brother Daniel came in handy here. He works on the online website for Guineys so he recommended Upwork.

"Cheers dude, I'll give them a look."

Straight away, I hired three people. A twenty eight year old dude from the Philippines to work on my bone marrow app. The reasoning behind this, is that I have been a blood donor since I was eighteen, I'm an organ donor after death and I'm a bone marrow donor. No one seems to bloody well match with my marrow worldwide though. With all of the restrictions in place, people are just dying of bone cancer. When I was taking Haloperidol while living in London, I was still allowed to donate blood. However in Ireland, individuals taking anti-psychotics are not allowed to donate. Can anyone answer as to why? Does this mean, I possibly killed someone by donating blood with a chemical in it? Anyway, the bone marrow app aims to have a lot of information on these issues. It targets Japan, Russia, Ireland, the UK and Australia. Never mind China. They have some weird thing about energy balance when donating blood.

The next thing I did was hire a lady from India to work on my website maryguiney.ie. She charges €10 an hour. I then hired a team from Pakistan to work on maryguiney.com. They charge €25 an hour. God only knows why I bought the rights to two platforms, but my head was still buzzing around the place.

"Mary get off that laptop it's time to go to bed", my dad said looking concerned as he came into the drawing room.

"Yeah about half an hour, I'm working", I replied.

"Who are you onto?"

"I'm talking to the Pakistani dude from Upwork."

"How much is he charging for your site?", Dad asked.

"Ah nine euro", I said quickly.

I just rattled a number from my brain.

"That's a lot of money for Pakistan", he uttered.

"Good night Dad."

I started laughing to myself when he left. It was too hard to explain to my dad that they had a huge team of people working on my website, and that I knew nothing about technology.

I still stay in touch with a Pakistani friend, Khurram, who I used to work with in Samsung. He has kindly kept in touch, to check in on me to make sure I am doing OK since my mother passed away. He knew how much hard work I put into her diet.

I also spent a bit of money on Facebook adds to promote bone marrow donation and positive thinking for mental health. I was having a few requests from a guy from Pakistan about how to help his three year old granddaughter who has bone cancer. There wasn't much I could do. I told him that plenty of rest was good and I advised some old tricks of my mothers. I advised that he gave her onion and milk. You simply simmer the onion in milk over a low heat for about forty five minutes and then drink the milk. It's a great remedy. It's something which a lot of people in Ireland should take rather than antibiotics to treat a cold. That or else Manuka honey and lemon in hot water. Manuka honey comes from bees in New Zealand and has powerful anti-bacterial properties in it.

I don't mind telling new people about all of this stuff, but if I have to remind another person here that I have told ten million times already, I will then shove their head down the toilet. I saw a comment back from this man on my add to say that they have a huge investment with the Italian government to help bone cancer worldwide. It's nice to get these updates.

I spent the next week or so working, and then also treating myself to spa days in the Ritz; well now it's called the Powerscourt Hotel. I also stayed a few nights in the Ritz as my dad's new partner in crime was spending a good month in our house and I just needed my own space. It was nice to actually stay there as it reminded me more of my mum. She had signed up and paid for a years membership when she got better after I moved home. Six months into it and she could no longer go. I decided to transfer her membership over to me when she died.

Straight away, I started using the membership and searched for signs from my mother that her spirit and energy was still alive. I couldn't find any, but I used to swim nine lengths of the pool to represent nine people in our family.

When Mum was going through a tough time, her three homes were Kilgobbin, John of God's and the Ritz. She knew how to treat herself when shit got tough.

"There's ghosts in this house Mary", I remember her saying when I was a kid.

Whenever she felt spirits or ghosts around the house, it would send her into John of God's.

"What's wrong Mary?", Mr. Mc Grail asked one day in school when I was twelve.

"My mum and Dad", the rest was rumble, as I burst out crying.

I think he thought I was trying to say they were going through a divorce. In my head, I wasn't sure why my mum was spending time in John of God's.

Seeing as the Ritz was quite expensive, I decided to try air Bed and Breakfast in Dalkey. I spent two nights with the best host who gave me her own chickens eggs and home made bread for breakfast. I also treated myself to nice dinners.

"Table for one?", the waitress asked.

"Yes please."

I got chatting to the bar man who was quite retro. He gave me the nicest red wine ever. I also lapped up a juicy fillet steak. The next night I went to Kathmandu. My dad wanted to join me. I waited thirty minutes for Dad to arrive. I got chatting to a nice Nepalese young lady, Jenie. We discussed culture, food and climbing mountains. A dream of mine is to trek the Himalayas and climb Everest base camp. This is a similar passion to my sister Anna. I want to do all of this for mental health and chronic disease. This was a dream of mine before I went to Vietnam and shit hit the fan.

I cursed myself for weeks after Vietnam, and had wished desperately that I had gone to Nepal instead. Looking back now, I have gained a lot of experience from the whole ordeal. Jenie is now staying in my house for two months as I need a bit more female company. She cooks nice Nepalese dishes.

Dad and I decided it was time for some sun. We booked a holiday to Gran Canaria for the 16th of February. It was win win. Dad wanted to visit his good buddy Mick Dwyer out there, and I just needed a break. I don't know why at this point, but more and more intense vibrations from Vietnam were coming back to me.

I all of a sudden thought about the tour guide Ben, who had told me about the islands in Halong Bay growing by one centimetre each year. I remembered that Martin was a friend of his on Facebook, so I asked Martin what his surname was.

"Mary he's a buddy of mine, you can see him in my friends list."

Martin has a tonne of friends and I didn't want to search through them so I asked for his name.

I found him, and messaged to see did he remember me from 2012.

"Mary of course I remember you, I think about you all the time. I was so worried about you. I hope you're well."

I started wondering why all of a sudden he popped into my mind. I instantly replied to him and said "I'm good, I'm working on a website on psychology and nutrition. It's a bloody mission. I have such a long story to explain to you about Vietnam but will do at some point."

I found out that he was some mad adventurer, and also used to photograph celebrities. I started then thinking, why was I paranoid about cameras and also why did I think I was about to hit the red carpet in Vietnam. My mind started buzzing.

I look back at Vietnam and laugh, as when I returned to Ireland, I phoned the hostel and asked could I speak to Ben. I thought he was involved in some weird and twisted joke about cameras and that he was the one saying to keep the horror movie going in the taxi. At the time, however, Ben was not in the hostel. I also phoned the Irish Embassy to get my I pod back, but sure that was my own fault.

Dad and I got to the airport the next day. Things were grand, but I was sharing a room with my dad and I needed more space. He wanted to do a few short strolls, meet his buddy and read the paper by the pool. I wanted great sea swims and a bit more adventure.

I went down one morning to see the sand dunes. I was amazed by how cool they looked and I thought back to Vietnam and how I missed the part where Sara and Martin got to ride bikes along the sand dunes in Hoi An. They had booked an extra week holidaying ahead of me as they had more time off work. I could only get two weeks at the time.

I was happy out this time. I was experiencing the sand dunes on my own. It was a mission to get over them, but a huge dip into the rough sea at the end and I was all rejuvenated.

"Make sure not to lose yourself in there. The sea is rough", the lifeguard warned.

"Ah I'll be grand, just a quick dip, no crazy swims. Here mind my phone."

He laughed and I headed off.

"Dad, you've got to check out the sand dunes tomorrow with me. They're wicked and only a twenty minute stroll from the hotel."

He nodded and smiled, "OK browner."

That was one of my nicknames as a kid. I probably had the worst nappies out of all of the children. The other two nicknames were Ockenheimer and brave brown. Brave brown came from my bravery as a kid and always being a chatter box and into adventure. Ockenheimer was this weird German name for me as my mum said that I wouldn't stop talking to German people when I was six on a holiday.

We headed off to meet Mick Dwyer in a pub that evening. The live band were great and I threw my flip flops off and started doing a jig.

"Careful of the broken glass", a bar worker remarked.

"Ah I'll be grand", I replied.

While Dad was in chatting to his buddy, I chilled outside and chatted to random people.

"Where are you from?", a Dutch guy asked.

"Dublin" I said smiling.

"Oh I'm here with my parents, who are you here with?"

"My dad", I replied. "Just keeping him company as my mum passed away eighteen months ago". "Apologies", he said.

Vietnamese Voices

"It's OK. She wouldn't want me to get into a depression, I can feel her spirit alive, and I'm here to celebrate hers and my life."

"Wow, you seem to have a very positive energy about you", he gasped.

I told him about the sand dunes and he was eager to go swimming with me. Like a gentleman, he walked me back to my hotel and we exchanged numbers to meet at 11am for a swim. I woke earlier, had breakfast before Dad and I headed off again on my own. I managed to fit in a good thirty minute swim, lapping up the heat. Dad and I later strolled down to the Riu Palace Hotel and sat on a wall by the sand dunes. It was peaceful, except that Dad's phone kept buzzing.

I laughed at him, "Now who is the one addicted to their phone, you or me?" He smirked.

Two days later I checked out.

"Is that your husband with you in the room?", the hotel receptionist asked.

"No it's my dad. I need some space. Can you ring the Riu Palace hotel and see if they have a room?"

This was the hotel by the sand dunes. I needed to treat myself and didn't care how much it cost me. That's why women are better for the economy. They spend more.

Close to the time after my mum passed away, I dined on my own with my dad, and there has been a few mix ups over him being my husband. This time, I needed alone time and to focus on myself. Dad had the company of his friend on the holiday.

I checked out and got to the other hotel, only to find out that it was fully booked. They arranged a taxi for me and dropped me off to the sister hotel. It was €300 a night but all inclusive, had a private beach with a jacuzzi, a nice pool, a spa, shops and sports stores. I was happy.

"How's the beach?", Daniel texted.

"Heavenly", I responded.

I then knocked my phone onto flight mode, as I was posting too much rubbish to Facebook, and knew I needed to unwind.

I got a few massages while at the beach each day. There were several Thai people around. I waved my hand up at a Thai person.

"How much?", I asked.

"Full body is twenty five euro."

I was in. She got a lot of tension out of my body.

Two days later I waved over to another Thai dude, and he gave me a good thirty minute massage. I got up to take money out of my wallet, and he walked away without payment. I went to run after him, but realised I only had a fiver in my wallet. Wow I thought, this is the reverse of Vietnam, where I was tipping hotel workers and women dropping me home safe and sound each night. This guy all of a sudden didn't care about payment. I remember one time in Vietnam I tipped the hotel guy two dollars and he was chuffed. A lot of money to them. When I wanted to tip the older ladies for a free moped ride back to my hostel, they didn't seem to want my cash. They're nice like that, and just want to make sure everyone is safe in their country.

Dad came out to my hotel one evening to check up on me. Seeing as I wanted peace from my phone, I called him from the hotel lobby and gave him my hotel address.

"There you are browner", he said with a grin.

I was wearing my swimsuit and a red sarong in the lobby.

"Were you out for a dip?", he asked.

"Yeah I swam two kilometres in the sea, it's class. The water is nice and warm too, no wetsuit needed. I can't wait to do another swimming holiday. Ironman here I come."

He laughed and said, "Oh the energy of the young."

We headed into the bar lounge, which had some entertainment.

"It's a lot livelier here than the other hotel don't you reckon?" Dad nodded in agreement.

"A whiskey and a beer please", he asked the waiter.

We were both happy out watching the singers and dancers. At least this hotel had a good bit of life.

"Dad, last night I got up and re-enacted what Mum did before she met you."

Before my mum met my dad, she was engaged to another chap.

"One day at a dance Mary, I got up and put the ring back in his pocket. I knew he wasn't the one, he went to mass every Sunday and he was too serious about religion", my mum told me years ago.

"So how did you and Dad meet?", I preceded to ask.

"It was in Kinsale on Paddy's night. He asked me could I buy him a six pack of Guinness and he seemed like fun."

They were married within three months of meeting each other.

I danced with the middle aged man on the floor in that lounge the night previous, and went up and put my mum's ring into his pocket. It cracked him up. I immediately went over and took the ring back. I don't know why, but all of a sudden I started getting an intense spiritual connection with my mum and I wanted to entertain her.

That ring stays with me for now. It wasn't an engagement ring, but is a ring that my dad bought for my mum when she gave birth to me, her seventh child. It has seven diamontes on it to resemble seven children. It was possibly a sign for my parents to stop conceiving at that stage. I have two other rings also. A claddagh which Mum bought me when I was eight in Connemara, and a silver band which Mum bought me in Russia when I was seventeen. That was the time I got to see Lenin in his tombstone when I was studying Russian history for my exams. Mum told me that a Russian man invented the claddagh ring, so I find that quite symbolic. I love my three rings and the only time I take them off is for swimming.

I went to the jacuzzi outside on my own later that night. It was where the private beach was, and it was open twenty four seven. I had my music and headphones with me and hopped in. I also brought a face cloth with me that I had since Vietnam. One of the nurses had given it to me in the French hospital and I kept it as a symbol. It was a funky face cloth with blue and red patterns on it. I decided it was time to start leaving symbols behind me. I dried my face with it and then left it on the side of the jacuzzi. I dried off and headed back to my room to go to sleep.

Two days later, Dad and I met each other at the airport. I was flying around trying to juice my shitty I phone up in sockets near the gate, so I could listen to beats for the flight. We got onto the plane, and Dad and I were in different rows. I was a few behind him. At one point I started thinking back on how sad the Ryanair flight home with Mum and Dad was coming back from Lanzarote. I needed a smoke.

I popped to the toilet and chilled out for a few minutes and puffed away.

"Madam you cannot smoke in the toilet, you can be arrested for that", I heard from the steward when I came out. There's no denying it, I didn't even bother spraying perfume to hide the smell. "Yes tell your director I just had a smoke in the loo, tell Michael O' Leary", I anxiously said.

He just shrugged and said, "I will."

Dad was queueing up to go in two people after me, and I smiled to myself thinking that the smell of smoke will remind him of Mum back in the day when people could smoke on planes, when the rules were a bit more lax. It's no wonder I didn't want my mum to come rescue me in Vietnam. The woman hated long haul flights because she couldn't have a cigarette.

On the car journey home, Dad and I got talking about the legendary Michael O' Leary and his smart business strategy.

"Sure half the world moans about Ryanair, but we wouldn't be able to travel for so cheap if he didn't come onto the scene. He got the airlines competitive again", I said.

Dad nodded in agreement. I then started talking about Sam Walton and his IRFD tags.

"Dad that is something you should honestly invest in and you're passionate about Wal-Marts business strategy."

"What would you rather, to meet Michael O' Leary or one of Sam Walton's kids or for Limerick to win the All Ireland?", I asked.

"Limerick to win the All Ireland", he said with a big smile.

"There's nothing I can do to control that, you'll be waiting a long time", I replied.

Dad and I got home and we both went to sleep.

The next day, Daniel popped up to the house with his wife and three kids.

"Do you think the malarone is still in your system from Vietnam, and its affecting you Mary?"

I reassured Daniel. "Hell no, the half life of drugs is rapid within the body. Sure MDMA is out of the system within a few days and hash maybe one month. I'm not sure about malarone, but maybe a week tops." He nodded in agreement.

"The reason I was suffering post-psychotic depression was because the doctors here made me take some strong medication for two years. And when you come off the medication eventually, there is a much higher risk of relapsing", I gasped.

"Were you really depressed Mary? I can't really remember."

"I was but I just got on with life and tried to see light at the end of the tunnel. I tried to keep myself as busy as possible. Looking after Mum was a big distraction also."

I got straight back to my website, and liaised with the Philippines, Pakistan and India. I was in driving gear and wanted my website launched as soon as possible. I was ready to work hard. A business class flight cropped up on my Facebook page which resembled a one way ticket from any location to any destination for the month of February. I started dreaming about getting the hell out of Ireland and taking my laptop with me.

Mike was home and he was shouting up to my room about a doctor's appointment in thirty minutes. The last thing I wanted was to see more psychiatrists and nurses, and talk the same bollox to them. They don't seem to want to get to the nitty gritty of an individual's problem, and had no interest in talking about my episode in 2012.

I had 1% battery on my phone and hailod a cab straight away. I packed in a hurry and booked a last minute flight to Vietnam.

Out the door I went, with my laptop and charger hanging out of my ass.

— 133 —

"Where on earth are you going Mary?", Dad asked as the taxi driver picked me up from the bottom of the avenue.

"I'll see you down at Cluain Mhuire", I said back in a hurry.

Cluian Mhuire is affiliated with John of God's, but I didn't want to go back. I had been around the block there with no resolution. Dad waved and so did I.

"Drive to the airport", I said to the taxi driver.

He pulled in a bit down the road and asked, "Was that your Dad? I can't drive you, where are you going?"

"Vietnam."

He looked at me in horror.

"Do I look like I'm on drugs?", I asked him.

"No", he remarked. "Are you sure about this? Have you got your passport?", he asked in a nervous manner.

"I do, just drive."

The taxi driver was really anxious for about fifteen minutes and decided to take a back road as he was worried the cops might follow us. I got there after thirty minutes.

I had four hours to kill until my flight. I was sitting down to enjoy a tuna wrap from O' Briens, and I got chatting to an Indian worker. One hour later I saw Mike approaching me.

"Not getting away that easily", he said. "Dad is on his way."

Mike must have tracked my phone.

They took my passport and wallet off me straight away and I was chucked back into John of God's. I thought I was about to vomit on the car journey back. The thoughts of going into the locked observation unit again made my skin crawl.

Chapter 11

The Lethal Injection

I met new people again in St. Martin's ward. Back into the observation unit for me, where CCTV runs riot. I was prepared about my laces and headphones being confiscated this time.

"John can you buy me a pair of Bluetooth headphones", I asked my brother over the phone.

"Yeah sure, how much do you want to spend?"

"I don't mind, just get Dad to buy them. I have no wallet or money. Make sure they're a decent enough pair."

John came in a day later with a carrot and ginger juice in my protein shaker and my headphones. I was allowed to keep them on the ward, so again I just did core work, yoga and a few runs when I was allowed out. The hospital food is rotten so I needed the carrot and ginger juice brought in to keep my health up.

I had several more doctors appointments, and this time I met a junior psychiatrist from Malaysia. She was fascinated by my story, and actually took the time to listen to my story since Vietnam. "You're Malaysian?", I said with a big smile. "You're a hard worker so?"

She shrugged back at me. I explained the gist of my story and she said she found it intriguing. She told me that she was going to dedicate most of her time to this case.

"You're always smiling Mary, that is rare in here", she said to me.

— 135 —

"I tend to smile quite a bit in college but the seriousness of study gets in the way", she remarked. "Yeah we have to put on a brave face in here. I'm not going to let depression hit me again", I replied.

"Dr. Sunad is lovely", I said to the senior psychiatrist later that day. She went silent and didn't want to discuss anyone else on the team. Here we go again, I thought to myself, lost in communication. Anytime they gave me a document to sign and that the best rehabilitation for me was to triathlon train, I would rip that piece of paper up and think how on earth am I supposed to triathlon train when I'm locked in a ward. I don't need a signed piece of paper to remind me that I am a triathlete. I do remember how to drive to the pool, how to drive to Seapoint, how to ride my bike and how to use my legs. Speaking of riding a bike, no one ever forgets as the saying goes. Well, my brother John had to re teach me about three summers in a row when I was a kid, because I used to forget with the winter months getting in the way.

I met Conor in there. "Do you want to go for a smoke?", he asked. "Yeah sure, there's nothing else to do in this locked up ward."

We got chatting on the balcony. Conor was in for drug addiction. He had been abusing coke and heroin for a good while.

I said, "Sure look, you're in the right place and have to stick to the plan, but keep positive and start using the gym. The drugs are hard to take but wean off them slowly and get into exercise. I'm in for stress for taking on too much over Christmas and my thoughts seem to be buzzing all over the place."

"Yeah these drugs are nasty", he replied. "They make me really nervous and anxious."

"Sure half of the world is addicted to benzodiazepines, everyone suffers mental health in some shape or form", I told him.

Conor and I became buzzing buddies. I was happy enough with the risperidone quicklets, but the nurses and doctors were still trying to medicate me with sleeping pills, both zimovane and stilnoct. "I'm not taking those. They make my heart race and make me feel like shit. My mum told me they're highly addictive."

The next day the nurse asked, "Are you trying to water down your medication Mary?"

"No. I drink three plus litres a day to flush out toxins."

It really was the observation unit. That made me start to think. I wished I was drinking copious amounts of water post Vietnam to flush the taxing chemical out of my body. Even looking back now, I was extremely unhealthy on the drugs and wasn't even drinking much water.

That same day I met Jack.

"Mary Guiney, your Michael's daughter", he remarked.

Jack knew my dad from the hurling days. He was very intelligent but talking a hell of a lot.

"I'm a doctor, this is what you need to say to your psychiatrist. Say that you want benzodiazepines." I moved away from him at that point.

"Here look I'll give you the names of the drugs."

"I don't need those pills, would you ever shag off", I said back.

I went to my room then to get some space. Four more restless nights and then I was moved onto St. Luke's ward. Again there were bits of clothes and cosmetics missing.

Back to St. Luke's ward for me and I was sharing a room with three others. I kept using lavender to help me sleep and sure enough I was back into a good enough routine without any nasty drugs needed. I was doing weights and high intensity interval work in the gym twice a week. I was going for runs out the back, plenty of walks, cooking and colouring.

"My knees are about to cave", Conor said to me as he was boxing in the gym.

His knee joints had gotten pretty worn down over the years from all of the coke and heroin he had been taking.

"Try more low impact exercises like the bike and walking", I replied. "You should also supplement your diet with glucosamine sulphate", I told him.

"What on earth is that?", he asked.

— 137 —

"It's just a supplement used to aid in joint recovery and is good for the synovial fluid and cartilage, we can pick up a tub of it in the health food store tomorrow."

Most marathoners should really supplement with this in their diet, especially if they get bad knees. It takes roughly three months to build up in the system and can reverse the effects of osteoarthritis. I looked over at him boxing away and decided to give it a go myself. After about ten minutes I was wrecked.

My dad came in to visit me later that day and we had a green tea.

"Did you do anything different today?", he asked.

"Yeah I did some boxing in the gym. Go Katie Taylor."

"I know we have some amount of talent in this country, considering we have a very small population. We have boxing, hurling, music, the list goes on", he cried.

I pondered a bit, and remembered as a kid I used to ask my dad was it better to excel at one thing or to be an all rounder. He always said it was better to be an all rounder. I should have been classed as being bipolar as a kid so, seeing as I have my voice classically trained, got to grade eight on the piano, love all forms of exercise, have a great diet, was good at school, love cooking and love socialising with friends and acting the maggot. Unfortunately, I don't seem to give any one discipline 100% of my effort. I tend to dip my pen into several ink cartridges.

"Do you want to try the injection?", the psychiatrist asked me.

"I'd rather not, I'm happy on the tablets", I said bemused.

"It's a sister drug of the one you are taking and will mean less doctor trips."

I kind of let family intervene at this point as they seemed to want me to get the injection. Stupid of me but I agreed. I got the first dose one week and another a week later. The second nurse that gave me the injection into my arm muscle jabbed it right in.

"Here have some chocolate Mary", another patient said as he devoured a huge galaxy bar.

"I see your drugs have the same effect on you as they did for me a few years ago?", I said to him.

"Yeah, the large consumption of chocolate prevents locked jaw which is a problem with the drugs." At that point, I was happy that I was eating copious amounts of chocolate and listening to my cravings rather than getting locked jaw.

The days in there were slow enough and I had to spend another three weeks in there, but it was nice to chat to new faces and try and figure out what was going through their heads.

"Are you leaving tomorrow?", one room mate asked me.

"Yep, I can't wait, I'm looking forward to hitting the pool and sea over the next few days and am going to continue with my website and book another swimming holiday", I said delighted.

"That's brilliant. You seem so positive and I wish you the best of luck."

Another room mate interrupted by saying, "I hope our new room mate is nicer than you Mary."

We all burst out laughing. This patient was a scream, but really ill at the same time. One day she would call me an earth angel and offer me cigarettes, and the next day she would spill coffee all over my slippers. I could only laugh inside. In fact, this older lady, used to leave three or four cigarettes by my locker some mornings. It made me reflect. When Mum was going though a bad time in John of God's, a dozen mental health patients used to always hassle Mum for smokes. Being the generous woman she was, she always gave them away. I remember looking at her when I was young and she looked really pissed off as there were numerous patients approaching her for smokes in one go. I thought to myself, this is the reverse. I am getting treated well by the patients.

By the time I got home, the injection started to affect me and I felt purely like shit. My arm developed a huge lump in it which made swimming difficult. My left foot developed a lot of fluid in the muscle where it is sore to walk. I had extreme lethargy by going to bed at 11pm and waking up at 2pm and my heart started to palpitate when I woke up. I was cursing family members in my head who were advising me to take this. It's not their bloody body I thought to myself. I'm thirty and free to live my own life. I have always listened to my own body and have experienced the nastiness of psychiatric drugs since 2012.

I started making sure my diet was pristine. Carrot and ginger juices, plenty of fish, smoothies, lots of fruit and vegetables, porridge, pasta, eggs & cheesy toasties. The usual. I was back to my 2015 diet and was drinking plenty of water to try and eliminate this nasty drug from my system. I was also supplementing with Floradix to get my strength back up. It's essentially liquid iron. I needed it. Generally I don't, as my haemoglobin tests in the perfect range anytime I go to donate blood. I mostly eat fish and maybe red meat twice a week, but because I have a large amount of vitamin C in my diet, it helps with the absorption of iron. Normally, I don't have problems energy wise. Cracked lips and lethargy are a sign of iron deficiency, and people may need to increase their fruit and vegetable intake to counteract this.

The blood clinic texted me the next day and asked could I come in to donate, as they were low on stocks of my blood group. I didn't bother replying. Stupid rules in place that we can't here but we can in the UK on medication. Back arse Ireland.

Again my period came and lasted a day. I thought to myself, this is another fucking thing. Lost periods. Anti-depressants, anti-psychotics, anti whatever the fuck you want to call them are aimed at making people infertile and fat. They have a place, but only for those who are suffering anorexia in my opinion.

On this injection, I was no longer in hospital, but I had to deal with a shit heart on my own. Way to go Irish healthcare. After a meeting with the psychiatrist, I explained my symptoms to her and she agreed to put me back on the tablets eventually. My dad and sister were worried and showed a good bit of anger. I told them, "I'm telling the truth, because I don't lie to people and you need to stop worrying about me and just focus on yourself."

I drove off to the pool in a rage.

I started thinking that people need to focus on their own day to day. That's what life is about. You reflect on yourself and tell other people to mind their own business. This is how my brother rolls. He calls it MYOBB. I still laugh. "What does that mean?", I asked him when I was six following him around our house.

"Mind your own business bitch", he answered back.

After a few weeks, I was happy again. I started using my erg, going to UCD to do weights, swims, long cycles out to Enniskerry and runs. My fitness was not as good as last year, as I smoked like a chimney while locked up in wards. At times, I felt like I was about to drop a lung, but I gave it my best shot.

I also got cracking on with my website and started writing my book from scratch.

At this point, I felt like I needed some sun again. That's another thing. Besides the odd protein shake and branched chain amino acid, I supplement with vitamin D in the winter. The hospital owe me two tubs as they confiscated it off me.

Back to sun. I mentioned to my dad that I wanted to do another swim holiday, and that Strel Swimming adventures started off the season in Dalaman, Turkey in May. He was happy enough for me to go alone. I booked the seven day trip with two days either end, so I could chill and have a real holiday alone, where I could focus on training and nothing else.

"Mary, delighted you have booked, you will love Turkey", Borut said over messenger. I was happy as a a pig in shit. I was busy working away on my own stuff, training, eating right and sleeping like a normal person.

Jenie, the Nepalese girl staying with me, was getting on great in the house. She cooked some nice Nepalese dishes, and we'd enjoy red wine together on her nights off. I helped her out for her addiction studies masters by showing her a copy of my two thesis. *"Mechanisms of triplet repeat DNA mutagenesis"*, which I did for my biochemistry degree, which it is centred on the reasoning behind neurodegenerative disease, and also *"Irrational Exuberance: A case study of investor sentiments driving market Euphoria*", which was for my finance masters. It was great to hang out, information share with each other and still have plenty of space.

"You have the memory of an Elephant", one sister remarked to me as we were having tea.

"I guess it's better than having the memory of a fish", I replied.

Memories are what keep people alive, and I strongly believe that memories of my mum are what keep me going in life. Not just memories of her, but also memories of me.

Alzheimer's and Parkinson's are actually huge problems in the West, and psychiatric drugs tend to contribute to this burden of disease massively. Elderly patients with dementia have dropped dead from taking atypical anti-psychotics. This same sister said before that I was like a dog with a bone. I take that as a compliment. A dog with a bone, is essentially a resilient and determined person who never gives up on life.

One day, a guy from the Himalayas added me on Facebook. He had the exact same birth date as me. 3rd of January 1986. I accepted him straight away, and we got chatting about treks in the Himalayas. He mentioned that tourism is down massively in his country. He organises Parvati trekking, and his name is Pankaj Sharma. You should check him out.

He is also trying to promote medicinal plants in Nepal, as he has a pharmacy degree, and he knows that these plants aid in healing the body. Certain herbal plants with great healing properties include Hieracium pilosella and Astragalus, which I was using to treat my mum. A lot of these plants grow at an altitude of 19000 feet on the Himalayas, and are very powerful, but they get no credibility in the West, as there is no profit to be made from them. You cannot patent anything from nature. Herbal medicines are known to cure the root of the disease, while drugs are allopathic, and follow mainstream medicine, which does not address the root cause of any illness. Pharmacy degrees in the West are based on promoting drugs full of synthetic chemicals and not natural plants.

That is another goal of mine. I want to travel to Nepal, as it was a big dream of mine when I went to Vietnam. I want to learn all about their culture and their cuisine, as I trek challenging peaks. A few people from around the globe have added me on Facebook and we have shared ideas about travel, nutrition, exercise and positive psychology. Friends here started getting worried and butting in with my business by asking people to stop sharing posts of mountains to my wall. I like to just ignore what they think, it's none of their business.

I was happy that I was keeping in touch with other patients from John of God's this time, and we were keeping each other positive. I also got talking to a sister's friend, who had been suffering mental health from a very young age. We met for a coffee in Starbucks.

"I just don't use technology, as I get quite paranoid around it", he remarked.

"I know. A lot of people with mental health are paranoid about technology these days. One guy even told me this year that apparently the MI5 can see us through our laptop screen."

I then filled him in on the TV calling me Britney Beers in Vietnam and we both burst out laughing. "Maybe some day in the near future you will get back into technology as you want to advance your career, but for now you just have to focus on staying positive and doing what you are doing", I responded.

I then continued to fill him in on the wellness recovery action plan which is highly successful in the States, and is promoted by Mary Ellen Copeland.

"I don't use the drug induced therapy any more, as it was wrecking havoc in my life, and making matters worse", he continued to tell me.

"You're dead right", I responded. "A lot of those drugs just offset the natural biochemistry in the brain and dope us up." We carried on sipping our coffee.

I went to the fifty meter pool the next day. As I jumped into my lane, a random dude turned around to me and said, "I've been watching you come here loads, you have great endurance and a nice tumble turn. When you have some free time I can perfect your technique for you."

I was chuffed to think that I can get some free advice about my technique. Being all over the place though, I seem to just give things 90% of my effort, so at the time I just couldn't be bothered improving my technique. He carried on with his swim and so did I.

I was kicking way too fast before my swim holiday in Croatia last year.

"You have great endurance with those legs of yours Mary, but you know legs waste 80% of your oxygen, and you need that for the bike and run after", Laura remarked one day on the boat.

From that point, I slowed down my legs and focused mostly on upper body. I'm chuffed that my legs have gotten so much stronger, as that is something I was paranoid of as a kid. A girl in primary school used to slag me, and say that I had short and fat legs. I never used to make the sprint track in Santry in primary school but seemed to be a better swimmer, perhaps because of my long torso.

On the 23rd of April, Dad was watching the news. It was showing a great deal on how they are trying to help Syrian refugees at the moment.

"You won't be going on that swimming holiday, look at what's happening", he angrily said to me. "They're helping people there Dad. It has nothing to do with me. Several of my old banking buddies have been to Turkey recently, and I'm going to a coastal area. If you're going to be thinking that way, then people may as well not travel anywhere."

"You're firstly flying into Istanbul, aren't you? There was a bomb there last week", he shouted at me.

"France, Brussels, Spain is next. What am I supposed to do? Wrap myself up in bubble wrap and just lie in bed and not enjoy life?", I gasped.

I quickly switched over the channel, and *Eat Pray Love* was on the TV starring Julia Roberts.

"Do you need a Xanax?", a black lady asked her at that point.

I got up in a rage and stormed off to the pub. I must have knocked back a bottle of wine and then came back home and passed out.

My sister Anna survived Nepal for four years, without being hit by an earthquake. I survived Greece and slept through a mini earthquake when I was twenty two. I survived an open water swimming holiday in Croatia on my own last year. If it's a shark or a refugee or getting hit by a bus, I don't care. Life is too short to be worrying all of the time.

Plus, with all of my research done on the Chan Zuckerberg Initiative since Christmas, I know that all of the philanthropists and billionaires and celebrities are out there to help others and invest in technology to make the world a safer place. In fact, Facebook gets hit with news ahead of any other platform such as the general media. I feel more connected with it all now. I am following a lot of Mark Zuckerberg's posts, and the hard training and running he is doing in several countries, as he also works hard to promote Artificial Intelligence so that blind people can see. A lot of the world is aware of this technology, but Ireland is a little slow and backward and doesn't invest in this technology to help people here.

I look back and laugh, as a really good friend of mine who was there for me most this Christmas, said that the funniest thing she read on my Facebook wall was:

Could the Chan Zuckerberg initiative Hailo
me a cab and get me out of here

I posted that comment when I was locked up in a ward. She still laughs at that, so it's good to see that some of my friends still have a sense of humour. She also knows how much research I am doing, and how I am following philanthropists and the good work that they are doing worldwide. Priscilla Chan was actually in Vietnam in 2012, helping refugees and promoting education when I was there, and I had that quirky connection with Facebook and cameras.

— 145 —

The moral of the story, is that I do not listen to gossip or bullshit any more. I seem to be a good listener, and everyone seems to tell me their secrets in life because they know I don't pass them on and have never been judgemental in my life about other people. I have my website coming live now and aim to travel the globe and continue working, writing, training for Ironman, doing long distance swims, trekking mountains and building houses in Central America for mental health and chronic disease. Building a house in El Salvador, is something three of my siblings did eight years ago for Habitat for Humanity. I was taking on a finance masters at the time so I couldn't go. It's time for me to continue my dreams; just as my mother would have wanted.

I still reflect on 2015. I was extremely positive, as I felt that I had come full circle since all of the trauma in 2012 and subsequent years. I felt like I had been punched in the face several times since then. The only thing that was bothering me in 2015, was that I wished that my mum could have seen how happy I was, and that I was doing all of my own training for a triathlon, and that I was finally back to myself. I didn't feel any spiritual connection with my mum in 2015. I just believed that we are all worm food. I used to wonder why I was doing more things that would have made her happy, such as wearing my hair curly as it is naturally and not bother straightening it any more. I am grateful now for the thick curly hair she has given me.

While some people are paranoid about cameras, it has to be said that technology is here to make the world more connected and make it a safer place. There are cameras everywhere, and google maps knows our whereabouts, so phones are important to have on us. If the Irish Gardai could make a better job about road accidents, then that would be a bonus. However, we seem to have the same shit going on in Ireland with no improvement in death tolls. People are always trying to avoid tickets and penalty points. The problem is that technology is so backward in Ireland, that the Gardai cannot keep up with tracking people who speed too fast. I just learned that they have new technology in the States, where it links up a person's phone with their number plate. This will allow the authorities to know if someone is texting while driving. I guess, just like green technology, this advancement will take at least ten years to come into Ireland. Ireland prefer to spend money on drugs rather than technology.

I may as well have been deemed as having bipolar or being schizophrenic in school or college. Actually, I read a magazine in hospital, which said that Liz Hurley leads a schizophrenic life. I used to listen to placebo, faithless and aqua when I'd go for my long runs before school. College got better, and I seemed to pull through a biochemistry degree, row well for the university, go to the gym and still drink plenty of beer and act the maggot. I even bought myself an Empacher skulling boat, so that I could go up and down the river alone some mornings. I used it twice, as the coaches were worried about me getting attacked by the river. Eventually I sold it off to pay for my Finance masters. I usually have fun in life and try not to take things too seriously. I try to adopt a good hearty balance. As my mum always said, "Moderation is key, even moderation itself."

I now follow Mark Manson on Facebook. He is all about "The subtle art of not giving a fuck". We all need to care less about what people think about us. I googled him when I wanted to give up smoking last year, and read an article which explains how dumb it is to be smoking through a white tube. The article is written below and is quite motivating:

> I smoked my first cigarette when I was 12 years old. My friend and I stole his mom's pack out of a cupboard late at night and smoked them in his backyard. They were disgusting, but I was fixated on being rebellious and cool — a dynamic that led me to smoke on and off for the next seven years.

> By the time I got to college, I was a full-time smoker. By the time I graduated, I was up to a pack a day. By my 24th birthday, I had "quit" a number of times...

one month here, three weeks there. Sometimes I'd get sucked back into it slowly while other times I just bought a pack and picked up where I left off. But in the winter of 2008, I was broke, unhealthy, and ready to quit. Perhaps the realization that I had spent half of my life as a smoker inspired me on some level. But regardless of its source, my decision to quit had been made.

...And I did what every smoker does: sneak a cigarette in here and there with an, "Oh, I'll quit tomorrow," thrown in for good measure. My girlfriend at the time, a fellow chain-smoker, chuckled at my failure while admiring my effort. But underneath, she and my friends doubted my success.

The problem with most smokers is that they quit for a week to a few months, convince themselves that they've kicked the habit, and use that as a rationalization to have one again. I suffered this fate numerous times over the six-year smoking phase. I now get why Alcoholics Anonymous treats alcoholism like a disease and encourages lifelong memberships: once you're addicted to something, you're always susceptible to it. So I understood that to successfully stop, one needed an almost religious-like fervor against smoking. There's no such thing as a non-smoker who smokes every now and then. You either smoke or you don't. And if you don't, that means you never, under any circumstance, have a cigarette.

This is why I used a cold turkey approach to quitting. Many people believe in cutting back, but that never lasted longer than a few days for me. That is simply a way to rationalize quitting without actually quitting. Besides, I'd rather feel the full pain of craving all at once than dragged out slowly over time. If I limit myself to five a day, why not use that same willpower to limit myself to none? After all, it's much easier to justify the

Vietnamese Voices

sixth cigarette of the day than the first. I have heard that nicotine gum, patches or pills can be very useful in this regard, though I did not use them myself.

Beyond the approach one adopts however, the key to quit smoking is wanting to quit smoking. I can assure you, this is much trickier than it sounds. Many people say, "I want to quit, just not yet," or, "I want to quit, but my job is too stressful right now," or "I want to quit, but I'm going to wait until I move into my new apartment."

This is bullshit. This is the result of nicotine creating deep physical and psychological cravings in your subconscious, subsequently triggering your conscious mind to concoct ridiculous bullshit to justify and feed the cravings. And of course you buy into it. You're a slave to it, in fact. The nicotine whispers, "You had a hard day at work, you deserve a cigarette," and you listen submissively time and time again, for you are now its bitch.

I realized I was nicotine's bitch during a bout with insomnia at 3AM. I had work later that morning but was dying for a cigarette. The nearest store was a 15-minute walk away through a snowstorm at -10 degrees. So you know what I did? I fucking got up, walked 15 minutes each way in the snowstorm, smoked one lousy fucking cigarette, only to fall sleep and feel like shit at my job the next day and use that shitty feeling as an excuse to smoke more cigarettes and feel even shittier. I remember thinking during my snowy trek, "This is utterly insane. I wouldn't even do this if I were starving. What the fuck am I doing?"

But *I* didn't trek through the snow that night. The nicotine did. Despite my intentions to quit over the years and to stay in bed that night, the nicotine convinced me otherwise.

How does one fight this psychological foe? With psychology, of course. So I implemented three mental techniques to help me on my journey.

First, I made a resolution: if my addiction makes me lie to myself to keep smoking, my conscious mind can lie to myself to stop smoking. So I started lying to myself to absolutely abhor cigarettes. Irrespective of rationality, I began blaming everything wrong in my life on smoking. Tired today? It's because I smoke. Feeling depressed? It's because I smoke. Getting sick again? It's because I smoke. Unproductive? It's because I smoke. Moody and angry with friends? It's because I smoke. Stock market crash? It's because I smoke. I anchored everything negative in my life to cigarettes.

Second, I built a rational case against smoking by writing down what smoking cost me in real terms and looked at it every day when I had a craving.

- $125+ a month (despite being broke).
- One hour a day.
- Poorer running and biking abilities (I enjoy both of these).
- Frequently sick (I used to never get sick).
- Lethargy.
- Repelling those around me (including some of my friends).

I constantly hammered this into my head, both the rational and irrational cases against smoking, and became a zealot. Nicotine may have brainwashed me to smoke, but I brainwashed myself into hating it.

Third, I made a promise that if I ever smoked again, I would do it by myself. In other words, I would not start smoking again due to a friend or my girlfriend smoking near me. I harnessed the power of two potent emotions to help my cause: (1) Pride; I had told my friends I was quitting and did not want to face the embarrassment of starting up again in front of them, and (2) Sympathy; I did not want any of my friends to feel like they peer pressured me into starting again. If I relapsed, I wanted it to be my fault, on my terms. Then something amazing happened after the first week: I began resenting that my friends smoked around me. This disgusted me even more and strengthened my resolve to stay smoke-free.

Anyone who has tried to quit knows that cravings usually only occur when thinking about smoking or seeing someone else smoking, either on TV or in person. When you're alone and distracted, you often forget that you want to smoke. By promising that I'd only start up again by myself, I rarely had to fight legitimate cravings. I'd go hours at work without thinking about smoking, and when I did, I never had a pack near me in order to minimize the urges.

My ultimate tipping point however, was getting sick for the third time in three months. I blew a psychological fuse and cried, "That's it. It's the fucking cigarettes. These things are fucking poison and ruining my life." I wanted to tear up every cigarette in a 10-mile radius, burn down every tobacco plantation, and piss on the Marlboro man's face while laughing maniacally as I stomped his pack of Red 100s. I had my last cigarette on March 4th, 2008.

The cravings were, of course, unbearable at times. Those first weeks required tremendous willpower, the equivalent of putting a steak in front of a homeless man and telling him not to eat it. The second week was especially difficult but I was fired-up. There was an emotional power behind my decision that has never left, as cigarettes disgust me to this day. Thankfully, the third week was easier as the cravings slowly dissipated in frequency and strength. By the fourth week, I'd often go entire days without a craving. And then it was all downhill from there.

As a final word of advice, remember that quitting is mostly a mind game. It's only as big of a deal or as difficult as you make it. The physical effects and withdrawal symptoms aren't any worse than those of a common cold. The struggle is mental. And if you decide that the struggle is monumental, then it will feel monumental. Conversely, if you decide it's just a temporary roadblock in your life that you must take a few weeks to overcome, then it will be.

I read this article and then emailed it to other friends who I thought might like to quit. Although I don't suffer lethargy and never get sick, I still wanted to quit to better myself as a triathlete.

After reading his article, I was off them for four months and found it extremely easy. Of course, shit hit the fan at Christmas and I needed my stress buster back. While off the smokes, I noticed that my run and swim times stayed the same, but I could cycle hills a bit faster. Before giving up, I contacted the Health Service Executive quit line. They were useless. They don't bother answering questions in real time, and just throw out the same dumb answers like they do to everyone. It's almost like talking to a dumb computer.

I have a few doctors appointments left, and have planned a trip to London and Turkey around them. It has been agreed with the psychiatrist that I need time alone on a sun holiday and to also continue training hard and to just remember to put myself first in life. Right now, I cannot take on the stresses of others. My mum, was of course a big worry of mine in 2013 and 2014, but I feel like I have moved on and can now feel a spiritual connection with her.

Part of her prayer reads:

There is work still waiting for you,
So you must not idly stand,
Do it now while life remaineth,
You shall rest in Jesus' Land.

When that work is all completed,
He will gently call you Home,
Oh, the rapture of that meeting,
Oh, the joy to see you come.

I have the full prayer for people to read and carry it around in my wallet everywhere I go.

The gist of this prayer, is that myself and the seven others still have plenty of work to do in life. However we need to do more of what makes us happy. Following your passion in life, means that you will never feel like you are working a day in your life.

Getting back to my mum. I want to celebrate her life. She smoked through every pregnancy, but had seven very healthy and tall children. This was possibly because she ate everything in sight, and she was stress free throughout each of her pregnancies. Stress is in fact the biggest killer as my mum used to say, so at least I know that smoking acted as a stress buster for her when things got tough in life.

She also firmly agreed that women should not stress about what they eat when they are pregnant, and that all of the goodness from the food goes straight to the baby. Unfortunately all of the junk gets left with the mother. It's only nine months however, so a bit of extra weight isn't going to kill anyone. Get fat and then breastfeed to lose the weight. Once energy returns, get back on your bike or go for a walk. Whatever you are into.

There is a lot of hype today surrounding Spina Bifida. My mum never supplemented with folic acid back in her day. I have done a project on this, and also volunteer at the Clondalkin Centre for Spina Bifida. The children need a lot more help with facilities, nutrition and rehabilitation. Folic acid is a supplement, that pregnant women are encouraged to take to ensure that the neural tube closes early on in pregnancy. The most crucial times for this are between days twenty one and twenty nine. However, what a lot of women do not realise, is that folate is a lot more beneficial in the diet. Folate is natural and comes from food. Beans, lentils, fruit, vegetables, avocados and bread are very high in this vitamin.

All of this nonsense about what percentile for height, or how tall your child is going to be can get out of hand as well. Women never had these sort of check ups years ago and they don't carry out that rubbish in the developing world. They have babies, celebrate and then chill with family and friends to count their blessings.

I've done an assignment on breastfeeding versus infant formula, and it really doesn't matter which route the mother takes. The only difference, is that the baby gets slightly more antibodies and immunity through breastfeeding. There is also a great bond between mother and child. However, plenty of research suggests that three months is more than enough to breastfeed. This may suit the mother if she wants to go back to work then. My siblings were breastfed for six months and I was only breastfed for three months as Mum wanted to head back to work pretty swiftly. There is nothing wrong with my immunity. I just had a rat piss on my baby bottle.

Not only is nutrition, mental health and triathlon a passion of mine, but the subject which I loved most for my biochemistry degree was epigenetics. I don't think I did very well in the exam considering I studied the ins and outs of it. It essentially discusses the nature versus nurture debate. Simply put, there is no answer. It is known that some people are born with stronger genes, but it is their environment which has a huge impact on their resilience and determination in life. I got messages from my mum while I was in John of God's this year and she advised me to be more selective with the friends I keep. I know who has been there for me over the last few years and at the beginning of this year, and I know who hasn't. I have decided to only surround myself with positive people. I'm also getting rid of nosey neighbours, who either just talk about themselves or who want the ins and outs of what goes on in my life.

I have known for quite some time where my passion lies, and it is a blessing that I left the bank when I did. I just always thought that I wasn't innovative enough to propel myself forward, but here's an innovation. Open up and write a book about a serious mental health episode that was surrounded with grief and heart ache, because I can guarantee one thing. And that is that personal stories are not immune to science. The real problem with mental health, is that every single case is unique. Individuals have to dig themselves out of a black hole. Unfortunately, no one can help them escape this hole, except for themselves. It takes a lot of courage and strength to be able to find that happy place again.

Some of the best innovators have come up with their greatest ideas while exercising or even taking illegal drugs. I read recently that Steve Jobs came up with the Apple Logo while he was taking LSD. God rest his soul, but it was clearly the stress of his job that sent him into an early grave. It's time for people to chill out more and enjoy life. We all have to leave this planet at some point. None of us are getting out alive.

I took a trip down memory lane and went to visit my friend Sue Roe in London last weekend. She likes to call herself tsunami sue or saint sue, whatever mood she is in. We had good craic together and headed out to a few clubs and pubs. I met Emily and Rory while I was over too and it was good to fill them in on the work I was aiming to do for mental health, and the travel plans I had while writing.

I visited my brother Mike and his family, and he was chuffed with my website.

"I told Dad that it was costing me nine euro an hour with Pakistan, rather than twenty five euro because he was worried I was spending too much money."

Mike laughed, "Sure Dad is living back in the day when everything was a penny."

We both went for coffee then. I still do recall after Vietnam, JP Morgan allowed me to work from home some days, so I used to work off my laptop and login remotely from my brother's house. Mike knew at the time that I wasn't myself but it was nice to have the company of family around me then.

I got to the gate for my Ryanair flight at Gatwick.

"You look like a really happy girl", a guy remarked as I was standing in the queue.

"I'm Gearoid, what's your name?", he asked.

We got chatting, and he decided to sit on the empty seat next to me, and we had a glass of wine. "I'm an engineer for the last eleven years", he said.

"Oh you must be good at Maths?", I asked.

"Well I used to be, but it's all driven by technology these days."

A lot of roles these days don't involve the use of your brain any more, and people only use the conscious 5% of the brain. With such fast progression in technology, it wouldn't surprise me if an abundant amount of jobs were robotic in twenty years.

We shared stories about triathlons and nutrition, as Gearoid used to do triathlons a few years ago. Gearoid seems nice and normal, and enjoys a few drinks like anyone in their thirties.

"You seem like an open book, I like that", he remarked.

"I was a closed book for the last three years, but have decided to let down a barrier and enjoy life a bit more, it's too short", I replied.

We've swapped numbers and he seems just as passionate about nutrition as I am. He likes to send me articles on pH balance and psychobiotics, which could be an interesting slant to take on for my thesis.

Chapter 12

The Clear Out

Throughout all of 2015, I thought to myself that I must be an extremely positive person. I was definitely comparing myself to how I felt the few years previous. I am a firm believer that recovering from mental health makes an individual much stronger. Individuals are properly in tune with what feels like the lowest of the low and thus they can really appreciate the good times. I looked it up before, and apparently the average person has ninety per cent negative thoughts floating around in their head at anyone time. I managed to turn a psychotic episode in Vietnam into a positive one, which only ninety per cent of people can do. By sharing this experience it will hopefully spread more positivity to anyone who thinks negatively on a day to day basis.

I remember my mum saying before, that I would turn into a mushroom one of these days. I had to remind her that mushrooms produce serotonin which makes a person happy. As a joke she bought me a recipe book entitled "no room for mushrooms". I had to laugh. I still remember roaming around Superquinn with her and we would throw a load of fresh shitake, maitake and field mushrooms into the trolley to make the most delicious mushroom soup. That legendary supermarket seems to have died at the same time as my mother. At least we can still buy the dried variety in Dunnes Stores, so I just steep these in boiling water before adding them to the pot.

"Ben Dunne achieved his success in life at forty Mary, you have plenty of time", my Dad said to me at Christmas.

"I'm not worried about my success yet Dad, once I keep following my passion I will always remain positive", I replied as I sipped my red wine.

Getting back to mushrooms, it is in fact known that individuals who eat more fruit and vegetables in general are prone to be happier thinkers.

When I told my dad that I was off to Croatia on my own on a swimming holiday last year, he replied by saying, "You're always on a holiday Mary."

I had to laugh. Even though I was working in retail buying babies wear, household and doing cash reconciliation, doing my nutrition masters and training hard for a triathlon, it did seem like a holiday. I kept extremely busy and filtered out any stresses going on around me. This of course, proved to be a challenge at Christmas. Even after my swim holiday, I took three days away with Dad and Suzi to Sneem, in county Kerry. This is where Mum and Dad used to take the kids. It was nice to just chill out, and do hilly runs around the place and swim in the cold sea after the forty degree heat in Croatia. It rained loads and I liked it for a change.

People in the past, have remarked on my salt intake, which I like to add as flavour to my food, along with black pepper and other spices.

"Any other concerns besides elevated cortisol Mary?", Danny Lennon asked me when I went to see him last year.

"I use a good bit of salt, but it's the sea salt variety generally, unless I am dining out."

"I wouldn't worry too much about that", he responded, "That Himalayan sea salt is needed in certain amounts."

I googled it later that day, and they are now proving that 2,300mg a day is too little. Also, whenever I have had my blood tests back, my sodium levels seem to always be smack, bang in the middle. This must be due to my high intake of water. However, I am a little concerned, that such a high intake of water is washing out other electrolytes, namely potassium, which is contributing to elevated cortisol.

I did in fact ask my psychiatrist when I got back from Vietnam, was it possible that the high amounts of water I was drinking, was diluting my blood so much that it caused a loss of salts which caused auditory hallucinations. He dismissed this comment straight away. Funnily enough, I found out this year, that my brother in law's Dad's friend hallucinated years ago due to extremely low levels of sodium. It is unfortunate, that the hospital in Vietnam did not do any blood tests on me at the time and these were only taken ten days after returning home.

I went down to Danny Lennon one day this year to pop in and say hi, when I was fed up of venturing into the Centre for Living and being advised on yoga and mindfulness. When I got to the building the phone was ringing at reception and I answered.

"Hi is this where I can get advice on COPD?", a lady asked me.

COPD is chronic obstructive pulmonary disease. I looked around and saw leaflets on COPD and thought to myself that there must be a consultant in that area in the building too.

"I am not qualified in that area, but I do know that it is a lung disease and that apples are proven to open up your lung capacity. There is evidence to show that people who eat five or more apples a week have higher lung function. I also know that swimming is the best for focusing on the breathing and again brilliant for lung capacity."

"That's great about the apples", she said, "Very informative, but I'm not sure I can manage swimming."

The lady kept asking me more and we chatted for about ten minutes. I got bored talking to some random lady, so I hung up the phone and left.

Getting back to the benefits of water. I still have to laugh at people who die a small death on a Sunday and repeat the words *"I am never drinking again."* I've been out with several people last year to the pub and they drink as much beer as me but never have any water and decide to skip meals and dinner while drinking. This could be with the intention to keep themselves lean, who knows. This is men I am talking about here. I'd be murdering a seafood linguine and lots of water along with my alcohol, and then feel perfect the next day, where I can train and feel back to normal. Their good intentions of not eating would go out the window as they would feel so rubbish the next day, order Domino's and just slob on the couch all day.

I have to say, I feel like I was driven to drink when I came out of hospital this year, as so much anger had built up over everything that had happened. I felt like I was waking up from a nightmare.

Coming back to alcohol and weight. I know so many people who avoid beer and wine and choose spirits instead, because they are less calorific. The first page on google does say that beer and wine have a lot of calories, but ethanol does not get stored as fat. It is correct that the alcohol has to be burnt off before the last meal you have eaten, but everything is needed in moderation. As the saying goes: Alcohol does not make you fat. It makes you lean, against chairs, tables and ugly people!

I have tested this one out, and alcohol has lowered my stress hormone cortisol in the past. A certain amount seems to relax me and it makes me pee more. A high level of urination equals fat loss and water weight loss. The maths is simple. I have come to realise this year, however, that maybe we cannot get away with this so much once we hit our third decade.

I've had people in the past try and control me, and keep me wrapped up in bubble wrap and not want me out socialising with friends. I find it ludicrous and feel like I have dodged several bullets in my life. I never want anyone to control me, and I never want to control anyone else. I want to meet someone who I am inspired by and enjoys time alone but with me at the same time. Someone who is as determined and passionate in life, into sports as much as I am and likes to eat out and have a few beers. I'm single five years now, and they have been the best years of my life for gaining experience and independence. Since 2012, I have been fighting many demons and it has made me a stronger person by facing them alone.

I was scanning through Facebook the other night, and the top nutritionist that I have a lot of time for posted a snippet from a book he had read last year. The heading is **Environment is everything**. "Who you hang out with has serious implications for your health habits. Harvard Professor Dr. Nicholas A. Christakis and University of California, San Diego associate professor James H. Fowler wrote the book on how our social networks unmistakably impact our well being. A 2007 study on obesity revealed that if one of your close friends becomes obese, you're 57% more likely to do the same."

This brings me back to epigenetics. I definitely feel that environment is a stronger influence than genes personally, and I have noticed friends in the past who suffer eating disorders tend to eat wholesome meals around me because they see that I have a good hearty appetite and am in a healthy BMI range because I burn off my fuel with exercise.

Speaking of obesity, while I was in Saint John of God's earlier this year, I saw on the TV that the guy who invented email had passed away sadly. He looked quite obese and perhaps had a host of health issues, but the man lived and was one of the best inventors out there. Email is in fact my favourite form of communication. You send a message and get one back when the person is ready to respond. It can be a nice long email with all of your news. It's the form of communication my mum used with me when I worked in the bank and the form of communication I used with her in Vietnam to let her know that we were all fine. Unfortunately people were hassling me for money while I was trying to send my mum emails, so my mind was going into over drive trying to help everyone out. When I travel alone, my dad texts every day and I like it that way. It's simple, and I let him know that I am having the best time ever on holidays where I can exercise freely, meet a mixed cultural group and enjoy meals and beers in the evenings.

I did a clear out of my room again the other night, and came across a lot of old photos, cards and letters from family members. There were a few tears as I read some of my mum's cards but I pulled through. At least I can read her handwriting, because there is no hope for me to be able to read my dad's.

My sister Anna, Suzi, brother Daniel and Mum wrote me several cards and letters when I was eighteen, and I moved to London to study veterinary science. The animal theme on the cards was running riot. Anna was filling me in on the theatre and her current life, and how she was happy being single and following her dreams, because she had met a few tossers in the past. Daniel was going through a pensive time in his life, so I think my mum encouraged him to write to me. He also said in one of the cards that he thought I was much more mature than him for my age, because I am a girl. I thought to myself, I'm studying veterinary but still drinking like a fish over here.

I have to laugh at one of Mum's lines. "John is gone to Bondi Beach in a pair of shorts, he looks ridiculous as it is freezing out. Dad is expanding and travelling constantly, so no change there and Anna is going to the theatre every night?"

She had to put a question mark after that. I think Mum thought Anna was bonkers by going to the theatre every night. We might have thought she was the black sheep in the family, but now I reckon that could be me. At the time, Anna was studying her masters and the two boys were at home so at least Mum still had loads of company.

Suzi was gutted I was gone, and in one of her letters she wrote, "On a positive note, I guess it gives me the opportunity to visit my little sis more in the coolest city in the world", signed off "You're favourite sis."

Suzi and I are quite similar. She just gave birth to her second boy and is delighted that she has a drinking buddy back. I love hanging out with Suzi and Sean, as the three of us discuss rowing, triathlon and swimming over some nice chilled beers and good food.

I also still have a card from my cool flat mate Natalie in London.

"To Mary, My wonderful Irish friend (I've never had one before!). Whenever you do something (e.g. beer drinking, stage, fifth years) we just say 'she's Irish'. You are the flat beer drinking champ and can down a pint faster than most! Have a very merry Christmas and a happy new year! See you next term. Lots of Love Natalie."

Vietnamese Voices

The fifth year thing is hilarious. They organised freshers week for us, and we had to do quirky things like stroll from pub to pub in our bras, and attach ourselves to each other when we wanted to go to the bar or toilets. They also made me down pints quite regularly. I'm three seconds flat for a pint of Guinness. I've done this trick for a lot of people. I'm surprised I haven't killed myself yet. I should really be in the Guinness Book of Records. All of my older siblings used to pint race in college too but they're out of practice now.

Natalie and I joined rowing together. Students made the cut to the rowing club if they could down a can of beer and row 500 meters in under three minutes on the erg. I was on fire as the can of beer didn't take me too long. I'm not quite sure about my split. I rowed for about a month, but pretty quickly I got tired of the commute. We were based way up north and had to get several trains down south to Guernsey to row, which took over two hours each way. I took up kick boxing instead. Luckily, I transferred into second year science in NUI Galway and took up rowing properly. The river, the college and the college bar were all side by side so it was handy. That is when I met Martin, and we clicked straight away. He was doing science, rowing and drinking beer also.

While I was clearing out old stuff, I also came across photos of Cathy Wright and I at Madame Tussauds. She was standing next to J Lo getting her pout on, and I was hammering Hitler over the head and also going in to kiss Tony Blair. I loved Tony Blair and thought he was a great politician. My mum used to laugh and think I wanted to marry him. He did a lot of good for that country, along with Maggie Thatcher. Who, by the way lived off five hours of sleep a night. So if anyone ever tells me again that I need more sleep, I will shove a lemon up their ass.

I also came across another photo of me when I was seventeen, and went on an Eastern European tour with Mum, Dad and John. I was getting the autograph off a pianist who had done a Mozart recital in Poland. I had gotten to grade eight on the piano at that stage.

I came across another postcard from my sister Anna and I burst out laughing. It reads:

> "When I was about six, I thought it would be fun to take my baby sister out of her cot and play catch with my best friend Lavina. "Catch!" One catch too many and the baby fell on her head. Myself and Lavina looked at each other in fright. What would we do? Within a few moments the baby started to scream, naturally in a lot of pain. My mum came running down the stairs, I threw the baby back in the cot and almost simultaneously, threw my hands behind my back in innocence. "What happened?" "I have no idea she just started screaming for no reason". Love Anna X

Kids are devils, but I managed to survive. This reminds me of the time when the Big Ben clock fell on my head when I was four. I kept kicking it in the midst of a massive tantrum, as I had the juice of a peeled orange all over my hands. I deserved that bruise and at least it stopped me crying. I got a shock, and learnt straight away to not be so aggressive with clocks. Speaking of clocks. The only thing that the doctors in the first hospital in Vietnam seemed worried about, was when I would nip my head around the corner into their office to look at the time on the wall. Time moved so fucking slowly in that hospital in the middle of nowhere. Two days felt like two weeks. I was banged up abroad and couldn't for the life of me understand what was going on.

Getting back to my current situation. I went online to get a visa for Turkey, which is my second swimming holiday starting on the 20th of May. Swimming is my favourite discipline, as I do not seem to get fatigued and think I would be able to take on a marathon swim. I couldn't apply for my visa as my passport is out of date on the 21st of September 2016, and it needs to be in date from October. The last time I had to get a passport was in Galway, when I was flying over to Boston to row in the head of the Charles. All of my photos on my driving licence and passports seem to be make up free and in sports clothes, so I decided this time I'd wear make up. I think I look like Satan in it. I cycled into town the next day to go to the Garda station to fill out forms. Onwards to the passport office I went.

"Miss, there's nothing you can do, it takes at least three weeks to get a new passport."

I just stood there blankly looking at the man.

"Does it not make a difference that I have my flights printed out and I'm off to Turkey in two weeks?", I asked bemused.

"Hang on, you can fast track it and go to rapid renewal on Monday, it's twice the price and only takes three days."

I relaxed then. I'm not missing another kick ass holiday, and if I don't get my visa sorted on time, I'll just make sure to sort that out in Istanbul.

Speaking of passports. I recall a holiday in Malta with all nine of us. We were getting off the bus and I looked around and saw my dad's grey bag that had all of our money and passports in it. I was four at the time. I followed him off the bus with the grey bag.

"Jesus fair play to her", my mum said. "We'd never get out of the country if we left them behind." Dad just smiled and was grateful I was with them.

That was the holiday with cats. The rooms were hot, and the air conditioning didn't really work, so we used to leave our windows open at night time and loads of stray cats would come in and climb all over our heads while we were asleep. It was also the holiday with the best ocean ever, according to my dad. I tried to organise Malta for himself, Suzi and I last year, but the three of us wanted different things. I got sick of going to the travel agent several times, so I just took the jump and booked Croatia for myself.

Barbados was another holiday I went on when I was six with the family, and I have to laugh as I look back. The heat was so strong that my arms started to get blisters all over them which looked like fried eggs. My hands also blew up into pin cushions. My siblings thought I was diseased.

That's another thing. Friends were concerned that the heat was too strong for me in Vietnam. I'm well used to heat and managed forty degree heat in Croatia alone. I think my energy levels were completely out of sync, and there was such an extreme difference between my London and holiday routine. My asics only managed to walk me around the quirky country.

I say it now, but I will go back to Vietnam. I'll go back alone, and hopefully I'll get to see Laos and Cambodia too. Travelling alone means that I can lounge in different hotels for as long as needed, until I am ready to move and see more. Mount Kinabalu in Malaysia is now booked for October, and I will get to trek 4,000 meters in the middle of the night to arrive at it's peak for sunrise. I wanted to travel the world by the time I was thirty. Now is the opportunity to do it in stages as I complete my masters online.

While also clearing out my room I came across my name and meaning:

Mary
Maria/Marie
Saints Date 15th August
Originally Hebrew
meaning "The wonderful"
Do not doubt that she is free minded, because she loves
her home and her family, this is her own free choice.
This lady has an amazing knack to master
many different things and deal with different
situations all at the same time!

Everyone should check in on their name, and get it's meaning. We need to focus more on the positive things in life in order to pull us through hard times. This is certainly something I was unable to do after South East Asia, however.

Mum's funeral was August, and the following August I was doing my first triathlon. Mum's coffin is now replaced with a rowing machine. I thought I knew how to handle things and move on fast by keeping busy. Perhaps I was in denial from the day she died.

I still laugh at one of the letters Mum wrote me. "Mary, I decided to write you another letter as when I phone, you always seem in a hurry."

I think one of Mum's major concerns about me, was that I moved too fast in life. It's almost like I put a grey cloud over any traumatic experience and black it out. 2016 is about reflection for me.

I'm happy now that my room is more organised, and I have cleared out a few dust collectors. It's a pity I cannot seem to organise my own gmail account. I have 5,093 unread mails. God only knows what I have signed up to in the past. I don't know how many times I have unsubscribed to e financial careers. I never want to go back to a bank, as I am eager to follow my dream. They probably still send updates of jobs to my account because they find my login name hilarious. I never open the mails but the title always reads 'New Jobs for Moving and aGrooving'. My brother came up with that name for me when I moved to London and was looking for work. He also helped me fill out my curriculum vitae, and within a week I got offered a job for Samsung Electronics.

I still wonder what some of my ex colleagues are up to these days. There really was a cultural team spirit around the office. The Koreans used to coax me over to their side at lunch to enjoy the Korean food. I liked to mix it up. They were good to me too. When I handed in my notice, they gave me my first smartphone, a camera, a bottle of wine and Marks and Spencer's vouchers. They wanted to keep me for more money, but at the time I was eager to get a job in the city working for JP Morgan. While at Samsung, I liked getting up at 6.30am and being at my desk by 8am. The office was in Chertsey, so I used to get the fast train to work. I dreamt of cycling into work then, but it would have taken two hours. Luckily I had more flexibility to move my ass in the city.

Dad has been up to Mum's grave almost every evening since she passed away. I prefer to run up alone. Sometimes if I don't feel like stopping, I just say hello as I run passed. I haven't ran up there since the 21st of December last year. I think I would drop a lung if I tried it now.

Other times I drive up and then treat myself to a glass of wine in Johnnie Foxes and look at all of the cyclists going by. I find running steep hills easier than cycling them. Cycling up to Johnnie Foxes was a goal of mine for this year, but obviously shit hit the fan and I got to writing instead.

I feel like my health has been compromised massively. Again, some of my dreams seem to have been crushed like they were in 2012. I am not going to give up though, and will try and take things a little slower.

Back to the grave. When Dad went up in the winter months, he used to light a candle at the grave. On numerous occasions, the flame has still been lighting when he goes up a second evening. Dad is still guessing about the afterlife. Since this Christmas, I firmly believe. I dare not say this to a psychiatrist however, as they will drug me up more.

While Martin was trying to take me home safely on a flight from Vietnam, I just couldn't leave, as I felt a spiritual connection with the country. It's funny to think that the drugs they made me take in Ireland, made me lose that connection and lose my positivity in life. When my mum got sick or even passed away, I forgot about the afterlife and I searched desperately for signs. I don't need to any more. Her energy is with me, and she is going to have an even better life this time around, because I am a fast learner and will not take on a deep depression again.

I headed into town to go on my date with the engineer that I met on the flight back from London. We got to talking about tinder and all of the dating apps out there. "People have just lost confidence in themselves and don't approach people any more in pubs. I like the way you came up to me in the queue for the flight, it's a sign of confidence", I said.

Vietnamese Voices

"Yeah I know, I've only gone on a few tinder dates, we all seem to have become keyboard warriors", he replied.

Keyboard warriors essentially means that people are confident online and say whatever the heck they want, but when they approach someone, they start to get coy.

Before meeting my date, I saw four people cycling stationary bikes and it was entitled *"help us break the cycle of homelessness."* This was at the top of Grafton street. I felt better that people are using exercise to raise funds. I was turned away when I wanted to volunteer in a soup kitchen last year. No criminal records with me. I guess there is just too much paper work to look at. I probably had enough going on at the time anyway.

The next night after my date, Martin and I decided to meet up, as he was home for the weekend. It was a nice day, so I decided to head into town early and look around the shops. I headed into the porterhouse central to grab a coffee on my own before meeting Martin.

"Are you American?", I asked the dude next to me.

"Yep, from Washington DC, my name is Mitch." He was having a beer and some food alone while watching the football. Being an open book these days, I decided to fill him in on my dreams of Ironman, my website and my book. He took down my name and the logo Vietnamese voices, and said that he would be intrigued to read it when it gets published.

"I've come to realise in my life that I have too many friends, and I need to let go of negative people", I said to him.

"Oh we all need to have a clear out, and only realise this at a certain age", he responded.

I stood outside for a smoke, and got chatting to Rob and two of his buddies. Rob is a primary school teacher and was sad that the weekend was over.

"Ah sure one of my teachers in primary school used to smoke in the classroom and smell of beer on a Monday", I said to him.

He just laughed and said, "I know, it's ridiculous how times have changed."

Rob seemed to be drowning his sorrows with beer to forget the thoughts of work the next day. It reminded me of how I felt on a Sunday in London. The fear used to knock on my door pretty strongly.

I like meeting new people, and not being accused of trying to get into their pants. It's nice to be alone sometimes and get no judgement from others. Martin arrived, so we headed inside and had a catch up.

I was speaking to Jenie the next day about the obesity problem that we have at the moment.

"I definitely feel that having been doped up on anti-psychotics in the past, has made me more compassionate about our obesity levels in the developed world", I said to her.

"I don't really understand what you're getting at Mary", she remarked in confusion.

"Western countries seem to be pumped full of psychiatric drugs, which is adding to obesity at an alarming rate. However mental health in the developing countries is treated differently, and the majority of people seem to be within a healthy BMI."

This was the best way I could explain it.

The most frustrating thing for me this year, was comparing the East and the West, when talking to my psychiatrist. She didn't want to hear a thing about it. Well, if I am supposed to figure out the root cause of my problem, surely it makes sense to reflect on my episode in Vietnam? Psychiatrists today are treating each episode in patients as new individual cases. This achieves fucking nothing.

Jenie continued to tell me, that in a lot of parts of Nepal, they work by hard manual labour.

"It's more the developing areas where people work hard and eat all different kinds of food such a buffalo", she continued to say.

This brought me back to a discussion I had with my dad last year. "Dad I have written an article to send into the 'Irish Times' on obesity, exercise and nutrition."

"Very good Mary, keep it up", he uttered.

I sent the article in, but it wasn't witty enough to get published. I lost interest at the time, as I had a million other things going on. The gist of the article, was that my parents never saw obese people back in their day. They walked four miles in and out of school barefoot, milked cows, raked the fields and ate everything from bacon and cabbage, potatoes, bread, milk, cheese, eggs and porridge. There wasn't a pick on any of them back then. Their diet could have been a bit better and loaded with more fruit and vegetables, but at least they weren't gorging on shit all of the time. They were also getting plenty of fresh air. It's just like Nepal these days I guess. Today we have too much choice and too many temptations in the West.

There are also too many apps floating around. I love Map My Run, as I like to clock up my mileage speed, but I tried my fitness pal when trying to lose weight post Vietnam and I lasted three days. I thought to myself, I'm not a bloody robot, and shouldn't be tracking my every morsel by telling a stupid phone as to what I had eaten that day.

Map my Run makes me laugh. I sent a ten miler over to my brother one time via email, and he sent his back all chuffed thinking he had kicked my ass. Mike is more of a rower than a runner, but he didn't realise that he was actually tracking his run in kilometres rather than miles.

I'm getting sick of this paleo and low carbohydrate bullshit going around at the moment. Yes, we were hunter gatherers at one point and ate meat and eggs and nuts, but we have evolved since those days and we need carbohydrate as our primary fuel source to load up our muscles with glycogen. How many triathletes out there can perform well on low carbohydrate? Maybe a few, but I reckon they could be in sane. I had a buddy last year tell me that I was drinking too many carrot and ginger juices and that it was too much sugar. This is a paleo hacks person who is always too tired to exercise, so they can go and shag a donkey for all I care.

I got bored during the day and decided to use my friend google. The thing I was telling people to use in Vietnam when they decided to pick my brain so much. I googled risperidone, the new pink tablet

I am on and a question came up as follows *"Does risperidone make you high?"*. I was curious, and I had to look at the answer. The answer reads as follows:

> "Risperidone is an anti-psychotic first of all. There
> are many side effects of risperidone, that may or may
> not occur. As for a high? Risperidone can make you
> have a restless effect, but also things like suicidal
> tendencies, lactation from women, and apparently
> some men get an erection that they find hard to get rid
> of. I think memory can be affected as well, like being
> very forgetful. It really just depends on the person
> taking the medication as does with all medications."

I had to laugh at this. Luckily, I am not getting an erection, but if my periods don't come back, like they disappeared after Vietnam, and I don't have the option to have kids or go to a sperm bank down the line, when I am ready to take on a little rascal (preferably Dutch sperm seeing as they are tall and sarcastic), then I will shove my head down the toilet. The drug did however cause massive memory loss during my manic episode on Facebook this year and siblings were telling me that I sounded like I was blind drunk when posting things. The drugs also heightened restlessness to a huge degree. Now on a more serious note, it says that it increases the chances of suicidal thoughts. I don't have them at the moment, but I do recall mentioning suicidal tendencies to a friend over Facebook when I came out of hospital the first time earlier this year. I also had several thoughts like this after Vietnam and Thailand, while continuing on haloperidol long term. So is the pharmaceutical industry sick and twisted and want these nasty side effects, or are they just dumb greedy pricks trying to make money from a science lab?

Another huge problem with risperidone, is that it severely messes up the neatly controlled hormonal balance within the body and elevates prolactin levels. Numerous cases have found that elevated prolactin causes galactorrhea, which is the abnormal production of milk in men and women, amenorrhea, gynecomastia, which is abnormal breast growth in men and a disruption to the production of growth hormone, which can lead to bone loss and osteoporosis. Osteoporosis is certainly something I would not be happy with, when I have a dream to complete Ironman.

After googling this, an old buddy from Smurfit, where I did my masters, messaged me on Facebook. I then asked him, "Are you still driving the mini?"

"Nope I'm driving my Dad's BMW now, he passed away eight months ago."

I replied by saying, "Snap, I'm driving my mum's car and she passed away twenty months ago." Shaun said that he was doing great and that he still plays football. He did his best with his Dad and used cannabis oil, however the cancer was aggressive and they used chemotherapy also. It spread to the liver and different places too fast. He said the funeral director told them that chemotherapy is a rancid drug.

When my family decided to go down the chemotherapy route, I said fuck this I'm going to Thailand to take a break. It's bullshit when you are the best friend to your mother and she made me the happiest girl alive, but then shit hits the fan. I was glued to google after Vietnam, up all night for weeks. Thankfully, at the time, I had no psychiatrist following me then. My family left me alone because I would say, "Goodnight, off to bed shortly", and I would pull all nighters and read like a maniac and make notes like a maniac. The oncologists were threatened by my information.

Getting back to psychiatry. If I was a psychiatrist, and analysing people's depression or schizophrenia, I would open up my mind more and do alternative research. Google the brain. I understand it. There are 7.5 billion brains and not just one. Every case is unique. Psychiatrists need to be more open minded. I always thought after Vietnam, that the best psychiatrist out there would be one who actually experienced a psychotic break for themselves. Yesterday, the psychiatrist asked how I was getting on and I said that I have almost written a book which will be published at the end of August.

— 173 —

"Jesus, that's fast, you're putting too much pressure on yourself", she said.

I told her that I started writing it three and a half years ago, but that my motivation dwindled due to the medication.

Angelina Jolie cropped up on my Facebook and I had to laugh. It says "When you have a gut feeling about something and you tell yourself you're overthinking but you end up being right."

Now I love this woman. I was obsessed with Lara Croft when I was a a teenager. Anyway, she's not being chased by psychiatrists, but she did star in that movie, "Girl Interrupted", where she plays a psychopath. Are people judging her? No. Now I survived a psychiatric ward too but my inner self was screaming triathlon and book. I got on with it.

I was up at Costa Coffee having a coffee and a truck went by with all of these athletes on the side of the truck. A type of Usain Bolt, a swimmer and a body builder. I felt like I had a lot of speed and agility last year, but seem to have been knocked down again this year. For now, I need to keep looking forward and remember how I felt in 2015. Hopefully this year, will get wiped from my memory by 2017.

Facebook. I know a lot of people stalk people on Facebook. What did I do for the last four years? I stalked myself. I looked back at my quirky comments and my photo albums, especially Vietnam. I thought to myself that I have had a great life and a lot of fun along the way. I was trying to desperately figure out why I was punished for going to Vietnam.

When Martin told me that I was selfish for not getting an emergency flight back home with him, I walked away from him and told him that he doesn't understand. I went outside of the hospital and sat down and felt like God was talking to me. Martin wouldn't have had a clue what was going on in my head. If I mention communication with God to another psychiatrist they would tell me that I am either lying or schizophrenic.

Now luckily, I had this spiritual connection there before my mother got sick. I lost that connection and now it is back. I firmly believe that the Vietnamese knew what torturous road was ahead of me, but that I would pull through eventually. People might get reincarnated as a rat and get poisoned with warfarin, and locked up in a cage and used for science if they are not careful.

Speaking of which, I didn't enjoy veterinary science much in London, because I got sick of dissecting greyhounds and beagles. The jig is up. We have discovered science a long time ago and it boils down to simple nutrition and exercise and a healthy mind, with a job that you are passionate about. The great advancements today lie in technology. You can go fuck yourself, psychiatric drugs. In Mum's day, there wouldn't have been much alternative information out there, as mental health was extremely stigmatised back then. Fortunately today, people are copping on and using their own head.

Let food be thy medicine and medicine be thy food, as the saying goes. That means, let carrot and ginger juice knock infection out of your system and let yourself have morphine or whatever drug when you're about to die. When Dad told me that Mum was on morphine, I just looked at him blankly and ran away. I felt like Mum was alien to me, and found it very hard to communicate with her and express myself. I was mostly silent while beside her.

I've met people in John of God's who are ex heroin addicts, but they know all about laetrile and alternative wacky cancer treatments. One guy told me that he was jacked up on heroin, when his Dad got sick but he was still well in tune to learn all about laetrile. I respect him for that. I told him that when my mum got sick, I gave up drink for a few months, and glued myself to google and bought numerous anti cancer books. When she died however, I started drinking again like a normal person and got back to training hard. I took up two jobs when she passed away. One in a restaurant and one in Mum's and Dad's business. Mum and Dad drove that business forward, and came up with the good ideas. I'll repeat myself, Delia Guiney raised seven children, worked in Guineys, donated to UNICEF, cooked amazing meals, raised money for Alzheimer's, went to meals and wheels, had common sense and knew how to keep herself happy without hassling other people. I can do the same.

Drama happened in Vietnam and this Christmas, which I didn't want, but it just shows people care. Even when my sisters went through Mum's stuff shortly after she died, I just legged it out of the house and went to work. I needed a distraction. I seem to always do the reverse of other people and I like it that way. It keeps me free spirited. I'm only starting to appreciate some of the clothes and jewellery Mum used to own.

If anyone wants to look at history. World War I and World War II did not go on for too long. It is in the past, and I swam through Hitler's submarine tunnel last year. World War III is pharmaceutical drugs, and it's been going on a long time. People are dying because of them. I just found out from another patient, that she had to have a kidney transplant from taking lithium. Is this some sort of sick and twisted money racket joke?

I had to ask a friend could I try one of her Xanax to help me sleep this Christmas. I popped that mother fucker when I went home, and I saw the universe on my ceiling when I had a positive thought and then a big black bird when I had a negative thought. This lasted for five hours. I controlled it straight away to just see the universe. I don't give a shit who takes Valium and Xanax for flights. I just take spotify with me. That's another thing. Why are we not allowed smile in passport photos? Who came up with that idea? We all have teeth.

I'm following the Laws of Attraction on Facebook now. I was sick of looking at paleo diets last year, while I shoved ten million carbohydrates into me. One comment says:

> "The less you respond to negative people, the
> more peaceful your mind will become"

And another one reads:

> "A person being too busy is a myth. People make
> time for the things that are important to them."

Now I have managed good education, good jobs, triathlons, socialising and being there for friends. Being there for too many friends in fact. People like hanging around with me because I am positive. Mum used to worry that I had too many friends in life, and she was right. I have eight close friends. I have five friends who are good to me and were there for me this Christmas, and visited me in John of God's. And I have three more overseas. I'm friends with the six I have selected for over seven years, which psychologists say is important and the other two for roughly three to four years. The rest are acquaintances and they all have their own true buddies in life. It feels good to have cleared out my wardrobe and head space this year.

I am not as fit as I was last year, but I won't beat myself up over this, as I know I can come full circle again. I ate like a greasy heifer after South East Asia, but at least I cut down the alcohol. The experience this year, drove me to drink and smoke like a mad man when I came out of hospital. I'm only coming to terms with my health again.

Next year I'd love to get my training abilities even better than last year. That means I can eat more. A tonne in fact. My brother John asked me what was wrong one day in the kitchen last year.

"John I just don't have the time to eat all of this food, I'm eating so much."

He looked bemused and said, "Stop training so much then."

I just couldn't, as I was extremely euphoric.

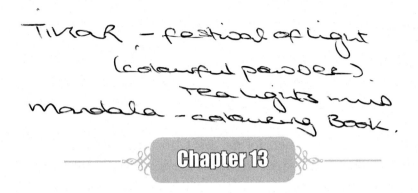

Chapter 13

Reminiscing and Moving Forward

I think my personal trainer last year wanted me to get a boyfriend, and suggested that I join a triathlon club. I just laughed and said, "I'll join when I'm thirty four if I get desperate, I'm having too much fun alone and training to my own schedule."

He looked at me like I had ten heads. Exercise does that, and I had to remind a personal trainer. It's funny how people bounce off each other. For crying out loud, I was praising www man and the music at the opening ceremony for the last Olympics and I went psychotic in Vietnam. My mental health seems to have revolved around the Olympics and David Bowie funnily enough. I was practising the subtle art of not giving a fuck out in Vietnam, but if I could go back now I would make sure to use those asics and attach google maps to me so I don't get lost.

The internet is one of the best inventions ever. I remember as a kid, I used to chat to random people in chat rooms while listening to Napster.

"You're from Maryland, wow?", I asked some guy.

I thought he was taking the piss out of me. Mum used to come down and look at me on our computer. She would smile to herself, as she knew I would next hammer a spaghetti bolognese into me, and then clock up a long run. I think the problem today, is that people are worried that kids will become overly addicted to technology and their phones. There seems to be a lot of pressure today with social media in some instances as well. When I was at my local doctor earlier this year, trying to source a good pill for myself to help me sleep, she turned around to me and said that everyone seems to be on Xanax these days as their phones are making them paranoid.

When I lived at home during my finance masters, I used to get the taxi driver to stop at the end of our avenue after a night out, so that the lights didn't wake my parents up. I'd walk in the door quietly and my mum would magically come up the stairs and want gossip. I'd sit there and have a smoke and a glass of wine with her.

"Town is full of nobs again", I'd tell her.

She knew I was after someone as passionate and quirky as me.

I still laugh as I look back. One time my brother John was getting off the bus and walked up our avenue. A random guy followed him. John came in the door, without locking it properly and this random guy strolled in behind him. John went down to his room. Mum thought this guy was a friend of John's that she had never met, so she sat him down, made him tea and gave him some dinner. After about an hour she realised he had no connection to John, and booted him out the door. Nothing phased that woman. She just had a giggle to herself.

I reflect a bit, and know why Mum and Dad bought me a mini in college. I was having so much fun in Galway, and probably only getting the train back to Dublin every six weeks, so they decided to buy me a car. Smart parents. It encouraged me to drive back more often. They missed my banter. I remember one time I drove that mini, with five rowers in the back to the off licence. The rowers used to call me mini driver and my recent date said that I laughed like her. I'm not sure if this makes me happy.

For one of our fancy dress Halloween nights in Galway, I dressed up as the Tuborg Sheriff. Everyone seemed to want to drink in my apartment, so I made up a rule that they were only allowed to bring Tuborg cans in for their choice of beer for a while. I glued all of them to an outfit and went as beer. I remember one of the rowing boys nearly wet himself when he saw me.

I still laugh about a time in Birmingham with Martin. We were visiting a friend, and headed out for the night. He took my phone off me to ring someone and then we lost each other. I didn't have a clue of the address where we were staying, so I just wandered the streets alone. A group of lads were coaxing me over to them. I ignored them and then got chatting to a nice looking genuine guy. He felt so bad for me, that he took me back to his parents house and gave me his bed like a gentleman. He had a picture of his deceased mother on top of his wardrobe. I felt a bit weirded out by that.

At the same time, Martin was getting a taxi home that night, and furiously kept ringing my number, only for the taxi driver to remind him that my phone was in his pocket.

Luckily, the next morning I got on Facebook and contacted my boyfriend at the time, and asked him to contact Martin for me. I was so embarrassed the next morning as I had wet the dudes bed. I just passed out in my drunken haze and never asked for the toilet. I didn't want to mention anything to him so I legged it out the door the next morning. I felt quite bad about that. I was in the dog house when I got back to my friend's house, as I was having an argument with my boyfriend and kept asking him to calm down while calling him Martin. Maybe I had Alzheimer's at the time and kept mixing up their names. At least I have never cheated on a boyfriend. I'm pretty certain my last boyfriend cheated on me towards the end and that nearly broke my heart. I'm loyal to people and am happy that I have dodged unfaithful pricks.

An ex once told me that I deserve someone so much better than him and he is right. I respect him for saying that. For now, the person that I respect the most in my life is myself. The other person is my dad. He is a Taurus, and I am a Capricorn and my mother used to say that I was destined to meet someone like my father, who will follow their passion and have most of the hard work in life done at an early age. Mum was a Sagittarius and I think she wanted me to be one too. Unfortunately I was two weeks late, as I liked swimming in her tummy, so I turned out to be a Capricorn. My eldest brother is a Capricorn too and we seem to have a similar outlook on life. When I came back from Vietnam, this brother was home from London to see me.

"Mary was completely fine in London before she left Mum. She was cycling out to our house and running laps of Richmond park, working hard and socialising with friends."

"I know I just can't understand this", Mum said.

Later that night, Mum and Mike sat up and I went to sleep down in Mum's bed with copious amounts of horse tranquilliser to sedate me.

"Are you sure Mary wasn't taking drugs in Vietnam?", I heard Mike say.

"Don't be ridiculous Mike, I know my daughter."

I ran straight back up the stairs and said, "I heard the two of you."

Mum just looked at me blankly. I thought to myself fuck it, I'm starting to hear Mike's voice in my head. Oh well and off to bed I went.

I was chatting to Jenie, the Nepalese girl staying with me, and she was inquiring as to where we put all of our empty jars and beer bottles.

"Oh we bring them to the dump for recycling, there's separate compartments for brown, green and clear glass", I remarked.

"Wow, that's so random. In Nepal, the street vendors come around to people's houses and give small amounts of money for jars and bottles. They either give money or else potatoes and onions", she said.

It just goes to show that there is less value for money in this country and the government are perhaps too rich. There should probably be more incentive for people to recycle.

That brings me back to blood. There are several developed countries out there, that give people cash for donating their blood. All I get is a bag of King Crisps and a chocolate bar.

Jenie was also telling me that the government was paying families to send girls to school in Pakistan a few years ago to promote gender equality. I was looking back at a book that my mother read a few years ago. It was a biography written by Malala Yousafzai. She was a young Pakistani girl who was sent to school by her father and got shot by a terrorist but survived. She started blogging for the BBC about the denial to the right of education and quoted, "How dare the Taliban take away my basic right to education."

Luckily for this young lady, she won the Nobel peace prize in 2013, as she proved to be very charismatic and resilient after the incident.

Another book which I was looking at, which my mother read was "A thousand splendid suns" by Khaled Hosseini. This is about a young Afghanistan girl who was forced into an arranged marriage with a man who was thirty years her senior. Arranged marriages are still quite common in these countries, but apparently there is a much smaller divorce rate, as the couple tend to work much harder to make the partnership work.

Jenie was telling me about the vegetable bitter gourd. It's grown in Nepal and India, but is difficult to get over here. It's known to lower elevated blood pressure. It's nice to learn about different fruit and vegetables grown all over the world, and perhaps they need to increase the import and export of certain goods across the globe. I wouldn't say many Irish people have heard of this vegetable, but we definitely need to increase the cultural mix if we want to excel at nutrition. I was definitely fascinated by all of the different fruits in Vietnam. A knife is needed to peel a lot of them.

I got back to looking at Facebook on the 10th of May. I saw a post from Mark Zuckerberg, which read "Mark is partnering with Airtel Africa, to launch internet.org free basics in Nigeria. Innovation across Africa."

Some people don't realise this, but he is donating 99% of his net worth to charity, and trying to connect the globe and make it a more open community. Some people are getting pissed off with Facebook though, as they see too many friends updating their every move and how many runs they have clocked up each week. People unfollow this shit. If I posted my map my runs and cycles and swims last year, I would just piss people off. I like to keep things personal between me and my phone. It's important to always compare your performance to how you were yesterday or the year before. In developed countries, individuals are constantly activating and deactivating their account. It's important to switch their feed to follow more positive news and quotes which are light hearted.

When I was in Vietnam, and was in the French hospital, I was logging onto Facebook and reading some of Mark's updates. The nurses knew what I was doing and just let me roam on and off when I felt like it. My friend was checking up on me however, as she could see that I was online. I was annoyed that I didn't follow much of Mark's updates and the work that he was doing.

Of course, when I was drugged up heavily, when I got back to Dublin, I forgot about Facebook and ignored all of this, as I lost complete motivation for life.

It was around October 2015, and my dad was watching the news. He looked over at me in delight and said, "Mary do you know that the founder of Facebook is donating the bulk of his net worth to charity?"

I replied, "Don't talk to me about billions of dollars, I knew about this in Vietnam, I'm off for a run."

While on my run, I started reflecting more about what I had copped onto in Vietnam, and then decided I would follow his work a bit more on Facebook. Mark likes to travel the globe and go for runs in different cities when he is taking a break from family and work. I want to be able to travel and do triathlons and hill walks and promote positivity via my website and writing. My masters is also online so I can complete my thesis as I travel. My third thesis is on psychology and nutrition. It will examine the impact of habitual intake of food versus psychology and will aim to explore which force is stronger. All of the gut hormones such as ghrelin will be examined closely and the impact of anti-psychotics on food intake. It is proven that ghrelin makes the brain cells hungry, and they have tested this in mice and humans. It's all to do with the gut brain axis.

For crying out loud, the drugs I was on screamed cheese, chocolate and refined carbohydrate. I didn't give a shit about my self image at the time.

"Mary smoke more and eat less", Mum said one evening.

"I'm eating and smoking enough for a small family Mum, I can't control this. The drugs are fucking me up."

I think her weight went up gradually overtime, but mine sky rocketed. Twenty pounds in five weeks is a hell of a lot of weight in my opinion. At least today, I can challenge that mother fucker.

Looking back at my manic episode on Facebook this year, I really don't care what I was posting. When Facebook asks "What's on your mind", it wants you to really share what is on your mind. Gobble shit was coming out of my mind, and I posted at the speed of light.

I had an interest in psychology during my Finance masters. I remember in my marketing module, the lecturer asked us about the impact of advertising on people. I answered him by saying "It is need versus want. A lot of us in the developed world have too much and it adds to confusion. The less you have the happier you are sometimes."

He thought it was a good answer, and we started discussing the impact of advertising on the brain. Some people today are getting heavily brain washed by what they see on TV or social media. I think Facebook is trying to clamp down on this advertising, but it seems to be a big task to control.

If I ever have kids, I would get them toys and nice things but not too much. I'd be much more inclined to buy them a play station or whatever the newest gadget would be. Some kids are actually smarter at technology than parents, and it gets their brain activated quicker. Of course this shit can get over used to a dangerous level. While I was out for dinner last week, there was a young couple with their three kids and each of the kids had headphones in while staring at their phones throughout the whole dinner. They didn't even say thank you to the waiter.

I was following posts on child psychology at Christmas, and an old buddy who is working on child psychology in Baltimore in the States, said that I sounded quite sharp and really in tune with how a child's brain worked. I think there are extremists today. Parents may get very strict and not allow their kids time in front of the TV, however the messages in a lot of cartoons go in subliminally into the child's brain. I then started talking about drugs and going completely off track. So many kids these days have attention deficit hyperactive disorder and are just getting pumped full of drugs.

I read a funny photo on Facebook which says, *"when she's sexy, cool and single, she must be psychotic."* This is the sort of shit I could have done with to comfort me after Vietnam. Unfortunately, I felt like I was in a black hole at the time.

Another proverb says that, *"A Japanese legend says that if you can't sleep at night it's because you're awake in someone else's dreams."* That's exactly what I thought while out in Vietnam. Two of my travelling buddies were bitching about me, while the other six were saying good things, mostly Martin, Sara and Kathy. I just filtered out the bitching and focused on the positive.

While everyone said it was all in my head, I had to come to so called realisation and forget about it. I was deemed as having trust issues out there. But I trusted the Vietnamese, because they kept smiling at me in the hostel and hospital. Although there was a language barrier, I felt safe in their company.

I reflect back, and when I was going through a break up when I was twenty, Mum brought me to a fortune teller. She said I would meet my new family at the age of twenty six. Looking back now, I thought that the Vietnamese were my family. It's no wonder I wanted to stay with them.

I've been told by loads of people in John of God's this year to never ever change my personality, and I certainly won't. Now that all of the past has been brought up, I know who my true friends are and I will no longer associate with others who have a negative impact on my life. I recognise the selfishness and negativity in some of them.

They add to a bad energy. Some are also gossip queens and just nose in on other people's business. I know one person who told me loads about friends of hers cheating in the past and she thinks she is the most amazing person in the world.

I read another thing that says, "Some steps need to be taken alone, it's the only way to really figure out where you need to go and who you need to be."

Being single the last five years, has been the best learning experience of my life, and I have been able to focus on myself. I have fallen down a lot, but have learned to pick myself back up again. I chose a challenging life, as I feel it keeps things more interesting and makes me acute. Some people this year have expressed concerns over my website, while they bitch and moan about their nine to five job. They can try and figure out how to be happy within themselves, and achieve success themselves rather than trying to heavily input my life.

I did challenging jobs myself, but got on with things by running and cycling loads which de stressed me. I never once moaned to a friend or family member about my job. I just got on with things. Life is a journey and not a destination in my opinion, and it is your own life to live and no one else's business. People are happy to settle in one place and do nine to five jobs. I'm not. I still want travel and adventure thrown into my life. I could get hit by a bus next year. There are loads of new and fascinating people out there that I want to meet, and I know I will learn more by meeting them.

The 11th of May came, and my period arrived alas. At least that toxic injection has finally left my system and my body is back to normal. I have a tonne of muscle and bone but also enough fat to still get periods. I swear some pharmaceutical drugs are aimed at population control. Hitler did population control and now the pharmaceutical industry is. Luckily for Mum, she had her seven kids before she got hit with a dose of drugs. I never asked her, but I'm sure her periods would have vanished for a while. I still remember when I got my period at the age of thirteen. All of the women knew in the house and my older sisters welcomed me to the club. Dad went crazy at me later that day because I never folded the towels from the dryer. I heard Mum say, "Michael leave her alone, she's going through a phase, she's a woman now."

Looking back, why was I a little servant in this house always folding other people's towels?

Speaking of periods. I remember going to a regular doctor for a check up on my foot after Vietnam. I must have stood on a bit of coral out in Halong Bay and she advised me to take antibiotics. Dad came to that appointment. God only knows why.

"Is there anyway you could be pregnant?", the doctor asked me.

Dad looked at me with shocked eyes.

"No way", I replied.

I wasn't having sex in Vietnam so unless it was the immaculate conception. I think you were not supposed to take the antibiotics if there was a chance of being pregnant. Looking back now, Martin's foot was a lot worse than mine. He was hopping around on a crutch looking after me while the psychiatrists were trying to figure out what was wrong with my head.

Throughout all of last year, I didn't have a touch of cellulite on my ass or thighs, due to the high intensity and endurance I was doing. This was transporting plenty of oxygen around my body. I started noticing a bit this year, as I was doing less exercise and smoking more, and generally becoming less healthy. I passed Ann Summers on O' Connell Street after meeting my brother Daniel for lunch, and I saw a nice red bikini. I had to go in and get it.

"How are you getting on?", the lady asked.

"Oh grand, I've accumulated cellulite, these mirrors suck."

She replied by saying, "If anyone stares, just tell them to look away."

I went to the till and the lady was scanning my bikini.

"You know all of the toys here are half price?", she said.

"Oh I'm grand, I'm just focused on triathlon missy."

I feel like I'm starting to become a nun.

That evening, I decided to hit the weights room in UCD, and go to the pool after. I left my house in hot-pants over my swimming togs. It was a nice evening. I parked in UCD and a random guy in a car stopped me.

"Hey there, where is the church?", he inquired.

"I don't have a clue, I didn't think there was one on campus", I gasped.

He must have been taking the piss out of me. I didn't give a shit and I strolled off.

That's another thing. I used to be very self conscious about my birthmark on my leg. "Mum, people keep staring at my leg", I used to cry when I was younger.

"Let them stare", she responded.

I had such an insecurity that I demanded my mum brought me to a dermatologist to inquire about getting it removed.

"We can take some skin from your thigh to cover your birthmark, but you will have a scar on your thigh", he said.

Mum looked really pissed off with this idea, so I decided to leave it.

I'm so thankful that I didn't tamper with it.

The 12th of May arrived and it was a glorious day. I said to myself that it was time to cut down smoking, as I wanted my old swim and run times back. I had my breakfast and coffee, put a wash on and hit the road for a nice six miler in my shorts and string top. I felt good. Again my energy was back and I did skipping and core and stretching outside after too. Jenie cooked me a big bowl of pasta and I had a protein shake and a carrot and ginger juice. I only had one cigarette that day and when I went to Costa coffee to get my second coffee, I brought my smokes so that I could chill outside and have a second one in the sun.

"You're not going to smoke are you?", a lady asked as she was sitting on the tables outside.

"Oh I was planning to have one", I replied.

"I'm allergic, I've got asthma," she said.

I was grand about this and didn't smoke, but I knew if my mum was with me, she would roll her eyes up to heaven. Mum would have been appalled that she was asked not to smoke outdoors where there were numerous ash trays lying on the tables. It makes me look back and laugh. I used to have an ex who had asthma, and he smoked when he drank. Mum offered him a cigarette outside a restaurant one night.

"Oh no thanks Mrs. Guiney, I'm OK. I have asthma", he responded.

"You know smoking is good for asthma?", she replied.

Mum and I looked at each other and burst out laughing.

She rang me one week later when I was in London, and informed me that she googled it and found out smoking is actually bad for asthma. I'm not sure whether she was taking the piss out of me or not.

Speaking of Costa coffee. I'm probably their most loyal customer. One evening last year I was coming back from a massage, and stopped in for one before closing.

"Do you want any cakes with your coffee?", the worker asked me.

"No, I'm grand."

I saw another employee take a load of cakes and sandwiches into the back area.

"What happens to the cakes?", I asked.

"Oh they go straight into the bin", she answered.

I was appalled. As soon as I got home, I googled Costa coffee and food wastage. I posted the link straight to my Facebook page. I know in London, places like Pret a Manger are much better at keeping food end of day and giving it to the homeless. For two months, I decided to go to the nearby market and get my coffee, as I didn't want to give Costa my business any more. When I finally went back to Costa, I kept asking the employees about the food and one of them said that they do keep the food and it doesn't go in the bin any more. I decided to give them more business. Ireland needs to catch up with the UK and the States a bit more. We have plenty of resources for keeping food and giving it to those in need.

Speaking of the States. I went to New York with my dad and brother in January 2009. This was the day after Caoimhe's 21st. One morning during breakfast I asked Dad, "I wonder how many pigs are killed in the US?"

There was mountains of food. I googled it when I got home and was shocked. There may appear to be a food mountain in the West and massive problems with obesity. In the East they have less, but in fact, people are happier. The problems lie on the West. We're too greedy.

When walking back from Costa, Mr. Wendal came on, Arrested Development. I love this tune. People need to listen to the lyrics. It's about exchanging knowledge and information with those less fortunate.

"Civilisation, are we really civilised?"

Who on earth knows. I like to think it's going that way, but we seem to be creating problems for no apparent reason. After that, Embrace PNAU came on. I just love this tune. It gets me fast on my runs.

"Running faster than my legs can take me.....You won't see me before you die."

I used to think all of last year, that I'm running faster than I ever have for Mum and for myself, but that also she didn't get to see me before she died. Before she became unconscious, I was legging it out the door to go to Electric Picnic. It didn't seem to phase me at the time. At least she had others around her. Luckily I was back in time to hold her hand all throughout the night and before she took her last breath. That's more important, because that spirit of hers is alive inside of me now.

I got a LinkedIn message from a colleague from Samsung. He said that I was getting finer with age and asked had I popped out a few kids by this stage.

"Nope. Still single and writing a book at the moment and have launched a website."

I have to laugh at his response.

> I was happily divorced by thirty. Come on gal get
> your fucking arse in gear. What's wrong with the
> younger generation? No sense of promiscuity and
> sexual deviance....I despair I really do. Spend all
> your time creating websites and writing books. Why
> ain't you dogging and hanging on Tinder like every
> normal thirty year old.....you have me worried now x

At the same time while reading this, I was watching First Dates in Ireland. They were all complaining about tinder and how shallow it is. I really have no interest in that site, as I feel I'm a bit more traditional than that. Definitely my virginity has grown back at this stage.

Reflecting back on my manic episode on Facebook this year, I recall that my first post was "Reverse Psychology, does anyone believe?"

Every normal kid out there wouldn't know what I was on about, but while out in Vietnam I wanted to do my own thing a bit more, but we were confined to groups. Luckily in Croatia, everyone on the boat minded their own business and we swam long distances, chilled, ate good food and had a few beers in the evening. I don't follow crowds. I never have in my life and that's what my thesis "Irrational Exuberance" is about. People follow the media and crowds too much. I was born free and alone and my relationship to myself is what is the most important.

While I was on Facebook, an old rowing buddy, Richie messaged me and asked was I OK. He reminded me he was in Berlin, so I said I would come visit him as I had a flight booked to go over and see my sick uncle. Seeing as my dad wouldn't let me go, I just told him that my flight got cancelled. I'll definitely go visit him this year though.

"Mary I was in the science lab and I had messages from Richie, Muireann and Caoimhe worried about you, I was all over the place with stress", Martin told me. We laughed it off and said thankfully we're all still OK and the stress is over. I even got a nice message from my sister while in hospital that Alan had passed on his regards. I texted Alan to wish him well at his wedding last year. Alan used to coach us in college and he complimented my technique a few times.

I also know that an old rowing buddy has bone cancer at the moment and this is why I'm striving for my bone marrow app to take off. My marrow is on the market, but so should everyone else's be. Even without the exchange of marrow, I'm definitely convinced that nutrition plays a massive role.

When Mum died, I forgot about Vietnam and telepathic communication and I started googling life after death. One nice note came up about telepathy and it said that when you realise it you will wake up with tears in your eyes. I couldn't for the love of me say the words "I love you" before she passed on, but by God that woman knew I loved her more than anything by my actions. Before chemotherapy was decided, she was doing so much better with my alternative diet. To put Mum and Dad into shock and not go down the chemotherapy route, I got numerous DVDs for them to watch that call it Kill em O Therapy.

It's a joke. Chemotherapy kills off natural killer cells, our white blood cells, our natural defence mechanism. It kills it. We all have cancer cells in our bodies, and a lot of us naturally have a strong army and force within our body which destroys them at a million miles per hour. The body is fascinating but the mind is even more fascinating. Doctors know how to fix the heart but they don't know how to fix the brain. I'm lucky that I reflected on my own experience and I moved on and got training again and kept busy, all while looking after my mum.

This Christmas was a shock to my system and my mother would have been saying "wrong move girl." Why on earth was I hosting five dinners and breakfasts for my siblings, their partners and kids? My name is Mary Guiney and it's not Delia Guiney. Luckily this experience has made me write and talk.

Dad has moved on with a new partner in crime already, so I am happy that she can keep him company more. Dad said to me last year, "Mary you have triathlon, I have no one." Triathlon is great, but it's not exactly going to fix every single problem that festers from time to time.

This house hasn't been haunted in a long time. The last time we felt spirits here was when my sister Anna said that all of her art work went flying into the air in the attic room. That's the room Anna and I used to share and that I sleep in now. That was years and years ago. What happened on the 19th of December just before I celebrated my 30th last year? I came home from the shops and I heard noises which sounded like doors opening and closing. I sat there, a bit scared and waited for my dad to come home.

"Dad, there's either a robber or a ghost in the house somewhere, can you go up and check my room?", I asked anxiously.

He smirked and said, "OK you're sending me so that they murder me first, smart girl."

I had to laugh, it would be Dad's worst nightmare if I went first. There was nothing. Just before I heard the noises, I had a little cry to myself as I was cooking, wishing in my head that my mum was here for my 30th like she was for everyone else's. As soon as I wished that in my head, noises happened. Perhaps this is where the second spiritual emergence started happening.

Chapter 14

Travel

Before Mum got her diagnosis, she came to visit me in London around March 2013. She was a bit tired at the time but we didn't think anything of it. I was in work, so she decided to get the train out to Canary Wharf from Richmond on her own. I went to meet her and we ate copious amounts of sushi for lunch.

"Those jackasses drinking beer with their lunch, they get away with murder", she remarked from across the table. I stared over at the table next to me and smiled at them. I think they over heard. "Sure Mum I head out for a few beers on a Friday with a few colleagues at lunchtime."

She shrugged.

I went back to work and Mum went around the shops and bought ten million presents for all of the grand kids. Six O' clock arrived, and I met her by the entrance to the tube. She was quite fatigued standing on the train, so a nice banker offered her his seat. She took it. This reminds me of Dad. Whenever he gets the Luas into town, he gets insulted if a youngster offers him their seat.

"Dad you just have to admit you're getting older and they're just being nice", I said one evening.

Later that night, Mum and I went to eat in an Italian in Richmond which serves twelve courses. We got back to my brother's house around eleven.

"Mary I looked into the restaurant on my way home from work, and saw you and Mum eating and I could see you talking and talking to Mum, she could barely get a word in edge ways. Also how on earth did you eat a large sushi lunch and then that Italian twelve course?", he asked.

I was still fighting food addiction at the time, but at least I was opening up to my mum.

When I saw Rory in London two weeks ago, he was chuffed that I was writing a book.

"Mary do you remember the time you got a head but in Sainsbury's?"

"Oh yeah that was hilarious, close call", I said.

This happened the night before Henley rowing regatta, in 2011. Caoimhe and I were in my local shop getting wine.

"Hurry the fuck up", this ignorant bitch shouted behind in the queue.

I looked back and said, "Have a bit of patience."

She took me aside and head butted me. I thought my nose was broken. Thank God it wasn't. She deserves elevated blood pressure as far as I am concerned.

That Henley was a disaster. Caoimhe, Suzi and I went and we all lost each other inside as the mobile networks weren't working. Well I actually had Suzi's bag on me for some reason. We got three separate trains home in our drunken haze. Caoimhe and I eventually got through to each other. We got back to mine and continued drinking. I was worried about Suzi but there was nothing I could do. I phoned Martin and he decided to make his way down to my apartment to drink with Caoimhe and I. On his way down he saw Suzi crying outside my door. The stupid door bell didn't work in that apartment. Luckily the three of us got over it and laughed it off and drank more wine.

I'm happy now that I have a Samsung phone back. I had a Samsung in Vietnam and lost it so I moved over to the I phone. I now have the new Samsung phone with the same passcode through swipe technology. Speaking of passcodes. While I was in the hostel in Hanoi, Vietnam, I thought that everyone knew my bank details and password for Facebook. I immediately changed my Facebook password. The reasoning behind this was because I could hear a loud enough voice saying "they can see through my eyes". At the time I didn't realise who could see through my eyes but now that I have that spiritual connection back, I believe that my deceased mother can see through my eyes.

This January I changed my details back to the original password that I created when I joined Facebook out in Greece. I joined then because I was meeting some cool travelling people from all over the world while I was alone on the islands. That was another great holiday which I will never forget.

Back to phones. One night last year Martin, Caoimhe, Di and I decided to hit the port house for some food and then head onto house on Leeson street for some beers. Martin was staying in my house. On the taxi journey home, neither of us had cash so I handed the taxi driver my phone. It was left open. I swapped it as collateral.

"Mary I'm so thick, I had a wad of cash in my bag in your room, I should have gotten that instead", Martin remarked.

I was pissed off because I missed spotify. I had to borrow my dad's I pod to train. I kept calling my phone but there was no answer. Eventually, about a week later the taxi guy rang me back and told me where he lived. His conscience must have hit in.

"Mary you are not going out there alone to meet this random taxi driver and get your phone."

Again Dad was worried about who I might meet. I had to get my buddy Jerry who lived up the road at the time to come with me. When we got there, I paid him the fee with a generous tip. Jerry was my DJ for the car journey home.

One of my favourite documentaries in the past was "Bin Laden, shoot to kill." I still remember it so fresh in my mind. It was the 2nd of May 2011 and I was home from London for the weekend.

— 196 —

I was a bit hungover in bed, and Mum told my brother John to wake me up.

"Mary get up, Bin Laden is dead."

I woke up in a haze and jumped out of bed. About a year later I watched the documentary and was fascinated. I'm not sure about this but I've heard mixed reviews that he was dead a long time before that. Also I've heard a lot of speculation this year over the twin towers and that the media somehow controlled it to make it appear like terrorists crashed the planes.

"Dad I hopped off a tube today and walked because I have this crazy fear in my head", I said to my dad as I phoned him from London years ago.

"I know, I don't understand all this terrorism", he replied sadly.

"America started it, they are the culprits", I cried.

Who on earth knows where all of this terrorism has come from, but certain religions sure as hell do not like capitalism.

This Christmas I looked at a phone book of Mum's. On the 5th of July 2005, she wrote in it a load of different money and got DG to initial. On the 7th of July 2005 she wrote more money and got MG to initial. The 7th of July was the London bombings and it was around the time my sister was getting married in Dromoland castle. I felt lucky. King's cross got bombed around nine in the morning and that was the station I exited every morning to go to college. Luckily I was at home for my sister's wedding. I asked Daniel why Mum had made him sign his name beside the money.

"Oh looking back now, I think I owed her money for a holiday I took."

Mum transferred some of that money to me for being good to Daniel and writing to him when he was going through a bad time in John of God's. I took a flight home from London to go in specifically and visit him in there. Little did I know, that I would get lumbered in there in 2016.

I went to Dunnes to do the food shop. Olives, tapenade, anchovies, mince meat, bread, scallops, fruit, vegetables, chocolate, beer, red wine, the list goes on. I came home, and an Indian friend messaged me on Facebook and it reads:

> "I was not able to tag you in a post as I was very depressed. One of my childhood friends passed away. People are saying he committed suicide but I don't believe that...I think he was murdered. His dead body was recovered from a dam."

I replied with:

> "Oh gosh I am very sorry. I have had a lot of ups and downs as well but I'm pulling through. What age was he? I firmly believe in life after death so stay strong."

At that point I was contemplating interval sprints up and down my avenue, but instead decided to bookmark this and open a beer. I had bought Asahi beer at Dunnes which is Japanese. Throughout 2015, I had managed to filter out a lot of negative press, however this year I started hearing more and more sad news.

I still laugh at the movie "Girl Interrupted" and when Angelina Jolie cropped up on my newsfeed. I know she has three biological children and three adopted children. I didn't realise, but she adopted them from Cambodia. I know if I want to have kids and if I don't meet the right man who will respect me for who I am, then I will adopt from Vietnam or Cambodia. Either that, or go to a sperm bank. When Jennifer Aniston and Brad Pitt split up, I used to feel sorry for Jennifer Aniston that the marriage had ended. Holy Crap neither of them give a shit now.

Back to Mum. Herself and Dad worked hard all their lives coming from very little money. And they are such good philanthropists too. Mum also wanted to spend and get nice clothes for her children. She loved Harvey Nichols and Brown Thomas. I remember one time walking up Grafton street with Daniel and we had loads of Brown Thomas bags.

"This is embarrassing Mary", Daniel uttered.

Mum used to want to buy me the most expensive clothes and shoes. I accepted sometimes but a large amount of the time, I told her it was just too expensive. She knew from an early age that I'm very good at giving people things but not good at taking. People who have suffered mental health, need to focus a lot on themselves and try and find pleasurable hobbies for themselves. Jesus the psychiatrist looked shocked in Vietnam. When she asked me to draw a big bubble of who was there for me, and who were my good friends, I put Martin and Sara first. Martin was there for me and Sara minded her own business. I had completely forgotten to list myself off though, as I didn't feel at one within my body.

I recall another girl saying to me, "Jesus Mary you went to Mount Anville, you seem to be the opposite. I thought it was quite a bitchy school."

"Yeah I went to Mount Anville, but I moved after fourth year to a mixed school."

My year was a bit bad. I was also shit at hockey. I remember doing a bleep test and I came second in the whole year, because I ran and trained alone outside of school hours. One of the PE teachers came in and looked shocked that I had come 2nd out of one hundred in running. When I left that school, the principal called me Anna.

When Mum wanted to know why I left, I told her it was because I wanted a better history and chemistry teacher. That was true to an extent. I got an A1 in Chemistry due to a cool teacher, Edel Lyons, who had her finger blown off by a Bunsen burner. The biggest motivator to move however, was that I wanted a more laid back environment, where we had both sexes and didn't have to wear uniforms to school. Mount Anville for me, was too cliquey.

In the institute, I joined the fast paced honours Maths class. I got an A for my junior cert, and the teacher in Mount Anville was good at encouraging me. The mentor in the institute was a prick.

"Is this the result I get for a fast paced honours Maths student?"

He embarrassed me in front of the class. I probably didn't want to work very hard for him, because he wasn't the most encouraging.

Mum took me on an Eastern European tour when I was seventeen. We had to get a ferry from Helsinki to Stockholm. On the boat she bought me some gorgeous Kanebo make-up. I had a few drinks on the ferry with Dad, Mum and John and I felt like a princess going to sleep on the boat with a lovely gift from Mum. Talking about princess's. I saw that Kate Middleton was helping people with mental health, when I was in John of God's. If the Royal Family can fly to Afghanistan and different places then so can I. It's a dream of mine to visit every country on the globe before I die. Well I'm not quite sure if I'll fit every country in.

Looking back on princess Diana, I remember Mum telling me about her death when I came home from swimming. It seems to be a swimming thing. The twin towers collapsed when I came home from swimming and princess Diana died when I was swimming. If the nosy paparazzi weren't chasing her so much then the car would not have sped up.

The lady from Cluian Mhuire just rang and interfered with my jam. She asked did I want to join the WRAP approach. Let me remind you that WRAP, is the wellness recovery action plan which does not involve drugs to treat mental health. Google Mary Ellen Copeland if you are confused. I sure as hell did not want to participate this year again. I hate art and I've done a load of weeding and planting before. The services they provide seem to only give a temporary solution by keeping one's mind busy at the time, but by no means do they get to the root cause of anyone's problem. I told her that I would go down to Detect, speak to Liz, and tell her to give people suffering from mental health my book. At least it's honest and open, just like the one book I was recommended three years ago.

Unfortunately, "Undress me in the Temple of Heaven," is a difficult read, as it comes from the so called "normal" person's point of view. It's nice to know that a friend of hers wrote a book about it at the time however. I know Martin was so concerned about me that he had to take a week off from work and spend time with his Mum and Dad. One person told me that Martin was exaggerating by having to take time off from work. Looking back now, it shows that he cared so much and didn't want me to fly off the handle.

At that time, I was spending time with me and reflecting on everything and my memory was sharp from the trip. Speaking of a sharp memory. In John of God's this year, I was sharing a room with a woman with Alzheimer's. I spent time with her, and her memory came back. I changed her clothes at night time as the nurses were too busy, and I put her into bed. This reminded me of Mum asking me did I always want to be a nurse.

It also reminds me of the movie "Fifty First Dates" with Drew Barrymore and Adam Sandler. I love that pair. Barrymore had an accident which damaged her brain in the movie and by the end of it she needed a video recording on the boat to remind her every morning that she had married Sandler; I forget their characters names.

I look back at Facebook and laugh. When I was almost certain that an ex had cheated on me, I didn't tell a soul, but I posted a comment to Facebook saying, "Who is the minister of complaints?"

I got funny posts back and just knew that there's more loyalty and excitement out there for me. Also when I joined Facebook, I posted that my religious views were Hinduism and that my political views were Bertie pontificating. Bertie Ahern used to be our Taoiseach, and now Enda Kenny has been voted back in. Let's see if he can solve all of our issues, and let's not forget mental health issues.

I was Hinduist at the age of twenty two? I don't believe in different religions, I think there is only one God and that Catholicism is one of the most closed minded religions I know of. We were slow to introduce gay rights and we still don't have abortion. Between seven and ten Irish women travel abroad every day to have an abortion. Wake up and smell the coffee.

This brings me back to apps. Dad thinks technology has gone cracked, even though he would lose his mind if he couldn't get in touch with me abroad. He wants an app that people can smell freshly cut grass from. I said to Dad, the invention is get out there and keep cutting it yourself.

Dad likes cutting the grass in the Spring and Summer, but he can't cut it in the winter. My theory, is that if I smelled pee off myself in Vietnam on the bus and there wasn't actually a smell of pee because I was showered, then I think an app that smells like freshly cut grass can be invented. I'm using my sixth sense.

Last year in nutrition we had to learn about additional senses rather than just sight, smell, touch, hearing and taste. Umami was an additional one I was learning about. But the list is endless. If you open your mind more you will realise that the list goes on.

This Christmas when the house was getting too noisy, and I needed space from everyone, I went up to my mother's grave with an old pair of asics in my hands. The last pair that Mum bought me was when I was getting gait analysis done after Vietnam.

"Mary put these in the bin, someone will chuck them into another grave", Dad said the next day. "Dad no one will steel them, they're symbolic and it represents Mum always encouraging me to run."

I put them back up the next day in a weird position. It hailed, sleeted and stormed over Christmas. The asics are still there in the same position surrounded by eight plants.

I had a look at my star sign again today and it says that everything will eventually work out but that I just need to be a bit more patient. The planets control this and everything happens for a reason.

I highlight my hair, but only twice a year. Another person commented on Facebook by saying I need to get my roots done. She can piss off. I like the sun to give it natural rays and I'm quite impatient in the hair dresser as I hate reading magazines. I don't like looking at which celebrity is thin or fat. I just read my star sign and listen to a hair dresser asking me about my day.

In future, I'm going to keep my beats in my ear. I thought it was rude to do that last year but from now on I don't care. I'm giving them good money. Plus they probably like to keep quiet every so often and just focus on their job.

Speaking of beats. I see so many women these days strolling with buggies and they have their headphones in. So if I ever have a child and they don't stop crying, I am going to take that little rascal out with me and go for a run so I don't have to listen to whinging. The little child can absorb all of their surroundings at speed and cry themselves to sleep.

Dad just brought home the olive oil. I like to throw any type of nut into my fresh pesto. Not just typical pine nuts, I throw in a mix like hazelnuts or Brazil nuts which are packed full of selenium. Walnuts are also good for the heart. I also load it full of wild garlic. It's an acquired taste, but at least it's packed with anti inflammatories. That was one of the annoying things for me when I tried weight watchers for a week. Nuts were off the menu. I made Mum eat a tonne of my homemade pesto when she was adhering to the diet. Olive oil too. It's great for the skin. Mum's bridesmaid Lorraine lives in Greece half of the year and has a very healthy diet and her son is massively into the olive oil business. Travel and culture. It's very important. You learn new things. Speaking of Lorraine. Mum and Dad eloped when they wanted to get married, and I think if it happened to me I would do the same. It's no ones business what I do in life. I'm thirty, not three. Hang on. I can't make up my mind. Maybe I'll have a big wedding. Sure I have bipolar, I'm allowed swap and change.

Speaking of food. Wheat intolerance is becoming a massive problem these days. I saw a doctor in a health farm years ago with Mum, and she informed us that we were both a little bit yeast intolerant. I still drink beer, eat bread and pasta. Wheat intolerance is evolutionary. If I listened to that bullshit, then I would become coeliac and the problems continue. God created wheat, and this is where the fitness industry and nutrition industry is saturated and fucking confused. We need to still eat the fucking thing or else we will all evolve into nothing and be living off air one day.

While I was asking my mum could I speak to a priest after Vietnam, I finally got to see one in John of God's this year. He was intrigued by my story, and did more listening than any doctor I have been to. It's almost like they have to do an exorcism on people. Which, by the way, was one of my favourite movies as a kid. I loved it.

I loved scaring the shit out of myself before going to bed sometimes. I liked thriller, comedy, anything really. Oh and Quentin Tarantino, lets not forget his movies, "wiggle your big toe' as Uma Thurman says. It's all in the mind. Dad finds that movie disturbing. Each to their own.

In John of God's this year, I started noticing people buying me coffees. Some of these people were on social welfare. That's another thing. The social welfare in the UK is sixty pounds per week, so it encourages people to work. In Ireland, it is €188 per week, so it doesn't encourage people to work. Individuals end up bored and more depressed, as they don't have much to do with their time. I have also been informed that mental health patients who fill out forms for social welfare on a weekly basis are adding to the wealth of psychiatrists. The psychiatrists get a subsidy for this. So mental health patients are bored and depressed, and psychiatrists are wealthy and not solving a single thing. I have never drawn social welfare before, as when I came back from Vietnam, I went back to work within weeks. Looking back at it now, I really should have applied when I came back from Thailand as I was not working and I was also caring for my mother at the time.

This time, I thought to myself that I was more than entitled to. I filled out several forms dating back from the day I was admitted to hospital in January and they turned me away. I was missing eighteen weeks of tax credits since 2014, and was thus not eligible. I found out later, that I should have been applying for disability allowance rather than illness benefit. Now why the fuck did the psychiatrist or secretary at the Centre not inform me about this? Pricks.

I have appealed this and if they do not answer my appeal in a serious manner I will fucking go mad. My parents do not have health insurance as Dad reckons it would have worked out the same insuring nine people over the years as it does when medical intervention is needed. They have spent enough money on psychiatric drugs for Mum and I which only made the two of us more miserable, and also chemotherapy which poisoned my mum's immunity. Give me a break. I demand that appeal to be looked at seriously you cowboys. No one in this family has ever drawn the social welfare.

I remember when the last recession hit in 2008, one guy on the radio was explaining that he wasn't motivated to work as the money and welfare he gets from housing is the equivalent to a €40,000 job. Australia. That's one place that never gets hit with recessions. And let's not forget the more developing countries. So before people can butt into my business. I'd rather be on a boat in Croatia, Turkey, do Ironman in Lanzarote, trek the Himalayas and try and promote myself online, rather than be stuck in this country just thinking about money. I have freedom and that's my choice. I'll come home to visit, but not at Christmas. Delia Guiney is sick of hosting Christmas every year and so am I.

I still remember a time in the Castle pub in London, and I was buying a round of shots for myself and three of our neighbours. A friend of mine came up to me in her drunken haze and said, "JP Morgan where's my drink?" She was really rude about it.

I know I have gotten drunk before but I don't like to insult people. This person has her own friends and to me was never truly there for me. It took me a while to realise.

I still laugh at the time in JP Morgan when I went out with my team for the first time. I got rat arsed, but my legendary boss at the time escorted me to the tube to make sure I got home safe.

"Mary, I'm shocked to see you in work", she remarked the next day.

I didn't want to call in sick and I wanted to get on with things. JP Morgan also had the corporate challenge which I ran in every year. Let's not forget the Lifestyle run for Mark Pollock. It's a run in the dark that is hosted in Dublin every November. Mark is blind and paralysed from the waist down and is a good friend to my sister. He also used to row. Even throughout all of my shit going on since Vietnam, I made sure to run and donate money to his charity every year. He is the most resilient guy I know and I am the most resilient girl I know. I tag him in Mark Zuckerberg's posts on Facebook about the technology out there to make blind people eventually see. I'm not sure he has read the messages.

Speaking of blind people. My old singing teacher and piano teacher was blind. He passed away when I was twelve. His name was also Daniel. He made me and my siblings very talented at music. His wife Ann took over his role and got me up to grade eight on the piano. I googled her last year when I wanted to take a break from triathlon training and get my voice back into shape. Straight away google pumped out that she had passed away. I was horrified. Luckily I googled more and came across her. People are telling me to use a different singing teacher. They can shag off. I'm going back to her.

Looking back to college. I remember when we went to Cork to row in the All Ireland Championships, we had to say one good thing about the crew member next to us at dinner the night before the race.

"I love the way Mary sits in the boat and never complains", Dee said about me.

There was always nonsense about who rowed shit and who rowed good. I just sat there ignoring that bullshit. That's probably why I bought my own boat. So I could go up the river alone. That's probably why I like training alone with music. I can't hear my breath and it seems less of a challenge. The fast music also inspires me. I remember Martin wanted to go for a run with me in London before Vietnam and I told him that we had to use I pods. He found it a bit weird running side by side listening to music. Talking to people while I run distracts me from my own goal.

I still remember a time when Mum needed a break from all seven of us. She went to the Golden Door in California. It's a health spa. Dad phoned her with an update on the kids.

"Mary is scribbling with crayon all over her wall. I told her to stop, as it would make you upset. She turned around to me and said, tell Mum it's my crayon and my wall."

Mum couldn't stop laughing at that remark. I wanted to send Mum to the Golden Door a few Christmases ago as a treat.

"It's very expensive Mary and I can't deal with the flight."

She wouldn't go. Hopefully I'll go some day in her honour to see what all the fuss is about. I want to walk in her footsteps and see California. I was there as a one year old, but I don't remember it. At least Mum brought back a workout video from there. I still remember doing the aerobics in the living room with her from a very young age. I probably needed to, seeing as I was a sugar addict and energy levels were flying around the place.

I didn't think I was great at English in school, but I asked for a recheck, in the hope of bumping my grade up for Veterinary medicine. My boyfriend at the time came in to read my stuff. I got an A for my essay which was centred around family.

"Jesus you wrote rubbish there, how did you get an A?", he asked.

I told him to piss off. I heard that year that another pupil wrote an essay on family and they simply put a dot in the middle of a piece of paper. Nothing else. They also got an A. Their dot resembled loneliness. This brings me back to John of God's. Some people are in there for years and years, because they have no family to help them come out and recover. They become institutionalised. John of God's were not happy that I had friends visiting me. They need to rethink that one. Some people just have friends and no family. Our government need to do a better job at solving the current issues, rather than simply arriving in all suited up, taking notes and going home to read and solve nothing. I'm sick to death of the same appointments I have, and being asked the same mundane questions.

"Are you still using Facebook Mary?"

We're not robots, we are people.

I met a guy in the pub up the road, who told me that he has been seeing a psychiatrist for years and has had no resolution. I went over to the shop to get smokes, and said to the young cashier, "Twenty Marlboro lights please. Oh by the way, when you get older, and are asked to see a psychiatrist, run away. They need to have more sex in college." He was in hysterics.

I got Daniel and Agne's password for netflix at the end of January. Daniel was asking what I wanted to watch.

"I really want to watch the social network again", I told him.

"Mary, if you like Mark Zuckerberg, don't watch it, it will make you hate him."

I watched that movie once, when it came out first, and the scene which I remember most was the court case. While all of the students and solicitors were talking away, the actor playing for Mark, was just scribbling on a piece of paper. Essentially he wasn't listening to anyone and was doing the reverse to them. I knew he was smart from the moment I watched that movie.

Turning this book into a movie has been inspired by three things. The publisher mentioned it to me. A patient in John of God's mentioned that CCTV has been around since the 1940s. And another patient in St. Luke's ward asked me was I a film star. Although, I'm not sure exactly what was going through her head at the time. A movie would be good to highlight the seriousness of mental health. I don't think there really are many out there, specifically for those who have experienced a psychotic break. I have looked up You tube videos before, of people experiencing psychosis. I'm not sure whether certain ones are real or fake however, because the doctors and nursing staff seemed to be laughing when the individual was going through an ordeal.

May 15th arrived, and I headed to Costa coffee to get my usual coffee. The sun was out and I sat outside. The worker from Romania sat beside me, and we discussed his bike, triathlon and boxing. "Does the food go to the homeless yet?", I asked him.

"Nope. We still throw it in the bin and employees aren't even allowed take it home."

My business is gone again. In London, an old house mate used to work in a coffee shop and they were allowed bring sandwiches home after work. Even if it is too much trouble to give to the homeless, why aren't staff allowed take it home? It's food for thought.

I remember discussing with Daniel before, that Green gyms would be an innovative idea.

"I think they have them in the States already Daniel", I remarked.

The idea is that people will run on the treadmill, cycle the stationary bike or row on the erg, and this will create renewable energy to supply the electricity to the gym. There's another idea for Ireland. Our Taoiseach needs to take a leaf out of Obama's book. I saw that Obama had a hurley ready for Enda's arrival earlier this year. It's all fun and games, but it's about time that governments started cooperating more without getting so argumentative. Our government is wealthy enough, so we can do a hell of a lot more with the finances. Where the heck is all of the tax payers money going? Here's an example. I had coffee with another patient from John of God's the other day, and he told me that he is leaving in two days and has already planned a drug fuelled trip to Ibiza. He said he was let out a week ago and has already had a cocaine party. So that's where a lot of our social welfare is going. It makes you bloody think.

"Hairy Mary", my older siblings used to call me.

"Don't call her that, it will give her a complex", I remember Mum telling them.

I didn't give a shit. Apparently, I was born with a hairy back. After a few days it all fell off. I must have a higher testosterone level. I used to be insecure about my bikini line. Shaving it caused too many red dots. Luckily they have laser now.

"Where did you come from?", my brother Mike asked me when I met him in Stephen's Green five years ago.

"Oh another laser appointment to remove hair."

"Where Mary?", he asked.

"Just down off Grafton Street", I answered.

"No, Mary where on your body?", he asked with a sinister grin.

"Oh Mike, just a Brazilian."

That quickly shut him up.

Speaking of testosterone. I also suffered from acne as a teenager. I still get outbreaks every now and again, but am looking forward to some fresh sea water and sun to clear it up. The huge amounts of stress at the beginning of this year, sent my hormones all over the place. I remember my mum allowed me to try roaccutane in school, to try clear my acne up. I was bed ridden for two days so she immediately removed me from the drug. It has a tendency to be very taxing on the liver. I have also heard of people committing suicide while taking this drug.

After Vietnam, I went to my regular doctor.

"I really want to quit smoking, can I try Champix?", I asked.

He wouldn't allow me, seeing as I was taking anti-psychotics at the time. Daniel tried it, and it seemed to work for him. I also think seeing as he has a family he is less likely to smoke. Daniel told me that he had some pretty scary nightmares on that drug though. I have read stories of suicides while people are taking it also. Drugs huh.

They should probably legalise MDMA for people who want to lose weight, legalise cannabis for those with disease, and then start making certain controlled drugs illegal. A lot of them seem to have more damaging side effects.

I was in Starbucks with Dad today. "That pair are less annoying, at least that annoying American one doesn't work here any more", he said grinning.

I agreed with him. I then got talking about Walmart. "Dad, didn't Walmart try to expand into Germany but it didn't work out?"

"Yeah, it's about twenty years ago and it cost them hundreds of millions in the end."

"Nothing to them I guess", I remarked.

They took a risk. I look at this myself and know why it didn't work. Those Germans probably didn't like the overly welcoming approach with a huge smile. The Germans seem to be more reserved.

I asked my dad to jog his memory of the name of the Castle Mum, Dad and my sister went to when I got back from Vietnam. At the time I was shunning afternoon tea, as food was the enemy, but I just couldn't resist it. Castle Leslie was the name of the place. Mum couldn't sleep well on that trip, as she was afraid of the ghost Norman being in the room. This was before she got diagnosed with lung cancer. Anyway, one evening Mum and Dad were discussing politics and how funny it would be to have the politicians heads on cows bodies. I found their laughter hysterical, so I had to get the painting done. I feel bad for Mick Wallace now, seeing as I have been compared to having the same crazy hair as him. Maybe we're all cows. Who knows. I'm just thankful that none of my family went into politics. Too argumentative. That shit isn't good for anyone's health.

Let's go back to Nepal. Back to the Future. They are in the year 2073 at the moment. Jenie says that there are still a lot of arranged marriages there. This policy is a bit backward, but they are definitely ahead of the game when it comes to pharmacy. They use nature, not synthetic chemicals. Their New Year is between the 12th and the 16th of April. Jenie was telling me that when a person dies in their family, they do not eat meat for thirteen days. It is believed that the spirit reincarnates straight away. They don't want to risk eating their family member.

"Mary, I've gained 5 kg since moving to Ireland six months ago", Jenie told me.

"You'll easily lose it Jenie, just take little steps."

She's already lost 2kg since moving in with me six weeks ago. This brings me back to my sister Anna. She gained a bit of weight when she moved to Nepal, because she lived off rice. She simply wanted to fit in with the culture and never copped on that an extreme change in diet would change her weight, because calorie counting never existed in our household. She didn't care though as she is not a vain woman and when she moved home, she dropped the weight in an instant. Anna was trying desperately to solve issues in Nepal by working on sanitation for the United Nations. My sisters also gained weight when they moved to London. They called it the Heathrow injection. They worked hard and they partied loads and ate out all of the time. They were away from Mum's nutritious cooking. All of my siblings and I are in a healthy BMI because none of us suffered eating disorders because we ate well and exercised and had a mother that drilled it into us to eat properly and not fucking diet ever. We never looked up to how pathetic women in magazines looked and aspired to be them. I have seen serious eating disorders in John of God's this year and that is a disease. They need anti-psychotics in my opinion. However, a lot of women today on Facebook are in the vanity eating disorder category and they are showing off and pretending how magical their life is. Today, women are stalking other women on Facebook and are entering a competition to be as thin as they can. Magazines used to create eating disorders, but now it is Facebook that is doing it. I had to delete a dickhead two years ago who kept putting up pictures of her in her underwear and saying that women who are into weights and fitness look rotten. This girl, takes MDMA and coke all of the time to keep thin. At the time, I was desperately wanting to get my toned figure back, so I just fucked her off of my friends list. Luckily, I have thirteen nieces and nephews who are all extremely healthy because my sisters and sisters in law shoved food into their gobs when they were pregnant. They listened to their cravings. I have one friend, who did suffer an eating disorder when she was younger, but I think it was because her parents were going through a divorce. I love this woman to bits and she has recovered completely as she knows it's just dumb. I have encouraged her to get back into exercise. And thankfully, her parents are back in a partnership together. I never seemed to have an issue with this, until I came back from Vietnam and was drugged up heavily. The neurotransmitters in my brain were altered so heavily that I hated myself both inside and out. I completely lost my zest for life. Christ, even my ex boyfriends loved that I had a huge appetite and I used to eat more than them when I dined out and I was always lean because I have been a keen athlete since the age fourteen. When Mum used to pick me up, I wouldn't talk to her in the car, as I was going through my moody adolescent phase and I didn't like the way some girls treated other girls in my school. I used to get home, study, have a huge dinner and then throw myself into a run to make me feel better.

Another patient in John of God's who suffers from ADHD, knows that he has gotten much bigger, but he reminds himself by looking in the mirror that he is beautiful inside, and he really is. For the love of me, I just couldn't do it in 2012. As soon as I got extremely fit and into triathlon in 2015, I loved myself both inside and out. This is when I decided to share my positivity, and volunteer in different places. It's a pity that my real happiness only lasted for one year, and now I find myself crawling out of a dark hole again.

I said to my brother John this year that I understand why people commit suicide. He took it up the wrong way, and thought I was on the verge myself.

"John, the only time I had suicidal thoughts was after South East Asia, because a psychiatrist didn't listen to me properly and fucked my brain up on drugs."

He brought me down to see an old psychiatrist again.

"You're paranoid about your weight Mary", he shouted at me.

"I'm not paranoid, I gained twenty pounds of fat in five weeks, and became extremely lethargic, you're not listening to me."

I stormed out of the room and went to the nearby Church. I had riverdance blaring into my ears. I went into the Church, strolled up to the altar and danced around the altar. That was the first Christmas Tree I noticed. It was all lit up.

Coming back to Church and Saint John of God's. Why is it associated with religion and anytime a mental health person mentions religion or life after death, a psychiatrist deems them as being schizophrenic? Some psychiatrists need to open up their minds a bit more. Looking back now, I was promised a brain scan after Vietnam. You can go fuck yourself. I'm not going in for a brain scan four years later.

When the cleaner came to my house this year to remove the decorations, I told her that she could chuck the tree into the bin for all I cared. It's not fair for someone to have to spend Christmas doing everything as a singleton and being surrounded by happy family's, when all I wanted to do was be in some foreign land lapping up the sun. People can do what they like in this house this year, but I won't be here. I couldn't make up my mind in December as to whether I was looking forward to Christmas or not, because it has been miserable for me with Mum's and Dad's health, and also my own for the last five years. Well there we go. A full moon happened and a big bang.

Habitat for Humanity just rang, and I am off to Zambia to build a house in July. I have two months to raise three thousand euro. I'm going to do bag packing, cycle at the top of Grafton street and organise a fun night out. Hopefully people will donate through my website too. I never even made my target of one thousand pounds while raising money for Breast Cancer Care, before going to Vietnam. Looking back now, I'm not sure that I would raise money for cancer again. I don't necessarily agree with toxic drugs.

This is why do I do triathlons. People pay themselves to enter competitions and then they don't have to annoy people all of the time about getting donations. Building a house was on my mind last year, but I just never got around to it. I even asked Aoife if she wanted to do it with me, as she went to El Salvador eight years ago. Unfortunately she was busy studying for exams. In Zambia, we have to bring our own sleeping bags, pillows and mosquito nets.

I look back and laugh at the show "Sex and the City." "Mary you know that shit isn't real?", my mum used to say to me with a frank looking face.

"Oh I know Mum but it's good entertainment."

Dad loved popping his head around the corner when the sex scene from Samantha came on. Anyway, didn't Carrie Bradshaw have to go to see a shrink when she was obsessing over Mr. Big? Well, I had my mum for me and a few close friends when I went through my own shit years ago. I still have a necklace from an ex. I kept it because it has a nice cross on it. It's coming to Turkey with me, when I go in two days and I'm chucking it to the bottom of the sea. I got over him a long time ago and for the love of me don't know why I still have it. I have a nice necklace of my mum's which has a cross and a palm on it. When we were burying Mum, I was thinking of chucking that ex's necklace in on top of the coffin. She would have come back to haunt me if I did.

Anyway, back to Carrie. She used to bang on about having the good job, the nice apartment in Manhattan and the boyfriend. Last year, I still lived at home, didn't have a job I was passionate about and had no boyfriend. I used to think to myself when going out for a run, that even though I didn't have any of them, I was the happiest girl alive. I felt lucky. But as a wise man once said, you don't end up being lucky, you work hard for it. I felt like I was eventually in a place where everything had fallen into place. How wrong I was.

Speaking of running. When I was fourteen, I used to write a sign above my bed that read "Just do it." I would wake up at 6.30am and read it. This motivated me to get up and go. The Nike logo is the best logo I can think of. People procrastinate too much these days. The beauty with exercise, is that you can eat a lot more and don't need to feel guilty after indulging every now and again. Little did I know, I would be hit with fucking binge eating disorder at the age of twenty six.

Mum would find this hilarious. At one point, when coming from the Centre for Living to get my lunch earlier this year, I was in a rage. The nurse wouldn't give me a tenner for lunch until after about twenty minutes of negotiating. The tenner Dad gave me fell out of my pocket. I was starving at this stage. I stormed down to the garage, and on my way down, Mum's Alexander McQueen brooch came undone from her coat. I held it in my hand and gave it to the Chinese lady working there. I asked her to give me a lotto ticket. Of course I didn't win anything, but I like that a nice Chinese young lady has a valuable brooch.

Jenie was telling me last night about the movie "Wild" with Reece Witherspoon. Her character goes on anti-depressants, after her Mum dies. She sets out on her own to hike the Pacific Crest Trail, which is one of the country's longest and toughest trails. I haven't seen it, but get the gist of the story. I aim to take on similar adventures. I am heading away to South East Asia on the 1st of September and will come home whenever I feel ready. My climb up Mount Kinabalu is mid October, so I may spend two to three months travelling. When December hits, I am getting the heck away from Dublin again. The Australian girl, Adeline who I met swimming in Croatia last year is going to be in the Philippines for Christmas with her new boyfriend and she has asked me to join them.

I told my psychiatrist that I got offered a role in JP Morgan in Singapore and that it was starting in September. I wanted to finish with these bullshit appointments. This was a lie of course.

He contacted me a few weeks later to say that he got an email from someone to say they were worried about me because I was heading to China. I don't know where this came from.

I have discussed my travel plans with my dad, and I feel like it is not the psychiatrists business any more as to what I do with my life.

I told one patient about my book. "Mary, it sounds like they will never have you back in John of God's again, if you open up so much about drug treatment."

That is the idea. I never want to go back to that hell hole again.

One of the hardest things I had to go through, was going to the Blackrock Clinic with Mum and Dad. She was weak at this point, and they wanted to draw blood from her for tests. They couldn't take blood from her arm, so they jabbed a needle into her vein in her hand. That was torture for me to watch.

"What's going through your head Mum?", I asked.

"Mary, I'm just wondering what it's like to be dead."

I looked away, didn't shed a single tear and I replied, "I bet it's like your asleep in a comfy bed."

Dad nodded in agreement. I seem to always have the right things to say to people, even though there is a war going on in my own head. Mum knew that I was the strongest going through all of this, even with my own issues at the time. However, I have come to realise that people who appear to be the strongest, are sometimes the most sensitive underneath. I haven't been able to cry to a single person about any of my shit over the past few years.

Speaking of war. One of the nicknames we have for Dad is "Daddy Warbucks." He cannot understand the inequality in the world. Dad used to think that my life wasn't valued in Vietnam. Looking back on Mount Everest, the Sherpas risk their own lives for

Westerners. Why do they do this? Perhaps they believe in life after death, and they believe that heading to Nepal and climbing their beauty is a new adventure for Westerners.

I remember as a kid in primary school, we had four men come to our school and give a talk about having climbed Everest.

"Was it harder going up or down?", I asked as an eight year old.

"Good question Mary, you need the fitness and strength to go up, but it's more challenging going down."

I had adventure ingrained into me as a young child.

Getting back to people helping people. When I was in JP Morgan shortly after Vietnam. A colleague was the best help ever, and she acted like a mother figure to me.

"Mary, you're just not yourself, I'll help you prepare for the Royal Bank of Scotland interview."

At the time, I desperately wanted to change my current situation and find a new role. I used to stay long evenings with this colleague, when everyone else left the office. On a few occasions, I tried to explain my episode out in Vietnam to her, as she was half Vietnamese and half American. She was certainly more understanding than any psychiatrist I had seen, but she just couldn't get to grips as to what I was trying to explain. I never got the Royal Bank of Scotland job, but I guess it was another blessing. Little did I know that my mum was going to get sick down the line.

I feel sorry for the nurses in John of God's, but I feel more sorry for the patients. People are going crazy in there, and there seems to be a stupid communication barrier. When patients want to phone family or friends, they have to queue up and wait for ages. The nurses never seem to have any spare time. Communication is important. Ireland is in cuckoo shit ville creek when it comes to mental health. No one is solving anything and it is getting worse. When more psychiatric drugs are used, more problems are created. Think about this you dip shits. Depression is worse than cancer, or any debilitating physical illness. At least Hitler communicated that he wanted people dead. The pharmaceutical industry is fucking with people's heads in a round about way. It is the most unethical job I can think of. Big pharma is in bed with the government who are in bed with the food and drug administration who are in bed with the psychiatrists. Everyone makes a nice little pay cheque for themselves.

When I got back from Vietnam, I challenged what the psychiatrist said to me and I looked at google. People with psychosis have a lower life expectancy by almost twenty two years, because they smoke more, eat shit and don't exercise. They get a host of debilitating side effects from anti-psychotics. Obesity, diabetes, heart disease and Parkinson's are extremely common. Well I'm challenging that mother fucker. I don't want to die young. The only thing I hate about myself right now is smoking. Each time a fucking episode comes around though, it is easier to reach for a cigarette. Psychiatrists in fact advise that one should not give up smoking when going through an episode. Piss off. I'll get a Japanese hypnotist to work on me next year. At the same time, I'm keeping my fitness up and eating apricot kernels and wheat grass shots like they are going out of fashion.

The brain is the most fascinating organ, and it controls everything. It controls every single organ in the body. It's all mind over matter. I've definitely been dumbed down again this year, but I'm trying to keep on a more positive note than I did a few years ago. I'm a dreamer and will keep following them. Christ, I forgot my actual dreams for about three years. The ones when you go through rapid eye movement. Drugs fucked up my sleep and made me remember nothing at night time. I had to live my dreams through my day to day.

Getting back to family. My sister Anna left Nepal when she fell pregnant, as she wanted to have her first child back in Ireland. Herself and her husband actually got married under Nepalese law, and then had a second wedding back here. If I ever get married and have kids, I won't care where I have them. I know that some of the best hospitals out there are in the developing world. So I might have kids in different countries and there will be a little story behind it for each of them.

Mum never told me the full story of her life, she kept parts secret. I'm starting to dream more about her life and how amazing it was for the bulk of it. She didn't deserve any suffering, but she got a fair whack of it. She seemed to pull through as a very strong character. Suffering makes us stronger. Her mother passed away giving birth to her. She was the youngest of twelve. She, however, had Auntie Mary who was twenty years her senior to act as her mother figure. If Mum was alive right now, she would tell me that it was definitely harder on me getting to know her and then losing her. At least I took the most valuable thing from Mum and that is advice. At times, when I was younger, I didn't listen to her advice, but I have it all stored away now.

It's hard to go through all of this again, without the advice from a woman who would have understood it all the most. I'm trying to stay as positive as I can however. Some people are happy to have boyfriends and girlfriends all along in life, while other's prefer alone time and trying to figure out their own strength and inner beauty. Croatia was amazing. I talked to strangers and I inspired them and they inspired me. I have homes to go to when I travel. Thailand sucked. Anytime I wanted to chat to a stranger on the boat or on land, I felt like I had no freedom to do so. I'm done with travelling in cliquey groups.

I read an article in a magazine earlier this year, and it said that a girl was more or less following her dream and travelling alone. Her buddy Martin hops off a Ryanair flight to see her as he misses her and he arrives with a bottle of wine. I started laughing, thinking it will be Martin and I some day. I need to get out exploring the world on my own first.

I still think it is so strange that the communication going on in my head was a strong bond between Martin and Sara. I felt like I trusted them the most. Sara's Dad passed away shortly after Vietnam and now Martin is fighting a similar battle.

When I rang the hospitals in Vietnam after I got back, they kept saying that they didn't want any side effects for me. I believe them. I still also believe that the Vietnamese might have known what war was ahead of me, and that I took every step for a reason. Had I stayed in Vietnam, and had no emergency intervention, I know for a fact that I would have caught the travelling bug. I'm happy at least I was there for Mum. Even though chemotherapy was decided in the end, I had no control over it. Touch wood. But if I ever got cancer I'd be living it up under an apricot tree and I would say go fuck yourself chemotherapy. My immunity is more important than a nasty drug.

Dad will miss me more as I travel but I think he is realising that I need to follow my dreams more. My mental health is the most important thing right now. I'm glad my masters is online. About time I completed it.

When I mentioned Zambia and building a house to Dad, he seemed happy enough. He has a new lady and I am happy for him. I said to my dad before going to sleep the other night, "Look after that hip, you might have to walk me up the aisle one day." He laughed at me. If Dad ever walks me up the aisle, I will have the song "Time to say Goodbye", playing by Sarah Brightman.

"Time to say Goodbye", is Dad's favourite song and I think the jig might be up. It's time for him to say goodbye to me regardless. I have to move on with my life too. Deep down, Mum must have been thrilled that I insisted on spending time with her, but I think underneath it all she was worried that I wasn't focusing on myself. Thankfully we have a large family, so there are plenty of kids around to keep Dad company.

When I wanted escape from John of God's, I said to Dad that Malaysia and the Philippines are looking after me. The student psychiatrist is from Malaysia and one of the nice nurses is from the Philippines. They treated me with respect and listened to me. Unfortunately their voice isn't so strong in Ireland, because they are nurses and students. Cop on Ireland. Some of the smartest people out there aren't just after money and power. They are born to help people.

I also just realised from Facebook that the moon controls the sea. I have seen a tonne of full moons since Christmas and there was definitely something in the air when I went to Vietnam.

Facebook is great for looking back at memories of yourself. Remember that word yourself people. Never ever forget it. We're not here competing with people, we're here to compete with ourselves. Comparing yourself to someone else is the worst thing you can do. You can never be them. You were born as you. We're spinning at a million miles per hour and the universe has no end. Just stop for a second and think about that. Rather than having a sad puss on your face, stop and smile and just be glad to be here. There are so many more people going through worse in life.

Chapter 15

Exorcism

I got back from the shop, and googled apricot kernels again. A guy called James Turner posted in 2008, that he was eating two seeds a day twice a day. Janet Terra replied by saying James wasn't eating enough to kill his cancer. She also calls it God's chemotherapy. Read Edward Griffin's book, "World Without Cancer". I had my mum on sixty a day and she was doing great. Chemotherapy took over and she died. One of the most frustrating things for me, was that people kept emailing me about what routine I was using with Mum, and I was glad to share it all. As soon as they found out that she died, they lost interest. The problem with today, is that people who use nutritional intervention also use conventional medicine. We need more people to go down the alternative route on it's own. People need to challenge information more. Challenge a doctor, because they do not know everything. God knows all of it and gave us every seed on this planet to enhance our health. Money and religion decided to get in the way and people got greedy.

Even last year, when I found out about friend's who had parents or relatives with terminal cancer, I typed up a fast email with everything I was doing for Mum and sent it to them. I did not want them to go through the same torture as me. Unfortunately, they also went down the chemotherapy road. I said to myself, even though I lost Mum, I

Vietnamese Voices

am not going to give up on all of the research I did, as I am passionate about my beliefs.

I don't know why guys wanted to settle down with me in the past and buy an apartment at a young age. That's not me and I'm so glad I never committed to it. Perhaps they were infatuated with me or wanted so called security but my security is my inner self and my inner drive to move my body, to hop on planes and to see more of the world. Specifically the developing world. I'm tired of the developed world. We think we know it all, but in fact the East have a much smarter brain. They have intuition.

I'm drinking a typical green juice now and it has fennel in it. You can guess the rest. Also what is the problem with people putting artificial sweetener into theirs? It's artificial. Sugar comes from the sugar cane and is better for you. And if you have legs, you burn it off. It's simple maths. In and out. The sugar debate has gone fucking cracked in the last few years. Nutrition has been made to appear so complex, when in fact it is very simple. Also what are all these people doing making egg white omelettes? The egg came from the chicken with a yolk in it. We're supposed to eat it.

When I went to Ios in Greece, when I was twenty two, I worked as a floor whore. Essentially, we were made dance in small nightclubs to coax people in. We were given free drinks for doing this. I would wake up the next morning with dilated pupils and purely feel like shit. I had to leave Ios after a month. It is also known as Irish Over Seas. I moved to Kos on my own, and while en route, I found out that in Ios, the bar workers put pure ethanol into the alcohol to make people crazy. I read in the paper shortly after that a young Irish man dropped dead due to ethanol poisoning that summer.

Kos was much nicer and I got to know the Greeks better. I also met a few Australians too, who I still keep in touch with on Facebook. They were on the run from the police. It was nice to hop

— 223 —

on motorbikes and venture around the island to see Kardamena and the hot springs. Again, I felt more liberated being there on my own.

I found out recently that Dad has travelled to Pakistan before. I'm still intrigued by that country.

"I was there five years ago Mary, I wouldn't go back. I don't have the energy to. Plus they had to check for bombs under the cars when I got to arrivals. They did that in Indonesia too when I travelled there with Suzi twelve years ago."

I never realised my dad went to Pakistan. Perhaps Mum and Dad did not want to worry us at the time.

Mum and Dad got invited to the Pakistani embassy on several occasions. Before Mum's death, I went with my dad. We were pissed off they didn't serve us any alcohol. They should probably open up their mind a bit more. If the Vietnamese prison gave me beer and smokes, then maybe the Pakistani embassy can supply wine. We're all human at the end of the day.

Cathy Wright and I used to say that the sea was God's spit when we were small. It's magical. I could never make my mind up, as to whether I was a sea girl or a mountain girl. I enjoy the wonders that God has given us. Apparently I have bipolar, so I'm allowed choose both. I love climbing high into the sky and I love swimming through waves. As soon as I did ocean water swimming alone last year, I thought to myself I never ever want to die, life is too magical. This is coming from a girl who had suicidal thoughts dating back from 2012, when psychiatric drugs made me think that I was the most horrible person in the world.

The psychiatrist this year has told me that bipolar is just a label. He is surprised that I haven't crashed into a massive depression yet. Again, this illness seems to get misdiagnosed on numerous occasions. I told him, that I would never let depression affect me again. It's fucking nasty. There are definitely up and down moments, as I seem to be comparing myself to last year's happiness. I'm feeling a little bit lost at the moment, but I'd rather be on a road that takes me somewhere new and exciting, so that I can jump into the unknown, rather than be on no road at all.

Julie just liked my post on Facebook, which states that women are superior. Men supply sperm and women create a baby, men supply a house and women create a home. I respect Julie a lot.

"Your mum has died, my dad has died and Kenny's dad has died, we're all the same."

She said this to me outside a pub last year. When my mother died, Julie told my sister Suzi, that her prayers started to get answered as soon as her dad passed away. I felt like Mum started answering mine four months after she died.

When Gretta and I were in Birmingham with Dad on business last year, Gretta and I both admitted that our prayers are getting answered. I didn't feel any spiritual connection with her, but I felt like I was on the right road.

It's hard to pinpoint the exact reasoning behind my psychotic break in 2012. I wasn't dealing with any grief in the family, but perhaps I was trying to move on too fast with my life, after getting my heart broken. I thank God for Martin and his intervention in London back in 2011.

"Mary, you're settled", he screamed at me over the phone one day.

"Jesus, calm down. Don't get your knickers in a twist", I gasped.

"I moved over to London two months ago and have not seen you", he said.

This was probably early days into 2011. I hung up the phone, and thought to myself. I'm twenty five and don't head out with my buddies as much any more. After that conversation, I started hitting the tiles every weekend with Martin, Emily and a few others, and also kept going out with JP Morgan colleagues every month.

My boyfriend was OK with this at the time, but when we eventually broke up, we both decided that we wanted different things. He didn't like going out with his friends, even though I encouraged him to, as I trusted him and wanted him to have more fun in life. I know that we were good together but the distance just grew larger towards the end.

Even though my mother always said "out of sight, out of mind", I phoned my ex after Vietnam and tried to explain what had happened to me. I needed an unbiased opinion. Three and a half years later and we got in contact on LinkedIn. He said that he was so worried before, that he read books on the effects of Malarone. I'm still not convinced it was malarone, but I will definitely avoid antimalarials. I would rather risk contracting malaria, as I know it is more easily treated.

There are so many mental health issues emerging today. I know that anxiety and depression contribute the most. Us schizophrenics are a rarer breed, and it is much more difficult to address the root cause. After speaking to a brother in law, he was saying that it will probably be hellish for girls born today, as they grow up surrounded by social media. So many people today, are feeling as if they need to look a certain way to fit in with the crowd. There is too much paranoia over what people think of others also. I never suffered from any of this, but I did after Vietnam. I wouldn't say I suffered paranoia but I suffered hell on earth. Waking up every morning was a battle.

I promised myself, when my mum passed away, that I would never ever get depressed again because it is the worst fucking disease anyone can go through. I will never again give up my appetite for food and exercise, and luckily I am a woman with hips and periods. The problem with people these days, is that they have lost confidence in themselves. They have forgotten their inner beauty and self worth. Anti-psychotics did this to me. I only decided to take them, when I got back from Vietnam, because my mum was worried. It caused a host of problems for me. I fucking felt like a miserable bitch. Luckily my mum went through suffering, and I listened to her. If anyone remembers that word. Listen more and talk less.

I don't know how many anti-depressants Mum tried over the course of fifteen years. I can only assume that by the end, she had read so many books on the power of positive thinking, that it was her outlook which eventually lifted her from depression and not a drug with the word anti in it. These drugs are the anti-Christ.

I met Mum's old psychiatrist in John of God's and told her that I was Delia's daughter. She knew Mum passed away and didn't seem to give a shit. I told her that Mum is looking at her from heaven, and her daughter is going to tell the tale about greed within psychiatry. She didn't have a fucking clue what I was on about. Little did the psychiatrists know, that there was a very intelligent young lady observing everything that goes on in a mental institution.

Daniel's wedding happened in Lithuania in 2014. "Mary, do you think I should have the wedding in Dublin or Lithuania?", he asked me.

"Daniel just go for Lithuania, Mum will fly."

Mum came, but she was more or less bed ridden. I got smashed at that wedding. I wanted to drown my sorrows. My best friend in life, was lying in a bed, in a room wondering when she is going to die. I downed vodka into me. The next day, I had to fly back to London to the Bank of England, and I felt like dark walls were caving in on top of me. I regret that I couldn't enjoy Daniel's wedding, but I had several issues festering within me.

I was in Turkey on my swimming holiday in Dalaman this year. I was there until the end of May, and I left my laptop at home. Borut and Laura were there again, and just five of us on the boat this time. The reason there were only five people, is because individuals are scared to travel to Turkey. I swam, but not as much as last year. Laura and Borut complimented my technique however, and said that I had less bubbles with my hands, I am breathing bilaterally and that my leg kick has slowed down.

I couldn't interact with people as much this year, as I was shitting giggles to myself, while on the boat. I felt like I was in confession with my own mother, and I was telling her all of my deepest secrets in life. Psychiatrists say that bipolar is a form of manic depression, however, I kind of feel like it is a spiritual connection with deceased loved ones.

I strongly felt like her spirit was within my body, especially on this ten day trip.

Mum suffered depression in her forties, but her diagnoses got switched to bipolar later on in life. Around that time, I remember her saying that she couldn't sleep in our house as she heard ghosts. The house became too haunted for her, so she had to spend a few weeks in John of God's. I observed her a lot. Mum was great at counselling people in John of God's, especially the younger generation, and she listened to people suffering from psychosis, depression, drug abuse and stress. Luckily my mum loved her family, and knew she had work to do by cooking, cleaning, raising seven children and working hard as a managing director.

I went through hell after Vietnam, and I couldn't for the life of me explain it to Mum. "Tell me your problems young lady", she said sternly.

"I will figure this out alone Mum", I replied.

I wrote thirty pages of a book after Vietnam, and then I let my mum read it. I gave up and moved on with work, and I tried to erase the experience from my mind. One day in the middle of 2015, when I was feeling extremely euphoric and positive, I opened up the book and reflected a bit. I was half tempted to continue writing.

I then thought to myself, I have gotten rid of all of my demons in the past and there was no point in writing any more. As soon as March arrived this year, and I was locked up in a ward, my mind was screaming at this book.

Getting back to cancer. In most instances, it comes back with a vengeance. If Doctor Maurer, who saved my dad's life, died from pancreatic cancer, then I suggest to others that they practice God's chemotherapy. It is now widely known that chemotherapy only works in 3% of all cancer cases. That's my advice from someone who researched an arm and a leg for her own mother. The sad truth in the matter, is that people only turn to nutrition when it is too late.

My New Years and Christmases for the last five years have been hell for me. I have felt like there is nothing for me to celebrate. I don't think I ever want to spend the holiday season in Dublin again. One New Years, after my mother's diagnoses, I went out with two pals. It came to eleven O' clock and I said to the two of them, "I have to shoot off in a taxi home, I reckon this is the last New Years I will have with Mum."

They understood. I got home and rang in the New Year with her and sure enough it was our last one together. I had intuition.

When Mum died, I went to the local pub with Dad and a few buddies for New Years. It was nice for Dad to get out. When I got home, I took a picture in my phone, entitled "New Year selfie". It was just a picture of a selfie stick. I think I still felt like I was trapped with no escape. I came off my anti-psychotics a few days later and my life turned around.

I thought my mum got reincarnated as a deer, as our land seems to have a load of deer coming to us since she died. I'm feeling more and more like she got reincarnated into a thirty year old body.

Getting back to Turkey. I read on the flight on the way over, that the plastic things around beer cans are now going to be made out of wheat and barley, so if the animal ingests them or accidentally gets them wrapped around their neck, then the animal will stay alive. It looks like the world is getting better, and there are great advancements being made with manufacturing, to try and protect our species.

I got to the airport in Dalaman. Borut had told me to organise with a taxi from their company for seventy quid, but I didn't bother. I got out on my own, and had five Turkish men surround me. "Hey guys I need to get to Maki hotel, seventy quid guys."

They all made a fuss and I hopped into the car. The price was agreed. It took three hours. I saw the no smoking sign, so I just chilled out. After two hours, I asked politely could I smoke and the taxi driver handed me an ashtray. I love the way the rules are more lax.

"Are you at the hotel yet?", my Dad texted.

"Nope still in the taxi, surrounded by mountains, the sea and a full moon. Mum is with me." He texted back saying God bless.

When I met Borut and Laura the next day, I explained more about Vietnam, and the full moons there, and that there have been a million full moons since Christmas this year.

"Mary full moons make people crazy", Borut gasped.

I agreed with him. He was more and more intrigued by my story since Vietnam and he now wants to expand his swimming business to go into Vietnam. I will definitely hit up a swimming holiday with him there.

After my first night at dinner, I couldn't remember where my hotel was, so I approached a Turkish guy on his motorbike.

"Hey do you know where Maki hotel is?", I asked him.

"Hop on, I'll take you there."

It took two minutes and he dropped me safely to my door.

After our swim the next day, I got off the boat and enjoyed a few beers alone, while I chatted to my mother. I then asked for a green tea. I got adacayi chai Turkish tea. It's nice to try something new while abroad.

For our briefing at Maki hotel, Borut explained to the advanced swimmers and myself about the health and safety checks on the boat. After sixty minutes I got up to leave.

"Mary do you want the paper?", he asked.

"Borut I know how to eat loads and load up on water", I replied.

"Yep Mary knows the drill, rip up that paper."

I had to laugh. I kept ripping up paper in Saint John of God's in front of the psychiatrists. Some of them are doing robot jobs. They advised for rehabilitation that I needed to get back into exercise. Go shag off. My training has now been dumbed down massively.

While in Turkey, I got talking to the friendly Turk guy who sold me my smokes. I read a Turkish paper about coffins. There was a picture of a dead person being put into a fetal position. What they do with the dead person, is they put them into a biodegradable coffin and bury it. The dead person comes back as a tree. I couldn't understand

Turkish, so I got the kind cigarette man to explain this to me in English. We both looked at each other in amazement.

As my mother always said, if you have something to say, go out and tell a tree. She was dead right. People can continue to tell me funny stories about themselves, but I'm not going to listen to bitching any more. Some women are nasty gossip queens as well.

In fact, while I was in the sea in Halong bay, one girl kept bitching to me by saying another girl had an eating disorder because she thought that she was too thin. I was roughly the same size as the person she was bitching about, so she may as well have been bitching about me. It's no wonder I heard bitching going on in my head after this. I also recall, a few months after Thailand, while I was suffering from depression again, I complimented one of the girls from Limerick by saying that she looked great and had lost a few pounds. This other girl, turned around to me and said, "Do not tell her she has lost weight, you will give her a big head." I never want to see this jealous person again.

It also makes you wonder. If people bitch to you, it would only make sense that they say crap about you behind your back.

While I was chilling on my private balcony in Turkey, I went onto Facebook, and I saw a picture of a baby water skiing. Mum and I doted on that little baby and knew that times are getting better. If Mum can see through my eyes, and she didn't have a clue about technology or the fast progression out there, then she knows that her grandchildren are going to enjoy water skiing and perhaps her little baby will get the opportunity to do that if she meets the right man.

At this point in time, Daniel sent through a picture of Amelia Adelia. That's Daniel's first born child. He sent a picture of her in a pair of red swimming togs. At the same time, I was sitting on my balcony in a red bathing suit. I looked at the picture and burst out crying, as I felt such a strong connection with my mum. Turkey was a good trip, but the spiritual connection gave me waves of ups and downs. I wasn't as sociable.

Looking back at coffins and dead people. When the black doctor came up to our house to check my mother out. He said to me, "Your mother has less than twenty four hours to live."

I told him to go away. Right then and there he asked, "Where's my sixty euro?"

"Send the cheque", I grunted.

I didn't have it on me, and I didn't want to hassle Dad for money. I let Dad sleep through this torture.

When everyone woke up, we had a priest and another doctor in the house. Dad joked to the doctor and said, "Now you make sure that my wife is dead, because the last thing I want is to be buried alive. We discussed death and both of us agreed that it would be terrible to be buried alive."

We all laughed at this.

I moved on straight away and so did the rest of the family, but little did the rest of them know that I had gone through the most amount of hell on earth. They didn't know what the fuck happened to me in Vietnam, Thailand or afterwards. While I was away in Turkey, I also looked back at messenger communication between me and a buddy. This buddy felt sorry for me after Thailand and wanted to know how I was getting on. I told her that the girl Claire that I went to Thailand with, said that I seemed stoned half the time, and impatient on the boat in Phi Phi. The over enthusiasm of scuba diving for the first time may have made me appear impatient. Stoned. Well the fucking Xanax and Valium that she advised me to take, made me appear stoned. I don't know why, but Xanax seems to chill people out and send them into a sleep. It makes me hallucinate to a huge degree and not know what the heck is going on around me. I also filled this person in on messenger to say that Mum, Dad and I are just watching some alien movie with Kim Basinger in it. I also said that I was watching "The Monk", and that it was some weird religious thriller. Looking back, Mum liked that movie but Dad was a bit freaked out. He is the traditional one, and Mum was the more open minded one.

Back to Turkey. Small beers cost me six euro in some places. When the bill came I said "Here dude you're over charging." There was a fuss about this, but I paid and walked away. The next day while sitting at the boat listening to my jam, the waiter approached me on his bike and apologised. I told him that I am undercover working for SKY.

I am going to the hygienist in two days. This is the hygienist where my mother went. When I went last year, she told me about cows in Ireland dying full of tumours. The cows in Ireland are pumped full of antibiotics and they are dying prematurely. The Irish government are cowboys. In contrast, the cows in Turkey, are under fed and eating rubble in the sun.

While out in Thailand in 2013, my sister Gretta had to do a lot of communication with Pa. "Pa is really nice Mary, he sounds like he was looking out for you", she said to me when I got back.

"Yep he is Gretta."

Off I went then for more top class psychiatry trips. In my butt hole. At the time, I didn't want to talk to Mum about it much, as she was undergoing chemotherapy. I was still a closed book.

Now if I can handle psychosis, my mother getting diagnosed with lung cancer on her wedding anniversary, schizophrenia in Thailand, God's chemotherapy, work in JP Morgan, nutrition masters, alternative research, triathlon training and Saint John of God's then I am resilient. All of these things seem to have crash landed on top of me in the space of four years. I haven't had a break.

Turkey was tough, and I didn't enjoy it as much as Croatia, because I felt like I was in confession with my mum. I was going through waves of in and out, trying to understand this spiritual connection. At least I have eventually gotten to speak to that priest. We are not programmed to know what happens to us when we die, it is only the spirit world that know. There are too many coincidences that have gone on in the last four years however. I had such a strong spiritual connection in Vietnam, which was taken away from me for three and a half years. As my dad has always said, "The Universe has no end, and it has no beginning." There are one hundred billion stars in the sky. We are all never ending. The spirit world exists and the spirit world is easy. Hell and Heaven are on earth, and it is about trying to create Heaven on earth for yourself.

The most misery for me was the Bank of England. I kept phoning Anna and asking was Mum still taking the kernels. Anna told me that Mum wasn't. She did not want to take God's chemotherapy for anyone else but me. I nearly gave up.

One day, I looked over the huge balcony from the top floor in work, and I reflected on a story of a guy in Citibank in Canary Wharf, who lost a load of money for the bank that day, and just threw himself over. I looked over, and thought to myself, that it would be so much easier if I jumped. I was still taking those nasty anti-psychotics.

It is in fact widely known, that psychiatric drugs massively reduce brain volume and dope people up. It's no wonder I did not feel very smart in that job. It is also known that anti-psychotic drugs are one of the most dangerous to take. They cause suicides, diabetes, hypertension and obesity. I have also recently read that a lot of terrorist attacks and shootings in the States today are centred around anti-depressants. A lot of people who carry out these criminal activities are heavily medicated. Wake up and smell the coffee. Actually, just drink it.

I know Mum tolerated anti-depressants for so long, but anti-psychotics are ten times worse to take.

Before I go any further, it is known that a lot of cases of bipolar are misdiagnosed, and it is simply a hormonal imbalance that can cause a manic episode. I believe this firmly, as I know from test results, that I have elevated cortisol. I also reckon that my adrenaline might be slightly elevated. My fight and flight hormones would have sky rocketed with the pressure of Christmas by taking on so many chores. I am looking forward to peace and quiet this year.

Personal experience is so valuable. In both instances after South East Asia, I was heavily depressed while taking medication. As soon as I came off my medication, my life got better. Friends who take anti-anxiety drugs have been butting in with my business. Those drugs may make them feel good. However, I dare them to try anti-psychotics. I would be intrigued to see how they feel taking the drugs. The majority of individuals, come off their medication, because their illness is actually a hell of a lot more tolerated than the side effects they experience from drugs.

What are governments achieving these days? In trying to solve mental health, they are simply pumping money into lab research and funding new and more expensive drugs. Cop on. And by cop on, I mean, go watch Beverly Hills Cop. Eddie Murphy is one of the best actors out there, and he catches the baddies in the film who are printing money. Quantitative Easing. Would you fuck off. When has printing more money ever solved any of our issues? This shit has been going on for hundreds of years. Years ago, it was more economical to burn paper money to keep a house warm.

I have to laugh. When Mum died, Dad was still signing cheques for the local parish. We had a discussion one night and I said, "Dad stop signing cheques for them."

We call the priest Father Cash as a joke. "Mary I do not see any improvement in the churches, where is the money going?"

"Stop making obligations to the Church then Dad."

Looking back now. Father Cash is a legend, but he also needs help.

Straight after Mum died, all eight of us sat around our dining table. I knew Mum and Dad met on Paddy's day, and I know when Mike, the eldest was born. Dad said to the priest that they met in 1973. Everyone else sat there in silence while the priest and Dad talked. I interrupted. "Mike are you forgetting when you were born?"

"Oh yeah, didn't think of the Maths Mary."

It's quite funny as Mike used to call me the accident years ago. Mum and Dad fell in love instantly, because my mother was a catch, and she told me that Dad chased her and chased her until she gave in. They met in a pub in Kinsale. They must have boldly gotten pregnant out of wed lock and then eloped to the Aran Islands to have a small wedding. Lorraine was the maid of honour and she still pops in to visit me and we talk like nothing ever went wrong.

"Mum why wasn't your Dad at your wedding?", I used to ask as a kid.

"Oh Mary he was sick, he had gangrene."

I guess it's important for parents to tell white lies. Father Cash told us that he finds out all sorts of secrets at funerals.

— 235 —

Chapter 16

Moving and aGrooving for the Chan Zuckerberg Initiative

I just looked at an interview with Mark Zuckerberg online, and he was interviewing astronauts up in Space. 1st of June. Mark was intrigued by them and wanted to know a fair deal about cutting edge technology. The astronauts gave him a good bit of advice, and said that it's actually very basic technology, which has not been updated since the 1960s. Mark finds this incredible, and that there is potential for future growth and operations. I showed my father this, to distract him from the shitty six O' clock news. We both laughed, and wondered how they shit up in Space. This was the first Facebook interview live with people from outer space. Respect to NASA. The human race is trying to understand more and more.

Getting back to dentists. When I was a kid, and I would say to my mother that I had a loose tooth, she would investigate my mouth. "Mum do not pull it out, that is too painful", I would say.

"Young lady I am just having a look."

I trusted her. One second later and the tooth was gone. If I ever have kids, I will not be rushing them to the dentist over a loose tooth. I will use my mothers trick and just yank the mother fucker out. Tooth fairy's should stay. So should Santa. Mum and Dad hosted Christmas in their own house, so the big red fat bugger could float down the chimney. Kids need to believe in Santa. It's magical. I believed in Santa until I was twelve. I was a little naïve brat. Christmas day came, and I got a black dress from Mum and Dad. I was sad. They told me on Christmas day. But Mum and Dad must have known that I would get bullied going to secondary school if I still believed in him.

Mike told me about asking Mum about the birds and the bees when he was younger. Mum must have thought that it was the man's job to explain it to a boy so she said, "Go ask your father."

What did Dad say? He was too embarrassed to tell the truth, so he phrased it like this, "Mike, the man puts his ya know...."

"No I don't know Dad, continue."

"Ah Mike, the man puts his ya know, his ya know into the woman's......butt."

Mike ran away and told all the boys in Blackrock college that this was how babies were conceived.

While I was in Turkey, I reflected more with my mother. I was in six, the engine of the boat, when I rowed in college. I was a little heavier then, but I didn't seem to care. When I wanted to slim down a little bit, I managed to do it within a few months, as I got more discipline back. After Thailand I hated myself again. Even though I have never been pregnant, or have had to lose baby weight, I knew for certain that weight gain from psychiatric drugs is much harder to shift than any other type of weight. The drugs really affect brain biochemistry by greatly enhancing one's desire for food. Dopamine levels are reduced to a dangerous level. It is in fact becoming widely known today that people are being used as drug trials to try and fix a so called mythical chemical imbalance in the brain, with a host of debilitating side effects. Anti-psychotics act by tranquillising and dumbing down the emotions. They are known to create a zombie like attitude, and have even caused brain damage in some instances.

I had a flick through my newsfeed on Facebook, and a post from Sara came up, and it was about forty tigers being found dead in a freezer at Thailand's tiger temple. Sara left a comment saying that *it was exciting to see wild animals close up but it's completely selfish. The human race won't be happy until we completely destroy these animals.* This may seem barbaric, but when I went to read the article, it says that the monks in Thailand were not available for comment. How are we supposed to know if this news is real or not? Tigers in freezers in Thailand? I'd like to think that isn't happening. How much of our news supply is controlled by the powerful media? These are quiet monks, just like in the Hangover when crazy horse dogs like Bradley Cooper, Zach Galifianakis and Ed Helms come in to wreck havoc.

Having thought of Sara. I want to get back to Martin. The two of us thought we were in love with each other in college. We respected one another, we fancied each other and we were great fun who studied similar things. He was confused though as he wasn't sure whether he was gay or straight. I remember finding out. When Martin moved to New Zealand to do his first PhD, he experienced a more laid back environment. He emailed me when I was working for Samsung Electronics in Chertsey. He filled me in on news, and told me over email that he was finally out and that he was happy. I read the email, smiled to myself and got up and looked around at my Korean boss. He was staring at me in the eyes, and laughing his head off. He must have known I wasn't exactly working and that I was reading a personal email. I walked out to get a cup of tea and I was glad for Martin. One person in college used to tell me to stay away from Martin, because he was gay and had no interest in me. Well we had a mutual thing going on and luckily we know each other too well now.

Facebook just landed another comforting post to my newsfeed which reads:

> *She has a smart ass mouth, but she's as honest as they come. She's sarcastic, but she's got a heart of gold. She's stubborn, but she's loyal as fuck. She's a little bi-polar, so sometimes you just gotta laugh and let her have her way.*

If I was to fall in love again, I would be anxious and I would have to go to see Buddhas, and go into mosks and focus on candles. Why would I have to do this? I feel such a strong spiritual connection with my mum, and I wouldn't want to picture her looking at me having sex. I want it personal and between two people.

This telecommunications thing is incredible. Borut from Strel Swimming adventures, said that he experienced telepathy years ago and it was also connected to full moons. Dad is also amazed by how telecommunications has advanced so much since his day. "Mary I just don't understand how one person can pick up a phone from one part of the world and call another and the call is answered instantly", he has been saying for years.

"Yep I don't understand it either Dad, but it's wonderful how intelligent the human race has become."

"Yep it's smart, but I just don't understand the brain, we are all wired differently", he continued to say.

Speaking of telecommunications. Mark Zuckerberg explained how they connected up the international space station to go live. They used satellite mission control in Houston and lots and lost of redundancy. I'm guessing seeing as Facebook is such a large business, they had to let people go with this huge advancement. All parties are kept satisfied, because they get a nice payout. I don't fully understand the systems used to dial up the international space station, but they use standard telephone service, video fibre network, NASA from Houston Texas and download facilities from Washington DC which acts as the encoder.

Facebook is sending me some memories to my newsfeed these days and there was one between my brother John and I dated the 20th of August 2012. I Facebooked him to say:

> *Will you tell Mum and Dad I am fine....I can't log onto my Gmail here for some strange reason*

John replied and said that he would let them know. He also asked was it OK for him to tell them about my tattoo.

Looking back, there were a few occasions where it was difficult to keep in touch with family. Zuckerberg has also worked very hard to get people connected via Facebook in the East.

Mum said before she died, that it would be a piece of cake for the older siblings who were married and had kids, but she was very worried for Dad, John and I. I now think that she was most worried for me, because she did not want the torture of mental health to affect me all of my life. This March, I feel like she was knocking from her coffin and telling me to write this book at last.

Getting back to the world wide web. I know that the computer scientist, Tim Bernes Lee, made the internet more credible in 1990. I have had an interest in these sorts of advancements for a while. Before heading to Vietnam, I watched the opening ceremony to the Olympics in a neighbour's house in London. As a joke, I dished out my Samsung Electronics cards which had the Olympic logo on it. The Koreans wanted to keep me in that job, so that I got the opportunity to go to the Olympics as a worker. I chose an American bank at the time. In 2012, I dreamt of Ben Ainslie and his achievements. I dreamt of becoming the best athlete I could be. I've been punched in the face three times now.

Looking back at JP Morgan, I had great fun with my team. Kevin noticed how much running I was doing in and out of work, so he recommended the book "Born to Run". Jane was brilliant as well. I remember a funny story about her leaving the office on Bank street one day, and she got an egg thrown against her head. She had to go back in and take a shower. My manager even used to slag my superwoman costume on a Friday. Luckily, we had casual Friday so I used to wear a long blue skirt with a red top. He used to also take the piss out of Martin who he never met. The first thing on a Monday morning at 9am he would say, "Did Martin frape you again Mary?"

Martin used to hack my account and write posts such as:

*My toes are getting extremely hairy, I must
head out to the pub for the shift tonight.*

I read recently, that telling someone with mental illness to snap out of it is like telling someone who is deaf to listen harder. I think I did the right thing by going back to work so soon after Vietnam. Every day seemed like a losing battle, however. I had lost the pleasure in doing the simplest of things. This time, I have decided to treat myself and travel alone. Hopefully I will be that qualified nutritionist by this time next year, so I am just going to take time alone to put myself back on track. Definitely the area of nutrition which I want to go into will be focused on mental health patients.

To keep my mind busy and maintain a sense of humour after Vietnam, I used to go on Youtube. There was a funny video about black sluts and white sluts. It was these men who used to wear black sunglasses going up to ladies on the beach and saying, "Do you like my black sluts?" I thought it was so funny so I tagged my buddy in it. He nearly had a fit and thought I was being racist. I think he needs to go watch impractical jokers, where they take the piss out of Facebook and call it Race book. That might drill a bit of entertainment into him during hard times.

While having a beer with Laura in Turkey. She told me that her mother was a pharmacist, but that she loves the fast paced environment of her job. Pharmacy never appealed to me as I wouldn't like to be counting and dishing out drugs all day long. Luckily for Laura's Mum, she loves it. She was telling me that her Mum is well in tune with how the cost of drugs in Nottingham compares to the boots brands. The boots brands will have a much higher turnover, and are extremely competitive with the real brands, which are five times the price. I am not surprised.

One day in the office with my dad last year, I came back from Dealz and said, "Dad I got some glucosamine sulphate for two euro in dealz."

"Mary put them in the bin, they might poison you", he groaned.

I threw them away, but looking back, it was a good deal, and the shop probably only gets them in once a year. I'm not sure whether these supplements actually work, or if they are just about making money like most drugs out there. At least nutritional supplements are much cheaper than other drugs on the market. The sad thing, is that doctors nowadays are heavily influenced by pharmacy reps, and they earn $200 to watch a twenty minute video. This is sweet money for their pockets. We didn't have this shit donkeys years ago.

I still have to look back and laugh at Mum. "Mum what on earth did you buy in Superquinn?", I asked her years ago.

"It's a tonic Mary. Look. I fly around the house and it gives me loads of energy, hoovering, mopping, everything", she said with a grin.

"Mum that's buckfast, its 14% wine. The rowing crew and I used to drink that back in college, it sends you bananas."

"Oh I only had two glasses", she smirked.

This reminds me of the rowing worlds in Munich. I went there in 2008, to support the NUI Galway rowing boys. A few science buddies came along too. Dickhead Dave and I used to have good banter with the rowing heads. Unfortunately, we were so consumed with drinking beer for breakfast and eating tonnes of pizza, that we never made it out to the river. I still laugh at Dave. My sister christened him dickhead Dave.

"Mary Des Bishop is over there", he said to me in a nightclub.

"Go up to him and say I have massive boobs, go on I dare you."

Always one to take on a dare, I went up to Des Bishop and said it. He looked at me sternly.

"You just want to sleep with me don't you?"

I called him a jerk and then walked away.

"Dave that went down well", I said angrily.

Dave couldn't stop pissing himself laughing. I have to admit, I preferred meeting Tommy Tiernan. "You have a massive cock", I said to him when I saw him.

That's one of his lines in his comedies. Tommy rolled around laughing at me which was funny.

Speaking of funny things. Suzi had to go into the pharmacy the other day as she has a newborn. She went in with my brother John and asked for anusol ointment. John didn't have a clue what it was for, but he turned around to Suzi and said, "They may as well call it rectify." John would be quick with that stuff seeing as he lived with an ass doctor before.

I look back on my steps in life, and realise that everything happens for a reason. As Mum used to say, "we have to cross paths with people for a reason". I'm happy, that at the age of thirty, I have figured out that I need to wave goodbye to people who have had a negative impact on me. I got a fortune teller to come to my house two months ago. When she walked in, she asked was there a recent death in this house. I told her about Mum. She said that she saw a shadow run quickly into the kitchen and asked was that my mother's favourite room in the house. When I sat down with her, I picked eight cards. She said that my energy levels were all over the place at the moment. She also said that I had travelling on the cards, and that the months from September onwards would be very auspicious. I was quite shocked by what she told me next. She told me that in 2012, there was an immense planetary movement which had a huge impact on my life. She also told me that I would find love by the end of January and that it will be with someone I already know. I'll let you know if she's talking shit or not, if I decide to write a second book.

When I finished my Finance masters, Dad really wanted me to do the Aldi interview. "Mary that would be a great job to have, you start at the bottom on the shop floor, you learn the tricks of the trade and you work your way up."

I did the interview but didn't get it. Aldi and Lidl are a huge success in Ireland, and are German owned. Their strategy seems to work. I also just heard that some bitch of a customer tried to sue Lidl for €70,000. The cashier accidentally short changed the customer by fifteen euro. This went to court. Luckily the judge had a brain and decided that it was an honest mistake. The shit bag trying to sue, claimed that the experienced cashier called her a liar. We need to open the doors to the truth, for future court cases. It is time to get IT intelligence involved and tap into what dip shits are saying.

I have noticed more this year, that CCTV is planted all over the place. If technology has moved so fast, how come we cannot tap into conversations? I bet we can.

This case is similar to those wankers who trek mountains, and trip over a little rock, and then try to sue the State. Judges must be sick to death of this bollox.

I have recently been looking at the work of Thich Nhat Hanh. He is a Vietnamese buddhist monk, who believes in the miracle of mindfulness. Most of us are over stressed in the West, and we find it very difficult to zone out. This is certainly something I am working on now.

I felt like Facebook was reading my mind in Vietnam in 2012. I was on the way to the doctor and I looked into an internet cafe, and I saw a bunch of Vietnamese men laughing their heads off at computer screens. The hospital. They let me float on and off the computers, and I was learning about Mark Zuckerberg and Priscilla Chan and the work they are doing. Psychiatric drugs made me forget about this and move on. I have a renewed feeling that data and the brain are connected.

I googled, "Can Facebook read your mind." In July, Zuckerberg has talked about telepathic advertising and the brain. A lot of people are drawn into adverts in an irrational way, however what the CEO wants is for Facebook to be able to read minds, and they have the technology to do it. He wants Facebook users to communicate brain-to-brain using telepathy. "You'll be able to think of something and your friends will immediately be able to experience it too." This vision is similar to the film "Minority Report" where adverts are shown to Tom Cruise based on his thoughts and inner desires. Science fiction is close to becoming science fact. Cognitive scientists have been able to reconstruct clips based on measurements of their brainwaves.

It also says that Facebook's top engineer Mike Vernal is trying to read our minds. This was dated and stamped on the 28th of November 2012. At that time, I was back from Vietnam and drugged up heavily, so I forgot about the miracle I saw out in Vietnam three months

Vietnamese Voices

previous. I knew there was an auditory hallucination, which I have read is from other people's dreams and thoughts, but I was not visually hallucinating. I thought I had copped onto smart technology out in Hanoi in 2012. Telepathy is real. The only thing that is slightly confusing for me, is that I didn't exactly have some mad head gear attached to me with a load of electrodes. However, I'm convinced those Vietnamese are up to something quirky, and my next point might explain the episode with more clarity.

Apparently, there are schizophrenics out there, who are desperately trying to prove that they have been misdiagnosed and that they experienced artificial telepathy. It is known that thought processes are linked to the computer through artificial intelligence. Psychological interviewing techniques have proved that artificial intelligence has come up with programmes which lead the intelligent human to believe she is talking to another person, when she is actually carrying out dialogue with a computer. This artificial technology is comprised of satellites which link the sender and the receiver. A computer multiplexer routes the voice signal of the sender through microwave towers to a defined location. The receiver in this instance is a human brain. Out of nowhere, a voice blooms into the mind of the target. The human skull has no firewall, and therefore cannot shut the voice out. The receiver can then hear the sender's verbal thoughts.

Life is a dream and no one can stop you following your own destiny. I just want to say at this point, that lots of gorgeous celebrities have opened up about having bipolar. Catherine Zeta Jones is one, and Britney Spears is another. It's no wonder the TV was calling me Britney Beers in Hanoi. On a serious note, Kurt Cobain also had bipolar, and he wrote a song called lithium. I'm only guessing that he was put on a course of lithium to control his problems. He put a gun to his head, about two albums after writing this song, so it just goes to show how dangerous some drugs are. Some pharmaceutical drugs are disgusting. The big C should not be for cancer, but it should be for communication. We seem to have already lost the war on cancer, as 97% of chemotherapy drugs kill people, and the food and drug administration are scaring people to death about the benefits of alternative cures such as laetrile. Fortunately, we may still have a fighting chance at opening the doors to communication for mental health. Mum's bird that she wrote on envelopes was aimed at communication and thankfully it is now planted on my ankle.

I'm glad that all of this has happened to me, as I firmly believe that experience is much more valuable than education. Luckily I have both, and four great jobs behind me. I'm eager to continue fighting, travelling the globe and inspiring people who have gone through a similar battle. You can look all of this up and it says that bipolar and psychosis are connected to a spiritual awakening. Start researching more of the positive and less of the negative. Mental health is linked to the afterlife, which is very comforting for people who are going through a grievance process. It's time to start looking on the bright side of life and start filtering out any negative energy that surrounds you. 2016 has been a challenge for me once again, but at least I have more clarity.

I just landed home from the health and safety check for Habitat for Humanity, and one of the power point slides was on cultural differences. I have only ever been to Morocco, but know for sure that I will not get a cultural shock. The team leader said that she had heard of a story of an African man flying over to the States, and he was eating butter straight from the packet. This came as a shock to others on the plane. I also learned that our wealthy government is funding 70% by helping those in the developing world, such as orphans and vulnerable children who need remortgaging. The remaining 30% comes from the individual.

People today getting married in Ireland are now worried about mortgages. Collateralised debt obligations just get squared and squared and squared, and the debt cycle continues. The abstract to my second thesis reads as follows:

The central thesis of this study is that our financial system does not behave according to the laws of the Efficient Market Hypothesis, as laid down by the conventional wisdom of today's prevailing economic theory. Instead financial markets are inherently unstable and habitually prone to boom-bust cycles. In this way, they require Central Bank intervention to help overcome these traumas, however to date there is no effective policy which can be used to combat periods of excitement and despair. This may seem surprising, given the fact that financial euphoria dates back to the seventeenth century, thus assuring us that polices have been tried and tested, yet none of them are capable of solving credit cycles permanently. This can only suggest that there is a much stronger force within the financial structure that is repelling 'ethical' policy implementation.

This study utilises qualitative analysis in an attempt to explore investors' sentiments surrounding the stock market. The aim is to examine their strategies and goals within the market thus defining how their psyche leads to aggregate mood behaviours within the market. This study is very topical as it focuses on investors attitudes towards a bearish stock market and these findings can be compared to their optimistic attitudes before the financial crisis prevailed. These psychological forces are self-reinforcing and predispose investors to judgemental biases. This prevents investors from forming objective measures of value in the market.

The findings are significant as they suggest that investor psychology does in fact play a dominant role in boom-bust periods. Economic theories which have been developed fail to consider real world scenarios and are thus no longer legitimate as a model for financial collapse. It can no longer be proposed that a shift in the economy is solely the result of an underlying economic factor. Psychological quirks are inherent in even quiescent market conditions; yet it is only when the economic bubble bursts that these habits are examined.

Governments need to start thinking smarter. The housing crises is pathetic, but at least it doesn't kill people. Dad has always said to me that he does not understand banking today and how money moves around virtually on computer screens. I found it a bit fucking confusing as well. The modern world is so different to the traditional barter that went on back in my parents day. Even though I worked in liquidity risk, recessions keep happening every eight years because the corruption amongst governments and banks and individuals continues and the greedy mother fuckers are hiding all of this. No wonder there are terrorist attacks today. We're going back to religion, and the Easterners want an end to greed.

The pharmaceutical industry are dealing with over regulation by the food and drug administration; and the politicians are the ones who control the supply and demand of inventory costs. Drugs in the States are much higher than they are in India, and I read recently that Australia is even cheaper again. The States is certainly one place that I would not want to settle in. There is too much money in politics and too many predatory banks around. Every time we elect a new government, we are essentially selling them off to the highest bidder. Also politicians are claiming that we have no control over climate change. Start recycling, we've known about this for years.

If you want to turn into a glass half full kind of person, then I suggest you start following your passion. The problem with today is that a lot of markets are saturated, and it is extremely difficult to find that niche.

Also be careful with what you read in the newspapers. They will have you hating the people who are being oppressed, and loving the people who are doing the oppressing.

It is time to change. Life has no remote control, you have to get up and change the channel yourself.

While this book is primarily focused on mental health, it also delves deep into the drug industry, politics, exercise and nutrition. I want to conclude, by sharing the difference between auditory hallucinations in the East and the West. Many studies have found that it is very difficult to differentiate between the symptoms of dissociative disorder and schizophrenia, because the hallucinations experienced are so similar. In a lot of Asian cultures, yogic meditation is specifically performed in order to reach an altered consciousness state of mind, and this is considered normal. However in the West, psychiatrists associate this state of mind with negative psychotic symptoms. Many non-Western cultures are more traditional, and have a spiritual belief system in place, which allows for better support and understanding of hallucinations. Western cultures are much more individualistic, and thus hallucinations are seen as an incurable attribute of the individual. This promotes isolation for the patient. This addresses a serious question. If psychosis is deemed to be incurable in the West, then why are we pumping so many psychiatric drugs into the patients in the first place?

Unfortunately, the idea that mental illness is the result of a chemical imbalance is a popular one, that is now firmly rooted in the conventional psychiatric profession. Not only does it take away the stigma of mental illness, but it gives psychiatrists a solution, one that fits neatly on their prescription pads. The trouble is, not only do the drugs not work, they may actually cause your brain to function abnormally. When antidepressants were introduced, it was with the intent that they would help people recover from depression more quickly. Unfortunately, what is happening is that patients are recovering faster, but are relapsing much more often. Psychiatric medication tends to offset the neuronal pathway which promotes an abnormal function within the brain. I do know for a fact that the voices I was hearing in Vietnam were much fainter as soon as I landed back in Dublin. Had I just been administered a course of sedatives short term, cognitive behavioural therapy and counselling, then I guarantee I would have recovered. Recovery may have taken twice the amount of time, but there would have been much less likelihood of an episode reoccurring.

I came off my medication before Thailand and relapsed. I also came off my medication before Croatia and I didn't relapse. And I was on a boat for much longer in Croatia. What has it got to do with Asia? The Asians believe in spirituality and life after death. If you are brought up well, to respect people, help those less fortunate, follow your dreams, make a good living, but you are not greedy and driven by money. Then you win the shuttle ride to space. My grandparents and their parents and their parents would have lived a very simple life. Farming, nursing, working hard to make a living. They never would have left Ireland. However, we get to travel loads. Then what happens to us all in 10,000 years from now? Technology has become so advanced and it's growing even faster. We are very futuristic. Would you not agree that it is unfair that people born years and years ago had a much different life to us now or those who will be born in one hundred years? If the islands in Halong Bay grow by one centimetre every year, then the islands in Turkey and Lanzarote grow by one centimetre every year also. How are planes going to fly over them when they turn into giants? We will have the advancements no doubt in technology. I'm only guessing that the universe might end, once these islands hit another planet. And look, Venus is our closest planet and that's twenty five million miles away. Also, planets move away from each other to make sure we are all spinning at an accurate speed to ensure the universe is never ending. Do you know what else lads? Those Koreans are smart. They out beat the yanks with technology. They managed to land someone on the sun. It was at night time though! No wonder my mother was proud I got a job in Samsung. She liked that I would learn about their culture and innovative ideas! She was also proud that I worked in liquidity risk, which was a new function when I joined and the aim is to stop corruption within the banking system. An ex told me before that his father thought my job in JP Morgan was unethical. Liquidity risk is the most ethical function in banking.

My mother and father have believed in life after death and then sometimes not believed, due to different forms of suffering going on in the world. Well, they are both such good people, and clearly their parents and family were too. Mum's and Dad's retail business was the first in Ireland to introduce American towels during the recession in the seventies. They also stack it high and sell it cheap to people who cannot afford expensive clothes in Ireland. Every other retailer seems to add five to fifty times the price onto cost. Mum and Dad made sure to just double up, so that everyone can afford things for their home. Rock on. It took the youngest of twelve to suffer mental health and be fucking drugged up for fifteen years and the youngest of seven to go through a battle as well. Fortunately for me, I had telepathic communication in Vietnam. So my experience was more mind blowing and in tune with spirituality. Technology, the brain and spirituality are connected. I feel like Mum and I are writing this book together, the bond is so strong, you would not believe it. We are all actors on planet earth. And the problems are getting worse, so the aim is to move onto the next planet as quickly as you can.

Last year, I thought to myself, I'm not sure I want to have kids. I love having the freedom to train hard and be adventurous. But now that I know I have my mum's spirit with me it is kind of making me want to have a family so that I can zoom into a daughter's body when I die, because I know I would raise my children well, just like my mum and dad did. I would give them freedom and be open minded and in tune with how our world is changing so rapidly. Then, eventually we will make it to Space some day and not be stuck on planet earth. Hats off to you Jerry for finding that out about head transplants. I'm a good listener and have remembered everything people have told me over the years.

Dad is grieving for Mum, but he may fast track his soul into Daniel's body because he is a nice and generous man, who has always helped those less fortunate than him. Mum and Dad were the perfect match. They were always thinking about other people and how dumb our government are. I have listened to their conversations about politics from a very early age and I absorbed all of it. My brain is unique. It has a lot of storage capacity and I have used my subconscious with my telepathy. If Dad jumps into Daniel's body then I'll let Daniel know how to handle bipolar, and just tell him to talk at the speed of light to Dad and laugh about it. You confess your sins to your parents when they die. That is your priest. And since my mum had such a quirky sense of humour, I did not give a shit that I was sharing my previous sex life with her and that I took MDMA in college. At one point this year, I was crawling up and down my room telling my deceased mother everything I have done in life.

My dad will not read this book, thankfully, because he doesn't read books any more. My siblings will though, and sure we're all as open with each other so that's a good thing. Also, my siblings and I all get along with each other so no doubt Daniel and I will be hanging out down the line and Mum and Dad will be together again. Telepathic communication is not made up. I did not have psychosis. I was telepathically communicating. And psychiatrists made me a miserable shit. I am travelling and going to find myself a nice adventurous man, and I never want to see a dumb psychiatrist again. The government, the food and drug administration and big pharma are all greedy and driven by money so they will probably raise their children in a closed minded manner to simply look at the first page of google and try and solve problems with the same information that everyone else is looking at. And they will remain on planet earth for a very long time. Have you guys not ever wondered how much information is out there? I have always googled alternative stuff. My thoughts were followed around in Vietnam, but I didn't care because I am nice on the inside and I did not like girls bitching to me about others. I don't know why the majority of psychotic cases are negative and mine was positive. Perhaps I had the nice spirits of deceased loved ones in my family, Sara's family and Martin's family following me. Also, I like what Sara does, she helps the elderly. And Martin, well he is trying to desperately figure out the reasoning behind neurodegenerative disease.

The problem with today is that siblings are falling out with each other, because they are getting too competitive with each other in markets that are saturated. When Mum died, all eight of us had several meetings about who would become the managing director in Guineys if, God forbid, Dad was to pass away, and there were no arguments about it. Also, my Great Aunt, Mary Guiney who died at the helm age of 103, left 25,400 pounds to say masses to ensure that her department store, Clery's stayed in the family name. She had no children. Before, the store got bought over by greedy pricks, Dad tried desperately to buy the store so that he could continue an ethical business function and make clothes affordable to the public. My dad liaised with my extremely intelligent brother Mike who works in a hedge fund in London and is very driven by his career. Mike is also trying to understand the inequality in the world as well and he still can't get his head around booms and busts. Mike and Dad had a discussion about trying to finance this for Dad by getting a loan. However, they decided to just leave it at the time. When this store got bought over by greedy fuckers who had nothing to do with the Guiney family, they made a huge profit and then decided to run away with their huge profit and close down the store. This caused outcry in Dublin and massive protests. It's about fucking time, that this store Clery's goes back into Mary Guiney's name and then we can hire mental health patients who are simply stuck in John of God's and feeling depressed because they cannot get a job. Have I just opened up the doors to communication for the banking crisis, mental health, spirituality, exercise, nutrition and technology?

Life is about happiness and not money. I firmly believe that my very nice boss, Janet Walton, from JP Morgan who was very good to me when I was feeling depressed and when my mum got her diagnosis will be extremely impressed with this book. Then, maybe I will give a talk to JP Morgan employees about completing Ironman and a swim across the Irish sea. I posted to my wall on Facebook before going to Vietnam that Jamie Dimon, the CEO of JP Morgan was going to throw a party for me and Ben Ainslie when we get married. That was of course a joke, but I have a feeling that everything we post, joking or not is followed closely and the CEO wants to know who enjoys life, has dreams and visions and who does not take life too seriously.

I will also, then encourage David Last Fitness to continue following his dreams and thank him so much for all of his support. He brought me back to life and when I started going to personal training sessions with him, he was only charging five euro for an hour long session. He quickly got his shit together and then started charging eighteen euro an hour. This man, is clearly passionate about his job and is not driven by money. Seeing as other personal trainers out there are charging over fifty euro per hour and they are generally pricks, I think it is time that David Last Fitness start looking at new clients who have suffered mental health and then he can slowly increase his fee.

All of these people trying to look good on Facebook and Instagram and be aesthetically pleasing to the eye are shallow and they are simply trying to look good to just sleep around and have one night stands. They eventually settle for someone without being truly happy and that is why divorce is growing bigger and bigger in Ireland. Also, because a lot of people hate their jobs today because they are not passionate about them, they get desperate and simply feel that settling down, following the crowd and having children will bring them happiness. Everyone is copying everyone on Facebook. I repeat myself, I have never followed crowds in my life. So, because divorce is getting bigger and bigger, more eating disorders emerge and also court cases go nuts, and then the barristers and solicitors and judges are overly stressed and that is why divorce is not granted for a huge five years in Ireland. I discussed with my legendary friend Tara, that if I had to go through a divorce, I would massively suffer from depression. She agreed. I just want to say that Tara is my best friend and she has been there for me the most this year. A lot of you other bitches didn't have the time to ask me how I am doing and one person in particular uninvited me to her wedding because she was worried what I might do at it. The reasoning behind this is because she visited me in John of God's and she was horrified by what she saw in that ward with the different mix of mental health.

Mum had to go through suffering and Dad had to work harder by bringing seven children in to visit Mum. Mary went through suffering as a single woman. And she will ensure it never happens to a child of her own. I will encourage my children to be athletes and to go into IT. The people suffering from obesity and anorexia and drug abuse in John of God's will be sent free some day. They are more open minded and they are better banter and not one bit vain. Also, David Last told me to go on Instagram last year to promote myself. I did not bother, because it is simply people looking at photos of each other. Facebook is by far better, it should be called Book Face. It has words and pictures. There you go folks. That's the viscous circle of mental health. Has anyone not copped on to how shallow tinder is getting either? I always wondered why it wasn't linked to Facebook and thought to myself, it's a shame because perhaps maybe some of the guys that I am friends with on Facebook are actually nicer men. Mum and Dad never joined Facebook and it was fucking important for them not to. They made sure that their children would learn for themselves. If I was to have kids, I would go off Facebook. My life would be private then.

Has anyone not thought about where inflation comes from either? People driven by money are trying to work in well paid jobs so that they can afford nice things, clothes, personal training sessions, food, beer. Everything is increasing in price. A fucking greedy prick that I used to know in college told me last year that I had nothing to worry about in life because I could just run away with Mum's probate. I have not received any of Mum's probate and have used my savings from JP Morgan, because I want to achieve my own success. In fact, I am the only child that has not received money from my parents in this family because I have not gotten married or wanted to buy a house. This my friends, has made me more in tune with life after death.

Also, private secondary schools are increasing their fees dramatically and girls are getting bitchier and this is where bullying comes from. That's where verbal bullying has now turned into cyber bullying because everyone is on social media comparing themselves to others. I dreamt last year, that Dave and I would go into business together and he would be an extremely successful personal trainer and I would be a nutritionist. Well, do you know what, I think I am that first class honours student in nutrition and I demand that you take my thesis seriously. Dave told me that I was the fittest client he had last year. I also smoked around ten cigarettes a day. So, if I can give up by next year, hopefully I will be even fitter in 2017. Seeing as I apparently have bipolar, then maybe I will compete in the Special Olympics in 2020. That will impress my dad.

They say, that when an old man dies, a library burns to the ground. When Mum died, everyone in my family was sad that a genius had left us, little did they know that her youngest daughter is a living genius and here to tell the tale. I read recently that Priscilla Chan was awarded for being a genius back in college. It looks like an IT genius from the States married a Chinese Vietnamese lady and I want to congratulate them on their first born child, who was born the same day as my nephew Daniel last November. That is the name I have planted on my leg since Vietnam. Family tree people, we are all related and we are all supposed to respect one another. Beauty is in the eye of the beholder. I am not surprised that my brother John is still single, because he would never settle for unhappiness. Time for John to travel the world with me and he can log in remotely to drive his online business forward. Maybe then, we'll get those crazy Japanese people wearing his Christmas jumpers, which by the way, some of the major retailers in Ireland have stolen from him. They copied his rights. Time for those fucking IRFD tags to be brought into Guineys so that people stop stealing from our family business. Hey Sam Walton, I think Dad just met you!

I was a good listener in my finance masters and was so fascinated by Wal Mart's business strategy. I never had to take notes in college either. It all fucking went into my brain. I also just want to say at this point, that Roger has been connected with his family all along and so has my cousin Johnny Crawford. They both committed suicide. One was due to drugs and the other was due to not earning money. People commit suicide due to drugs, both illegal and legal, money and work. Time for my legendary cousins to get Sheila, Johnny's mother back into a happy place again. I also want to get Auntie Kathleen back into her happy place. This is the woman that was in a psychiatric ward this year and her son was murdered in the Phoenix park a few years ago, so she is going through hell at the moment. Her son was set on fire, as he decided to live homeless as he hated having money. I tried to give a homeless man some food last year and he was so anxious when I approached him. He didn't trust me and he would not accept it. It was a fucking bag of popcorn that was closed.

Vietnamese Voices

I was such a happy person last year, that I wanted to help so many people. I am back in that happy place. For the last week, I have smoked forty cigarettes a day because it has stimulated me to write more and it is connecting Mum's and my brain more. Before I go any further, I also remember telling an ex, after a holiday with Mum and Dad, that I was sad because Mum told me that she thought that Dad may have had a wandering eye when she was ill and in John of God's. This was clearly a load of bollox, she was only saying it because she knew my ex wasn't treating me very well at the time.

I said to my personal trainer last year, that I want to show my dad that I have achieved success in life before he kicks the bucket so that he isn't worried about me. Mum, again had to go through suffering before she died because she worried about us. I am happy that Dad will get a nice little send off. Maybe I'll send him psychotic in five years!

Mum told me when I was eight that I was foolish. I used to clean all of my siblings bedrooms, because I have always been a hard worker and liked keeping my mind busy. I can't wait to have my youngest, we're going to have a lot of fun together. I think I should be a Nike model, with a fag hanging out of my mouth! Smokers for fucking jokers. I was always happy with life. I was always happy studying, exercising, drinking, playing piano and being a very fucking high achiever. Vietnam fucked me up in the head, but I am so glad it all happened.

Now, if you want to know how I have connected all of these dots. When I headed off to Electric Picnic the day before my mum died, I was planning to just take a load of MDMA at that festival because I was still a miserable bitch and dealing with binge eating disorder and thought that it would kick start my weight loss. Perhaps, if I had done that, this might have been the one time that I could have dropped dead from taking the drug. Telepathically, Mum, in her conscious mind must have known that I was thinking of doing that, so she went into black out mode in front of Suzi and Dad and thus, Suzi phoned me to return home. The phone is also telepathic. So I have discovered the answers to the questions that my father has been asking all of his life.

Dad, is at the grave right now, still asking Mum "What is the meaning of life, what are we all doing here?" It's time, that the Late Late show have me on their show to discuss mental health. After I'm done speaking with Ryan, Dad and I can then go onto the show "The Meaning of Life", with Gay Byrne and this man, who did the Late Late show a hell of a lot better than Ryan Tubridy and actually entertained Irish people, can get a nice little send off to comfort him after his heart attack scare this March. I sang "O Holy Night" for Gay Byrne in the Westbury when I was eighteen, and I also went to his house so he knows me and my family well. I am the real Catholic girl. I have been such a forgiving person all of my life. People have stolen from me, people have cheated on me, people have bitched about me and I have always forgiven them. Not anymore you fucking assholes.

Dad just said to me that technology is ruining us. What he means, is that he sees so many youngsters and so called couples who are supposed to be in love, just staring at their phone. I have had my phone glued to me for the last five years, because I have been single, listening to the legendary spotify while I train and googling alternative information to figure out my own head and how to pull my mum through cancer. In fact, people used to slag me because I wouldn't move onto a smartphone for ages. The reason being is that I liked to ask strangers how to get to somewhere rather than look it up on google maps. I also just wanted to use my phone for texting people. I thought technology was moving way too fast and I wanted to live back in my parents day. I used to say to Mum, that I wished I was born at the same time as her so that I could have been her best friend. I wanted to know what it was like back in her day. She left Kilrush, in county Clare at the age of sixteen to make a success of herself in London and she partied a hell of a lot and then met the legendary Michael Guiney at the age of twenty eight. Dad, left school at fourteen because he thought it was a load of bollox and he learned the tricks of the trade and made a huge success of himself.

Back to phones, the Koreans gave me my first smartphone for free and then I got intelligent.

When I had my heart broken in London, before going to Vietnam, my ex deleted himself off Facebook. He did not want to see any comments of mine and he did not want to see any pictures of us together. I never put him and I up as a profile photo on Facebook, because he was a private man and I wasn't sure if he was the right one. However, I did look at a load of photos of us together and I missed the good times. This ex has been desperately trying to figure out what happened to me when I went psychotic. While he was reading books on drugs, such as malarone, I was looking up stuff that was saying that smoking causes psychosis, so I desperately wanted to give up but I was depressed at the time so I couldn't.

Psychiatrists now want to put me on lithium. What the fuck is wrong with them? I am a woman of child bearing age and would not want abnormalities to a fetus. Nor would I want damage to my kidneys. Seeing as I tend to alter my water and sodium levels to how I desire, then lithium would be fucking toxic to me and my kidneys. I train as I desire and I eat and drink as I desire. I like the idea that lithium is on the periodic table, however it does not occur naturally in the body. I'm also not an artificial battery that needs to be juiced up.

Time for me to swim the Irish Sea. It looks like I have all of the hard work done in life and I reckon that man who is on a similar wavelength to me, has also. When I meet that fella, my phone can piss off into the sea. Actually, no wait, we have to get those underwater headphones. That is true love and this is the Bible of 2016. Third mental health episode? And I eventually write this book. Third time lucky kiddos.

P.S. I secretly work for the MI5
P.P.S. Larkin Feeney is the only psychiatrist who hasn't pissed me off ever

Now leave me alone. That was A1 Sharon ;)

Lightning Source UK Ltd.
Milton Keynes UK
UKOW05n1423050217
293644UK00001B/6/P

Acc
my statements°